Praise for *Venus Envy*

"Loved it from the first line. Full of delightful snark and lots of heart!"
—Melissa Senate, author of *Questions to Ask Before Marrying*

"Witty, charming, and surprisingly touching. Don't miss this delightful novel!"
—Beverly Brandt, national bestselling author of *Match Game*

"Sexy, clever, and fun, *Venus Envy* is absolutely delightful from beginning to end."
—Jane Porter, author of *Flirting with Forty*

"Charming. Puts a fresh spin on the classic fairy godmother story, and Venus—catty and generous with her barbed wit—is cut from different cloth than the standard well-behaved fairy. McKelden's sharp sense of humor pulls plenty of weight."
—*Publishers Weekly*

"Inventive . . . Witty, funny, and truly original, McKelden's romance is a standout."
—*Booklist*

"A great twist on the fairy godmother story line . . . laugh-out-loud funny . . . A fantastic debut novel."
—*Romance Junkies*

Tor Books by Shannon McKelden

Venus Envy
Venus Guy Trap

Venus Guy Trap

Shannon McKelden

TOR®

A Tom Doherty Associates Book

New York

VENUS GUY TRAP

A Tor Book
Published by Tom Doherty Associates, LLC
175 Fifth Avenue
New York, NY 10010

www.tor-forge.com

Tor® is a registered trademark of Tom Doherty Associates, LLC.

ISBN 978-0-7653-2335-4

First Edition: January 2010

Printed in the United States of America

0 9 8 7 6 5 4 3 2 1

For Jon, Jessie, and John Michael.
You guys give the best family hugs!
Love you forever!

Acknowledgments

Thanks to The Knight Agency: Deidre Knight, for everything you do, I can't thank you enough! Your faith in me and your nudges to make me the best I can be are all very much appreciated. Jamie Pritchett . . . you know why. The words "above and beyond" should be permanently etched beneath your name. And to everyone else at TKA for your dedication to us writers. It's wonderful to know I could go to any one of you for support. You rock!

Thanks so much to the Tor/Forge Team: Melissa Ann Singer, for your hard work in helping me sculpt this story into its final form. Melissa Frain, for answering all my last-minute questions with a smile in your e-mails. To all the people behind the scenes, who brought this book to life. And last, but not least by any means, to Jane Herman, copyeditor extraordinaire, without whom one of my characters would have received an "enormous bouquet of FLOORS."

And finally, one last thanks to Deidre Knight. If it weren't for your wicked way with a rhyme, this book would have been called *Venus Man Trap*.

Venus Cronus

It's not every day that an actual *sign* seems like "a sign."

Most "signs" are things like, you know, your treadmill breaks, which is clearly a sign that you really didn't need to do all that sweaty exercise anyway.

Or, that boutique you love has Donna Karan on sale for, like, two percent off, which is *soooo* a sign that you need to pick up that new little black dress you've been dying to indulge in, even if it's still over your budget. (Not that you should let a little thing like a budget ever stop you from treating yourself to wardrobe indulgences, anyway.)

Or, when you find yourself slaving on Earth as a fairy godmother—when you're really a goddess who should be enjoying a life of luxury. That's a sign that your father, who may be King of the Gods, is also a pigheaded ass who doesn't understand you at all, and is just flaunting his authority . . . well, that's not important now.

What's important is that I have seen a sign. A real sign. One that says "Mount Olympus Books." This is most definitely a sign . . . if you disregard the "books" part, which I do, because, really, all those words cluttering up perfectly good paper? Not so much my thing.

Mount Olympus on the other hand? So. My. Thing.

This can only be a good sign. Not only is there a real sign denoting my favorite place in the whole cosmos—home—there's also a window display dedicated to Greek mythology. With, I might add, a prominent showcasing of my favorite statue—the Venus de Milo—which even makes me *more* willing to overlook the blatantly un-PC use of the term "mythology" when referencing the goddesses and gods that make up me and mine.

Not that there aren't some gods and goddesses who I *wish* were myths. Starting with Daddy Dearest.

A rumble of thunder warns me to get my thoughts back on track.

Fine. I duck into the bookstore, a bell announcing my presence, dragging my bags behind me, in case Zeus should decide to soak me with a rainstorm out of spite. I have better things to turn my attention to anyway. Like getting on with fulfilling my quota and getting off restriction. Is that not the stupidest thing you ever heard? Putting a grown goddess on restriction? I'm far too old to be grounded just because Daddy was "disappointed in my behavior." I'm disappointed in *his* behavior, too, but do *I* get to do anything about it? No.

The only way to get off this Zeus-forsaken planet and back to Mount Olympus is to pick another godchild—like I haven't already had hundreds over the last two millennia—and find her a match made in heaven.

So, with that in mind, I prop my suitcase against the wall beside the door and take in my surroundings in a clinical, yet professional, manner. I decide that taking seriously my job (read: punishment) as a fairy godmother is necessary. However, I cannot overlook that I appeared for this particular job in front of *Mount Olympus* Bookstore. Coinkeedink? I think not.

At first glance, the store is deserted, and I see nothing to reveal my purpose here. It's a bookstore. They sell . . . books. I try to avoid books. I read catalogs. Reading books seems like a waste of perfectly good shopping time, in my opinion.

"I'll be right up," a voice drifts up the stairway to the right of the front door. Running parallel to the front of the store, it leads down to a lower level—probably full of more books.

I shudder. "Don't hurry," I instruct the voice. It's not like I'm going to buy anything anyway.

Suddenly, it occurs to me—

If Zeus thinks he's getting me to give up shopping and become a bookworm, he has another freakin' think coming. I know his tricks. I know his schemes to try to change me. And it's not going to work!

Following the scent of strong coffee to the left, I find the front counter, so I meander over there. A short-haired black feline is curled into a ball in one corner. On my best days, I don't care for cats. They're too . . . lower-life-form for me. (Oh, and lest you think I am prejudiced against cats . . . I don't much care for dogs, either. I'm an equal opportunity pet hater.) This particular cat isn't earning any brownie points, either, as he's raised his head from the counter and is staring at me. And not in a friendly way. Like I care. I'm here to find a godchild, not to win a popularity contest with hairy beasts who just shed all over my designer togs.

A stack of business cards tells me I've arrived in Bander, Oregon. Never heard of it. Obviously I'll not be hanging with the glitzy and sequined famous here. A year-at-a-glance calendar on the wall behind the counter (with all the bygone days meticulously crossed out and another day about six weeks from now circled boldly with red pen) reveals that it's nearly mid-May. Six months from the time I finished up with my last love life makeover. Thank goodness, being immortal, jumping around in time doesn't have quite the same discombobulating effect on me as it would on humans if they were to do the same thing. I've bounced around so much over the last two-thousand-some years, I couldn't possibly give you an accurate timeline of world history. It's like being on a loop-de-loop roller coaster sometimes. Except I'm looping through time.

Anyway, back to the ever-present present. The rest of the store reveals books, books, and more books. Arranged . . . alphabetically? Artistically? Astrologically? I wouldn't know. It's not like I've ever purposely entered a bookstore before. Multiple broad windows and a set of French doors run along the entire wall opposite the front door. Beyond them, I can see a deck and, beyond that, the ocean. A few cozy settings of chairs face the windows. Like for people to sit and read in, I guess. Whatever.

Twirling, facing back toward the front of the store, I notice a sign on the wall near the stairs indicating that customers will find the metaphysical section downstairs, as well as computer manuals and various and sundry other inconsequential subject matter. Upon Zeus, why would people want to buy *computer* manuals? Computers are another waste of time that could be spent on valuable retail activities—unless, of course, you're *shopping* online. And I highly doubt anyone would need a manual to perfect online shopping techniques. It's simply a matter of point, click, and checkout. Not too highly brain-taxing.

Voices drift up the stairwell again. Probably discussing which boring old books to waste their money on. Hey, if they have American Express accounts wanting use, I'm more than willing to take some credit off their hands at any boutique in town.

But I have more important things to think about right now. Finding a new godchild. Fixing whatever's wrong with her. And getting the heck back to the *real* Mount Olympus. I need a plan. Because I'm bound and determined to do it right this time. To follow the rules (which I'm aware will require actually reading the rule book more thoroughly; still, it's a sacrifice I'm willing to make if it means I'll find out what I've been doing wrong all these years). I'm going to ace this love match, I just know it!

I go back to looking around, waiting for another sign, and growing more bored by the moment, until I remember why I entered the store in the first place—aside from digging its name. The front window display.

I can't suppress my little happy dance when I spy that the back of the display window is open. It contains several glorious picture books with such titles as *Venus, Goddess Extraordinaire* and *The Art of Aphrodite,* as well as framed prints of various artists' renditions of *moi.* While my mind continues to plan firmly my next step, my ever-so-eager ego can't help but shiver with joy that someone who works in this store obviously has an obsession for all things goddesslike. Or at least Aphrodite-like. And, after all, isn't she—me!—the most *significant* goddess?

Anyway, I need to choose a new godchild and, unlike my last Extreme Love Life Makeover, when I picked my godchild at random (she liked my Gucci bag, what can I say), *this time* I will not use such frivolous means to choose a project. This time, it will be all about level-headedness and common sense.

I barely stifle a squeal and reach into the window display to snag the Venus de Milo replica. Clutching the statue to my breast, I savor the flood of memories that could potentially make me do something really stupid. I *loved* posing for this statue . . . the original one, I mean. My godchild at that time had been a housemaid in the home of a sculptor. It had been the best makeover ever . . . mostly because the little waif's boss had taken a liking to my, uh, *form,* and the focus had turned—rightly—to me. Oh, I got that job done, of course. And I'd done it with gladness. With joy. Maybe because I had been adored and worshipped. Maybe because . . .

Concentrate, I think. But I don't let up my grip on Mini Me. I'd last seen a reproduction like this during a match I'd made years ago. A good match. A happy match. I need another one of those. I need to get my groove back.

This time, I vow, I will choose the perfect godchild. Based on study and contemplation. After interviewing candidates and giving the process much thought and deliberation. Only then will I—

"Is Aphrodite your favorite goddess, too?"

I whirl around to face the speaker.

And I know instantly, that *this* time, I will choose a godchild who obviously *idolizes* me like I haven't been idolized in Far. Too. Long.

❧ 2 ❧

Haydee

I couldn't help but flinch when the customer clutching my Venus de Milo replica turned around.

She was a knockout. *Hot,* as Paris Hilton might say in her breathy little voice. Stunningly high cheekbones and doelike eyes. Lashes of that unnaturally long length usually—depressingly— reserved for men, much to the disgruntlement of most women. She was the fairy-tale definition of perfection.

Except for the streaks of inky black mascara running down her face.

But even that didn't make her *un*attractive. Maybe it was a Goth thing. Small coastal towns like Bander don't typically attract a Goth crowd, so it was possible I was painfully out of touch with today's up-and-coming trends in cosmetics.

"Are you all right?" I reached for her elbow to steady her. She really did look like she was going to pass out or something. Only it looked like happiness, not depression. Which didn't really fit the image her tear-and-mascara-streaked face presented.

"You're it!" The woman's face lit up even more, if that was possible. "You have to be."

"It?" I shot a quick glance at the front counter to make sure the cordless phone was handy, in case I needed to call Howie, the sheriff. Zeus, my cat—who wasn't really supposed to be curled up on the counter—watched us through narrowed eyes.

"You obviously get me, so you have to be it."

O-kay. I put on my most professional face, lest I show my complete confusion. "Can I help you find something? A book maybe?" I gestured to the Venus she held in such an iron grip I was a little worried it would snap in half. "Sorry, the statue's not for sale. It's from my personal collection."

"Oh, of course not. Once you have one, even a copy, you'd never part with it." The woman held the Venus out at arm's length to admire her. Her smile faded as she ran a finger along one of the stubs where an arm had once been. "Whoever broke off her arms should be shot. My arms are one of my best features!" She held up one arm to demonstrate. "Wouldn't you agree?"

"Sure. They're . . . great." The customer is always right. And in this case, she really was. She *did* have great arms. She wore a pale blue, sleeveless, stretchy top that showed them off. I wondered if she frequently held them up for public scrutiny.

My thought was interrupted by the ringing phone.

"Excuse me one sec." I headed for the front desk, relieved to escape for a few minutes. This one was just a little too odd for my taste.

I watched her from the corner of my eye as I picked up the phone. "Mount Olympus Books. How can I help you?"

"Uh, Haydee?"

"This is she."

"This is Bill Blankenship. From Love Harmony?"

I turned my back on my customer, as if she'd care that I'd stooped so low as to sign up for an online dating service. "Great to hear from you, Bill. I'm looking forward to our date tonight."

"Yeah, see, that's the thing . . . I'm not going to make it."

Not going to . . . "Are you sure?" Maybe he wasn't sure. Maybe he didn't really mean to blow me off. Because I really needed this date. None of the other six Love Harmony dates I'd been on panned out, and I was out of prospects according to my True Love Match Profile.

"Of course I'm sure," he replied, his voice a bit irritated. "Why would I have called otherwise?"

"May I ask what changed your mind?" Maybe this could be salvaged. Maybe we could just go out another time. After all, we'd gotten along so well the last time we'd spoken on the phone. We'd connected.

"Look, my wife's in labor, okay? That a good enough reason for you?"

When the phone went dead, all I could do was stare out the front window of the store. What had just happened? How in the heck could I have just spent two weeks getting to know this guy by e-mail, not to mention several hours on the phone, only to have him not mention the fact that he was *married*?

Note to self: Just because a guy looks good on paper (or computer screen) doesn't mean he is.

I gently replaced the receiver and practiced deep breathing as I turned around and surveyed my calendar. I had six weeks. Or rather, six weeks, five days, and eight and a half hours . . . until I needed to be married. Or else.

Okay, "or else" was a bit dramatic, but it felt like "or else." It felt like worse than "or else." It felt like . . .

I couldn't breathe.

I'd followed The Plan to the letter since I was sixteen, when I had *needed* The Plan to put one foot in front of the other after my mom died. It had been the only thing that got me out of bed in the morning, kept me in school, stopped me from going crazy with grief. The Plan had been the only thing that kept me going on several different occasions over the last almost seventeen years. The few times I'd deviated from it . . . disaster.

I would never stray from The Plan again.

And The Plan stated that I would marry by the time I was thirty-three years old. Which was in six weeks, five days, and eight and a half hours.

I probably shouldn't have waited to start actually seriously looking for a man just three months before my deadline, but hey, things got in my way. Like trying not to think about dating and what a complete and utter disaster it had been in my past.

Besides, I had a contingency plan . . . an alternate, I guess you could call him. Patrick.

Patrick.

Dammit.

Fighting off an anxiety attack, I grabbed the phone again and called Curt, my weekend employee, who I'd begged to work on a Friday night, since my evening employee, Kim, had asked for the night off. And so I could go on this hot date. So I could get engaged. So I could tie the knot. Which might just all have happened if I still had a date with Bill from Portland. Who wasn't Patrick, which was a point in his favor right off the bat.

Only his *wife* had gone into labor.

I left a message on Curt's voice mail, hoping he'd get it before he headed over. Maybe he could still salvage his Friday evening. He was only seventeen, young and resilient, and still had plenty of time to think about things like serious dating.

Unlike some of us.

"*Ahhhhhh!!* Why didn't you tell me I looked like this?"

I turned to find my apparently still unstable customer had discovered the burnished gold mirror my feng shui–crazed friend Joan had hung in the space next to the French doors, opposite the main entrance. It was supposedly meant to scare evil spirits right back out the front door, should they happen to make their way into the store looking for reading material.

"Sorry." I dropped the phone and plucked a tissue from the box behind the counter, figuring I'd give her another minute before getting back to my own life crisis. "Isn't that kind of an awkward thing to tell someone? 'Oh, by the way, you cried all your mascara off?'"

"I wasn't crying," she snapped, snagging the tissue from me as soon as I was within reaching distance. She made a guttural sound in the back of her throat as she leaned into the mirror, dabbed the tissue onto her tongue, and went to work at the stains on her cheeks. "I was . . . I have . . . allergies. Why in the *hell* isn't this coming off? And why is *non*waterproof mascara even still manufactured?"

"Seems waterproof now," I offered, meaning to inject humor into the situation. I needed humor at this moment or *I'd* be tempted to cry. "Need another tissue?" I dashed back to the counter to get her one, catching sight of the list I'd started yesterday. A list of possible places to find a husband just in case my date tonight didn't pan out. The list was very short and now mocked me from the countertop, reminding me that the chances of Mr. Right waltzing into my bookstore—where most of my social interaction took place—were slim to none.

Tick, tock, went my mind clock.

"That's what I get for becoming all stupidly emotional," the woman across the room muttered, apparently forgetting she'd just blamed allergies for her makeup mess. I returned to her side and passed her another tissue. She finished with one cheek—the blackness of the mascara streaks had now been replaced with streaks of scarlet from scrubbing—and turned to tackle the other. "The rule book was definitely right about getting personally involved with humans. That will *not* be a problem in the future, I assure you."

She really didn't seem to be talking to me specifically, so I didn't try to interpret. Rule book? Not getting emotionally involved with humans? Who else would you get emotionally involved with?

She finally turned from the mirror, the damage marginally repaired. Not that anyone would notice. Everything else about her screamed confidence and beauty. Her outfit was obviously quality, with a flirty flowered skirt that swirled above her knees like butterfly wings. Whereas my jeans were fairly new and serviceable, but boring. (No one dressed up in Bander, a laid-back tourist town through and through.) The spiky heels on her feet would have rendered me incapable of walking. And her hair—cumulouslike clouds of loose blond curls draping her slender neck and shoulders—made my serviceable brown ponytail seem drab. She looked like one of the princesses in the books I'd devoured as a little girl. Like the princess I'd once vowed to grow up to be . . . you know, before real life crushed those fantasies.

Great. Just what I needed. A confidence crumbler when I had a big date tonight.

Only I *didn't have* a big date tonight anymore. Bugger.

Sighing, I tried to forget about my fast-approaching deadline—and my alternative if I didn't find another alternative—and concentrated on my customer instead. If I'd been a traffic-stopper like her, maybe I'd already be married, and this wouldn't be an issue at all. Maybe I needed a trip to Bander Spa & Beauty for a few highlights, a facial . . . a quick liposuction.

I finally stopped checking out the me I wanted to be—which was making me more stressed by the minute—when I found her leaning toward me, eyeing me with what looked like anticipation. She stuck out a long-fingered hand with nails that looked like they'd never missed a date with the manicurist. Feeling like a small-town girl next to a glamour queen, I reached out my hand with its serviceably short nails. She shook like a man, with purpose and a firm grip.

"I'm Venus," she announced, apparently sticking around the store now that she looked more presentable, though she appeared to have no interest at all in books. Which was too bad. I could almost always use extra help around here.

"Ah, Venus. That explains why you like my Venus de Milo so much."

"Something like that. And you are?"

"Haydee Miller. I own the store." I plucked a business card from the counter and passed it over.

"Miller?" She looked at me oddly a minute, like she was trying to remember something . . . then her eyes grew wide and twinkly. Then she shook her head and frowned, more at herself than me, it appeared, before continuing solemnly. "You're looking for a man."

Whoa. Did I look so desperate that strangers could tell? A glance in the mirror revealed I just looked panicked. Maybe because I was.

I waved absently toward the phone. She must have overheard my conversation. "I did have a date tonight, which I had to cancel. But no big deal." Except that it was.

"No worries." She grinned again, flashing perfect white teeth. "Tell me about it. What's your plan?"

"Plan?" Interesting choice of words, almost like she knew me better than she possibly could.

"Let me guess . . ." My customer whirled delicately and began strolling around the room, picking up various items, then replacing them quickly when they didn't interest her. "You dreamed your whole life of owning a bookstore." She examined the Book of the Week display, featuring the latest book by Stephen Colbert, before grimacing and dropping it back on the table. "Though, seriously? Why not something fun, like . . . shoes? You totally should have gotten into shoes."

"Shoes aren't really that big a deal to me."

She sighed. "Pity. Had I been meant to work anywhere, I'd have loved working in a shoe store. Anyway . . . now that you have the dream career, you're ready for the man. And kids. The full package of True Love!"

Well, we didn't have to go that far. Dreaming of a handsome prince sweeping me off my feet had pretty much disappeared with puberty and life's realities. "I do have a plan," I told her. Might as well just blurt it out. After all, maybe she had some ideas. "I basically charted my whole life when I was seventeen . . . for a counselor at school, when I was having a really hard time." No need to elaborate that my mom had recently died, and my dad had buried himself in grief until he hadn't even known I existed anymore. Depression had so consumed me, I'd been practically paralyzed. "I planned out when I'd graduate, what I'd major in. When I'd have saved enough money to open this store, buy a house, a family-friendly car."

I resettled the pens and pencils in the Welcome to Bander mug on the desk, kind of like resettling the memories I had floating around in my head. "At first I thought The Plan was lame . . . but it worked. I got through that hard time, made it through high school and college, got my MBA, and I've had the store now for five years, and it's pretty successful."

I stopped talking, suddenly struck by how easy everything up to this point had been. After some false starts—then some deviations from The Plan during college that had nearly sunk me into depression again—I'd followed The Plan to the letter. The house, the car, the store. None of those things had been difficult. I'd never dreaded running my own business. I'd looked forward to it, completely confident that I could do it. A couple years later, when I'd saved the down payment for a house, there'd never been even a flicker of fear about having a mortgage or what homeownership meant. As long as I stuck to The Plan, everything turned out fine. I could move forward with confidence. I knew what to do and when to do it.

Without The Plan? I got hives even thinking about throwing away what had basically been the guiding light of my life. If I ditched The Plan, how long would it be before I couldn't get out of bed in the morning? Before I stopped socializing? Before I let my business deteriorate because I had nowhere to go and no guide to follow?

"So, anyway," I continued, "I turn thirty-three in six weeks, five days, and"—I glanced at my watch—"eight hours. On June twenty-fifth. I'm supposed to be married by then. Only I haven't really dated, *really*, in like, ten years." God. That was the most pathetic thing I'd ever had to admit out loud.

But it was true. I hadn't had a serious date in ten years. I'd had six—now seven—online dating disasters, the last of which I hadn't even actually dated. It had taken me two weeks to accept Bill's invitation to dinner because the last six had only served to discourage me. But Bill had been different. I'd had a good feeling about him. Before I knew about his pregnant wife.

Venus didn't even try to stifle her gasp. "Ten years?" She sank into one of the reading chairs scattered throughout the store, her perfect teeth worrying at her lower lip and her brow collapsed into a frown.

She didn't have to take it so personally. It was my problem, not hers. "I mean, I've dated a little in the last few weeks." A male stripper, the biggest jackass redneck I'd ever met (who practically had the cops called on him during dinner for harassing the lovely Mexican woman waiting on us), and, of course, now the married guy. "But I need to get serious. I need a husband."

Finally she squared her shoulders and nodded. "I can work with that."

I laughed. "Wanna be my dating coach? I bet you have a trick or two up your sleeve." Surely someone so beautiful knew some tricks us "girl next door" types didn't.

"I'll be better than your dating coach," she counteroffered, flipping a cascade of blond curls over her shoulder in a practiced move I'm sure had caught the eye of many men. "I'll find you the perfect man. One hundred percent satisfaction guaranteed. With no money required, of course, because that would be unethical. Although a place to stay might be nice. Anyway"—she popped out of the chair, practically quivering with excitement—"I'll be your fairy godmother."

"Ha! I stopped believing in fairy godmothers about the time I stopped reading fairy tales." About the time my mom died and my dad . . . well, anyway.

"Maybe it's time you *start* believing again," Venus snapped, hands on hips, looking at me with disapproval. "You need something, and I can provide it."

I opened my mouth to tell her . . . I don't know what. That I'd take her help? That she was a little too weird for me? I can't know for sure what I planned to say, because before I said anything, the door chimes sounded.

I turned to greet the new customer—

—and in walked my contingency plan.

3

Venus

During my moments in front of the mirror, trying to make my-self presentable again, and wandering around this store, noticing self-help books practically choking all the other books like weeds, I decided two things. Well, three, actually.

One, this Extreme Love Life Makeover is going to be differ-ent. I'm going to make it different. I am going to really put in an effort to be the fairy godmother I've been forced to be. Because, I figure, if I have to be it, I may as well be it as fabulously as I *be* everything else I be.

And two, I am going to read the whole damn Fairy God-mother Rule Book. And not just skim it like I've done in the past. I'm going to read every Zeus-forsaken word of it. Because there has to be something I've overlooked. Zeus doesn't do anything without a reason—usually a reason that benefits him. I have a feeling he's hidden clues in the rule book that I need to find.

Which leads to resolution number three. My last godchild's *feelings* are what led to the mess of mascara I almost had to resort to dermabrasion to get off my face. They'd also led to the near-catastrophic almost–end result of my last makeover, which I'm not eager to repeat.

This time, I'm going to be very careful. Brief mental scouting missions only. If it gets too hairy, I'm out of there.

I return my attention to the man coming in the door, while sending feelers out in Haydee's direction. (And, yes, I'm perfectly aware she hasn't exactly agreed to accept my services yet. But really, what choice does she have? I'm the chooser, she's the choosee.)

Vanilla. If I have to give the guy a flavor, he's vanilla. Not bad in terms of flavors, just not very exciting. Brown hair, brown eyes, bare face (not even a shadow, like he's not old enough to shave yet, though he obviously is). He doesn't look like an athlete, but he's not porky, either. He's wearing a white lab coat with an unidentifiable stain on it.

Which, I realize, as Haydee's thoughts tickle my brain, is the proverbial last straw for her.

Under the pretense of needing coffee, I step over the black cat—who has nothing but a stub for a tail (freak!) and has planted himself at my feet for some unknown, and probably devious, reason—and cross the room as quietly as possible. I want to see my godchild better.

To use my hair as a shield, I bend over the table and peek through the strands at them as I pour a cup.

"Patrick." Haydee's smile is as plastic as Barbie's. "What're you doing here?"

Have you ever seen someone bracing themselves? You know, like for a big slobbery dog to jump on them? Or for their Great-aunt Myrtle to pinch their cheeks? That's what she's doing. She's bracing herself.

And she's not breathing. Literally. The closer this Patrick guy gets, the shallower Haydee breathes, until she completely stops altogether as he leans in to kiss her. She dodges the bullet and takes it on the cheek.

Maybe the guy has B.O.?

"Thought I'd take a break from neuter-and-spay day to check out the latest in the mystery section."

I see a black streak of fur shoot across the store, disappearing through an open door. Almost like he understood the implications of "neuter-and-spay day."

"And, you know, see how things are with you." He looks hopefully at Haydee, who takes a discreet step back, now breathing through her mouth.

"Oh, great! Why don't you . . . uh, go ahead and browse? I'll just . . ." She frantically searches until she locates me and then waves in my direction. "I have another customer."

Patrick flashes a toothy smile in my direction, then nods. "No problem."

Figuring maybe I should carry the coffee charade through to the end, I stir in some milk from a tiny pitcher that's been nestled in an ice bath, and then plop in a half dozen sugar cubes.

"Who's he?" I ask when Haydee joins me. "And why don't you breathe when you're talking to him?"

She looks startled. "You could tell that clear over here?"

"I'm very observant," I tell her, taking a sip of the coffee and grimacing. Needs M&M's. "So, who is he?"

"My contingency plan." She sighs, closing her eyes and shaking her head slightly. "If I don't find another guy to marry . . . Patrick's it."

I lean around her, checking out the guy across the room, who seems thoroughly engrossed in reading the back of a soft-cover book. "No, he's not."

Haydee does some glancing of her own. "He's not bad, he's just—"

"Not The One."

"We made a pact," Haydee continues. "Last year on my birthday. All my party guests, except Patrick, left the party to go home with their spouses or boyfriends . . . or to hook up with a random guy from the bar because they're too bitter about men to have a meaningful relationship. And then my dad came in for a beer and waved at me from the other side of the bar without even coming over to wish me happy birthday, because he's still too busted up about my mom dying seventeen years ago to remember stuff like that."

She clears her throat, and I flinch at the rush of sadness coming at me through our connection. I chug a slug of the ghastly coffee, hoping the distraction will slam the brakes on the emotional bus crash that's about to happen.

But she gains control again and continues. "I've known Patrick for years. He's our veterinarian." She gestures toward where the cat had been lying on the floor, but he's long gone, having streaked into the backroom as soon as he'd heard Patrick speak. The cat equivalent of holding his breath? "He neutered my cat."

Which explained the cat's animosity toward him. But not Haydee's.

She steps around me so she can keep an eye on our topic of conversation and continues speaking in a hushed voice. "We ended up sharing a couple pitchers of beer. Like, a couple pitchers *each*."

"True Love."

She starts to protest, then gives up. "*Anyway,* Patrick and I drank way too much, and shared too much personal information. We're a lot alike. We both want a family, but we're feeling our age, I guess. Misery loves company, you know? So we made a pact. If neither of us finds anyone by the time a year goes by— now only six weeks, five days, and seven and a half more hours— we'll marry each other. We drank to the pact. And then we slept together to seal it even more. He took it way more seriously than I did—the pact, I mean—and sometimes I think it would be okay, that we'd work out. And other times . . ."

She groans softly and sinks down onto a box behind the front desk, where Patrick can't see her. "Deciding that a guy can't be

The One, solely based on the fact that he smells like his work, is superficial and lame, right?"

I'm totally confused now and almost just reach into her head for the information I need, before she takes me on another round-about path to the final truth. But there really is no time like the present to stretch my long-unused intuition wings.

"You'll have to be a bit more clear," I tell her. Hey, intuition can't work without something to work with.

"Patrick Butler smells like a veterinarian's office."

Which is logical since he's a veterinarian.

"I probably smell like new books," she continues. "Though why that might be a turn-off to anyone, I can't imagine."

New books have a smell? New one on me.

"We kind of had a fling for a few weeks. I thought maybe it would work out. And then he ran over my dog backing out of the driveway one night." She scrunches her eyes closed as if to block out what I'm sure would be a sad memory to a pet owner. Then she opens them and glances to make sure we're not being eavesdropped upon before lowering her voice even more. "It was totally an accident. Bear darted out behind the car before I could stop him. Patrick was *really* nice about it. He was so sorry and car-ing and sympathetic. He drove us to his office and . . . and did what had to be done to make sure Bear didn't suffer. Then he took me home with him, you know, so I wouldn't have to be alone in the house without my dog. I woke up the next morning in Patrick's bed, and all I could smell was, like, disinfectant and new puppy . . . from years of hanging out at his office. Which re-minded me that he'd killed my dog. I mean, put him to sleep."

"A mood killer."

"Exactly!" Haydee covers her mouth when she realizes how loudly she spoke. She starts again in a near whisper. "Exactly. And then? He offered me a new dog. Who does that? It's like telling a grieving mother you'll get her a new child to replace the dead one."

As if finding the analogy particularly upsetting, my godchild pales. Closing her eyes a moment, she finally gets a grip on herself and continues. "It wasn't like he murdered Bear in cold blood. He did the right thing. But it's not something that goes away. It's been almost a year, and I still think of it every time I see him. Or smell him.

"So, I made my excuses. That I needed time. That we had to be free to find our soul mates without distractions like dating each other."

"But he would have liked to skip that part and just marry you," I guess.

Haydee peeks around the corner of the desk to make sure he's still busy, and I use my Oscar-worthy acting skills to look enthralled with my nasty coffee in case he checks up on us.

"Yeah. I think that's exactly what he'd like to do. But I don't think I can. I think . . . I think we made the pact in haste. Because we didn't want to be alone. I just . . . I don't think I can marry him."

Of course she can't marry him; he's not The One. I know these things. "So, what you're saying is that you need to find the right man in six weeks, five days—"

"And seven-whatever hours."

"No problem." I give up on the paper cup of putridness and deposit it in the plastic-lined trash can beneath the table. "If you're looking for a man, I'll find you one."

"I don't want just anyone, though," she says, with another glance in Patrick's direction. "He has to be intelligent."

"Exactly!" I agree. "Someone willing to hold your handbag while you shop."

"Someone with similar values."

"A sharp dresser."

"Someone responsible."

"Someone *romantic,*" I press, steering her away from the boring list of must-haves she probably feels obligated to recite.

"Someone financially secure," she adds.

"Someone who makes you hot!"

Been there, done that. The words hit me as though she'd spoken them aloud, only she's staring at the floor at her feet.

"Stability is the most important," she finally says, looking up to stress her seriousness. "The best isn't the best if there's no stability in the relationship."

"Fair enough," I tell her. "I'll add 'stable' to your list of requirements."

"What requirements are those?"

Both of us startle when we find Patrick standing at the counter looking down on us.

"Oh, nothing," Haydee leaps up to help him, quickly taking the book he's chosen from his hand. Holding her breath, of course, just in case a freak wind blows through the store and she finds herself downwind. "Just . . . reading . . . requirements."

"I'm a *huuuuggge* reader," I lie smoothly, silently amending that my reading is limited to clothing sale flyers and price tags. "*Huge*."

"You came to the right place then," Dr. Vanilla says to me, then turns his longing eyes back to Haydee. Uh, oh. "Our girl Haydee here has the best books in town."

"The only books in town," she corrects, before ducking down behind the counter for a plastic bag . . . and taking a deep breath while she's out of sight. "And flattery won't get you a discount."

"Being your husband will, though, won't it?"

Haydee and I both freeze. Me in the middle of inspecting my nails, her in the midst of shoving his book into a bag.

She finally breaks the ice with a forceful laugh. "There's still time, you know, Patrick. The love of your life may be right outside that door." She points to the sidewalk outside . . . where an elderly lady is hobbling by pushing a walker. A squeak issues forth from Haydee that sounds like half-laugh half-strangulation. "Well maybe not right this second."

"I think I'll hold out for you," he laughs.

At least the guy has a sense of humor.

Haydee doesn't share my thoughts, I can tell by the look of distress on her face. Silently, she runs his credit card, waits for him to sign the slip, then closes her drawer. While they take care of their transaction, I nonchalantly lean over the side of the counter, feigning extreme interest in a small box stuffed with colorful bookmarks. What I'm really doing is checking the odor situation. My nostrils twitch, as I take a subtly deep breath. Hm, he does smell like antiseptic, and a bit like . . . not sure what, but it's probably related to the vile-looking yellow stain on his jacket. Though it doesn't bring back any memories of pet euthanasia for me—I've never had a pet, thank Zeus—it's still not something I'd like to smell on a regular basis, I think.

Transaction and sniff test complete, we all stand there awkwardly for a moment. Patrick's eyes dodge back and forth between Haydee and me and back again, Haydee's between Patrick and me and back again, and mine, well, you get the idea. It's like a three-way tennis tournament.

Finally, Patrick takes a deep breath and focuses on Haydee. "So, do you have plans tonight?" He waves in the general direction of the street. "I was planning on getting dinner at The Clipper. You could join me."

"Uh . . ." Haydee's mouth flaps open like a fish on dry land.

After an awkward moment, I rescue her with a quick brain forage. "She has to work."

Patrick recovers quickly from my curious jump into the conversation—after all, I'm supposedly just another customer.

"Maybe after the store closes?"

"Oh no, not then, either," I tell him.

Both Haydee and Patrick turn in my direction this time. Equally surprised.

"We have some business to discuss."

Her eyebrows disappear behind her bangs.

"You know," I tell her, flashing her a "play along and I'll save your ass" look. "That *thing* we were talking about?"

Though my new godchild is a little slow, she finally gets it. "Oh, yeah! You're right. Sorry, Patrick, it's really not good to-night."

He looks so disappointed, I feel a little bit sorry for him. Or I would if I didn't need him out of the way to get any work done. Maybe I can hook him up as a side job—a bonus, maybe. I'd get props from Daddy for making a match out of the kindness of my heart. Wouldn't I?

"Another time then." With a quick wave, he disappears out the front door.

I examine the state of my pedicure. "He's not so bad," I say.

I look up to find Haydee staring at me, her eyes wild with panic. "So," she says, "what would you charge to be my fairy god-mother?"

❧ 4 ❧

Haydee

What in the world had I done?

"There're fresh towels in the cupboard in the bathroom," I said, standing in the doorway of my guest room. Where my guest was unpacking her Louis Vuitton suitcase. "And more in the hall closet if you need them."

I'd let a complete stranger into my home, all because she managed to convince me in the past five hours, while we chatted between customers, that she was the best matchmaker in town . . . this town or any other on Earth. And maybe it was my complete desperation to find a man—besides Patrick—that made me believe her.

And let her move in with me.

My friends were going to shoot me for my foolishness. But what choice did I have? I needed to find a husband ASAP, or I'd be stuck with a man who was nice enough as a friend, but who would forever remind me of the death of my dog. And truthfully? He just didn't *do* it for me. But Venus seemed perfectly confident that she'd be able to find me a husband within The Plan's time frame. So I accepted. Desperate times and all that.

Granted, it seemed a little unusual to provide room and board for a matchmaker, but then I'd never actually hired a matchmaker, so what did I know? She was apparently new in town, having just been "dropped off" today, according to her, after having recently been up in Washington. She needed a place to stay and was willing to work on the barter system. Instead of cash for her services, she'd take room and board. Which could have been code for "scout out and rob blind," so I'd tested her out by giving her a fifty-dollar bill to go pick us up some dinner since Curt had jumped at having the night off, and I couldn't leave the store. I figured if she disappeared into the sunset with my money, at least I'd know she was dishonest. She came back.

But that could totally have been a ploy to get into my good graces. And my house. What was fifty bucks when I had a house full of antiques that had belonged to my mother?

Biting my lip, I glanced down the hall toward the stairs, wondering if I should lock up the china and silver somewhere. If I was ever going to relax, I'd have to keep my guest with me in the store all day, I guess. God, I was such an idiot. I mentally smacked my forehead.

"Second thoughts?"

I jerked my head around to find Venus closing the dresser drawer on a huge stack of lingerie she'd just deposited. "Uh, no. No. Not at all."

"Liar."

She was nothing if not blunt.

"I suppose I should have expected this," she said. "All my godchildren are the same."

She really took the "fairy godmother" branding thing seriously. From a business standpoint, I totally understood. It was catchy in a fairy-tale-ish kind of way. Instead of calling herself a matchmaker and referring to her clients as, well, clients, she'd adopted the *whole* vocabulary of the Cinderella story.

"However, I do have to say you're a better dresser than my last," Venus continued, gesturing at my pink-and-green-plaid boxers and white tank, my standard nightwear. "I'm grateful you have more fashion sense than that one. She made her entrance in paint- and dust-stained jeans and a baseball cap."

She was a difficult conversationalist at times, this one. I gathered, though, from bits and pieces of this afternoon's chats, that she was speaking of her last client, Rachel. Who she'd matched with a guy named Luke. A hot firefighter. I suppose I'd take a hot firefighter as a husband . . . though I didn't think we had any hot firefighters in Bander.

"At least you aren't disgracing the female population by being seen in public looking like a slave laborer. Though, really? Loafers? Heels are so much more slimming for the calves."

I glanced down at said calves, which I'd always thought were pretty decent. I tried to keep in shape, running and volleyball on the beach on occasion. Did they need to look slimmer? Really?

"Anyway, I have high hopes for you," Venus went on, having forgotten my less than slim calf muscles. "Especially since you don't need a fashion makeover along with a relationship overhaul. Just that much less work for me."

I figured I'd better get the real scoop on this whole matchmaking process now that we wouldn't be interrupted by customers every few minutes, so I crossed the room to sit in the comfortable reading chair I'd tucked in the corner by the window.

"So how does this all work?" I asked, pointing to the leather tote she'd set on the bed. "Do you have forms for me to fill out? To tell you my likes and dislikes and hobbies?"

"It's not nearly that difficult." She dropped onto the bed, kicking off her shoes. "See, I was born to do this kind of thing. Hooking up humans," she added, seeing my confusion.

When the clouds didn't suddenly clear from my expression, especially since this wasn't the first time she'd used the word "humans," she sighed, then glanced around the room. Her face brightened when she noticed where I'd set the Venus de Milo replica on the bedside table, thinking it would make her feel at home. She'd made it pretty clear at the store that she had the same feelings about the statue that I did. It had been my mom's favorite, and she'd given it to me on my sixteenth birthday, when she knew she probably wouldn't make it much more than a year before the breast cancer got her.

For a while, I'd been really angry that she'd given it to me. It meant she was giving up, that her death was inevitable. Only years after she was gone had I realized she'd wanted the statue not to be just another item in the house to be gone through and forgotten. She'd wanted me to know she *wanted* me to have it.

The statue had meant something between us. Mom, a writer—and a mythology buff, who'd passed her love of it on to me—made up this story about how she and a friend had been in a museum the day she met my father. They'd both been admiring a replica of the Venus de Milo. It had been love at first sight, and he'd asked her for a date. Mom's friend, who Mom insisted had been the *real* Aphrodite, which I believed until I was older, told her he was The One. She accepted the date, and the rest was history.

I knew it was just a story. But it was my favorite story as a little girl. As a romance novelist, my mom had been all about Happily Ever After. *Both* my parents had been, though in different ways. My dad, Lawrence Miller, had also been a writer—the Nicholas Sparks of his time, I guess was a good comparison. While his bittersweet love stories often didn't end as happily as my mom's, for which she teased him mercilessly, they were still stories about love. I'd asked her once if she ever thought she'd run out of happy ideas. She'd replied that as long as love existed, the river of ideas would flow. It had worked for her up until her death.

That's how long it had worked for my dad, too.

Venus plucked the statue from the nightstand and crossed the room toward me, greeted by a low growl from Zeus. She glared at him, then raised the statue she had cradled in her hands. "I was holding an apple, you know." She set the statue on the tiny table next to my chair, where it seemed to glow a little in the lamplight. "In my left hand. I was starving and just wanted to take a huge juicy bite of it. But Alexandros kept saying, 'Not yet, my love, not yet.'"

Her voice drifted off, and I nodded absently, not really comprehending . . . not for the first time in our short acquaintance. As I watched the statue, which now looked totally normal, my heart contracted a little. Like a million other times in my life, I wished my mom was here.

"So."

My head and attention snapped back to Venus. "So?" I tried to remember what we'd been talking about and failed.

"The fairy godmother thing?" Venus prompted. "I'm going to prove it to you."

"You really don't have to." I plucked Zeus off the floor and onto my lap, where he stared suspiciously at our guest, unsoothed by my attention. "It's a brilliant marketing plan, I admit, but you don't need to carry it out as if it's real."

"*Pfff!*" Venus rolled her eyes. "I have no idea what you mean by 'marketing plan.' I *am* a fairy godmother, though, believe me, it pains me to say so."

Because choosing a marketing plan that "pains" you is a good idea, why?

"So how do you find the right guy for your clients?" I finally asked, just now realizing that she was in an unfamiliar town, so it wasn't like she had a database of clients to draw from. Even if she had the stats on every available Bander male, *I* was hard-pressed to think of any one of them who might be marriage material. And I knew them all. Hence the brief and futile attempt at an online dating service.

"It's a goddess thing."

Not the answer I'd expected at all. "A goddess thing?"

Venus grinned and pointed at my statue. "I'm her. Venus . . . well Aphrodite, if you want to get technical. Which I prefer not to. I go by Venus now . . . mostly because it pisses Daddy off—"

"Daddy?" She was clearly a few chapters shy of a novel.

"Zeus," she stated, her mouth twisted like she was sucking lemons. "God of Sky and Thunder, Ruler of Mount Olympus?"

I stroked the cat under his chin. "Hear that, Zeus? Ruler of Mount Olympus. But you knew you ruled the bookstore long before I did, didn't you?"

Venus stared at the cat. "What did you call him?"

"Zeus. He came with the store when I bought it. So I named him after the god, of course."

Venus glared at him. "I can think of a dozen other gods more deserving of a namesake. Although I suppose the real Zeus has a lot in common with a black cat . . . like being bad luck."

A rumble of thunder rattled the windows behind me and the statue wobbled precariously on the table.

"What in the world?" I jumped up, ready to slam the window closed to avoid getting soaked. But stars twinkled in a cloudless sky.

"Oh, *sit,*" Venus instructed, waving dismissively at my worry, then leaned in to whisper, "He just doesn't like to hear the truth."

"He?"

"*Zeus.* Aren't you following the conversation?"

I used two fingers to rub the spot between my eyebrows, which was starting to ache. I think it was time to stop talking about fairy godmothers and true love. "You know, really, I should get to bed. You're probably tired, too." I turned to go, but not fast enough.

Venus thrust the statue in front of me. This time it really was glowing. Warm yellow light emanated from it. I blinked and glanced at Venus the person. "What is this?"

"Touch it," she instructed. "Fairy Godmother Rule #462, under the subheading of Proving It, says, 'Use of a special object for the purposes of proving existence is acceptable. However, reanimation of inanimate objects for entertainment purposes is strongly discouraged.' Though I may be entertained by this, it's not *only* for entertainment, so I'm unlikely to get slapped on the wrist for it."

With no clue what she was talking about, but curious as all get-out, I set Zeus on the carpet, and reached out to take the glowing statue.

The moment I did, a feeling of warmth spread through me, making me feel like I was the one glowing. I hadn't felt anything like this in . . . years. Like a warm hug, it wrapped me up and pulled me close. The scent of vanilla swirled in the air.

My mother's scent.

I closed my eyes to savor it. As soon as my lids closed, a movie projected itself in my head.

My mother hauls in a box from the porch, excitement in her voice as she calls out to my father and me to come quickly.

Daddy is laughing and swinging me up in the air before Mommy even manages to slice open the lid with a knife in her shaking hand.

I know to be excited, since we've done this before, only for my dad. This time it's Mommy who pulls a book from the box full of lots of others just like it. Her first book.

With tears in her eyes, she clings to it for a minute before turning it for us to see.

On the cover is a beautiful blond lady with lots of curls that I think looks like a princess, even though Mommy told me she's really a goddess. She's holding out a present. The Gift of Venus. *I've heard the title of the book many times as my mom wrote it. I run my hands over the bumpy lettering on the cover, petting it, loving it because I love books and I know my mom loved writing this book.*

She tells Daddy she loves him, tells him their story is finally told, which I don't understand, but I don't much care because everyone is happy and smiling, and I love them so much.

Suddenly, I remember and tug on Daddy's sleeve until he leans over to let me whisper in his ear. We have a present for Mommy, for when her book came.

He puts me down and I race to the closet where we hid the present.

When Mommy tears off the bow and the silvery wrap, she starts to cry again before pulling out the statue of the silly almost-naked lady with no arms that my daddy had assured me Mommy would love, even though I thought he should find one that still had its arms.

"I'll never forget her," Mommy whispers, and I know she's talking about the goddess on the cover of her book. The goddess who introduced my mom and dad and made them fall in love.

As the movie in my head faded, I still saw the book clearly, and the pieces fell into place. As the Venus de Milo in my hands began to shake a little, I raised my eyes to the woman in front of me. The Venus my mother wrote about in her first book. The Venus my mother insisted introduced her to my father.

The Venus I never realized until right this second was very real.

❧ 5 ❧

Venus

I see the moment she gets it. And catch the statue as it slips from her fingers.

It stops glowing as I step back across the room to return the statue to the bedside table, then retreat to the attached private bathroom—no sharing this time!—giving my godchild a moment to recover.

When I've freshened up, I peek back out the door to find her still rooted to her spot.

The emotions are shooting off her like geysers, along with all the identifying info I need to know about her. Name, age. Her need for marriage that's grabby in its urgency. She's set herself a time limit through a plan she seems to put a huge amount of faith in. She wants it now, but nerves, worry, and confusion make her feel as if she's been thrown into the deep end and doesn't know how to swim.

But, I can tell . . . this one's gonna be a snap! *Wanting* my services is a step in the right direction.

Then, the next set of feelings bombards me. Pain. Sadness. *Ouch!* Peeking around the corner of the door, I try to read her.

Finding out I'm real—and that I had something to do with her parents—seems to have set off a string of emotional explosions in her, though I don't know what it's all about yet. There's this big wall of pain that hurts when she gets anywhere near it, so she stays away. And if she doesn't look behind it, I can't, either.

Which is just as well. I can tell it's way too raw. No way am I going through that again.

Rule #1000: "A fairy godmother shall protect herself at all times from becoming emotionally involved with humans . . . or suffer the consequences."

With my last godchild, I broke that rule and became way too emotionally involved. I delved too deeply into all I could see of her past, her fears, her unfulfilled desires and it had nearly been my ruin. I broke a—*the*— most important fairy godmother rule. Mostly 'cause I never read the whole rule book (how many rules did one actually *need* in a lifetime?), so I'd missed that little detail. (Which, as stated before, I will be remedying in the very near future.)

There aren't going to be consequences this time, though, because nothing like that is ever going to happen again. I'm sticking to the rule book, especially when it comes to that particular rule. I'm keeping my distance, remaining neutral, objective.

As Haydee's messy human feelings take to the disco floor of my mind, I find myself getting dizzy, sweaty with the overload. It's like a panic attack. Grabbing onto the nearby counter, I mentally slam shut the door between us.

It takes a minute before the feelings subside. My heartbeat goes back to normal. My breathing slows. Crisis averted.

Haydee's still standing by the window, staring at the ground with her arms wrapped tightly around herself. Feeling my eyes on her, she raises her gaze to meet mine. For a second she just stares at me in wonder.

And then her face blossoms into a smile.

Got 'er.

A moment later she's dashing toward the bathroom door where I'm standing. I open my arms to accept her ever-so-grateful hug . . . only to have her veer off, making a beeline out the bedroom door.

I just pretty much showed her a guarantee of my legitimacy, my absolute ability to hook her up with the guy of her dreams, and she's ditching me?

Stepping out into the room, I wait.

A moment later, she returns with a book in her hands, which she thrusts in my direction.

"That better not be some self-help book of crap," I tell her, snatching it away from her, "because I do not need any human psychologist telling me how to live my life. I'm just fine, thank you very much, and will be even finer when I get home to Mount Olympus."

There's a hot blond chick on the cover holding a brightly wrapped present.

"That's you," Haydee says, grinning brightly.

I squint down at the book, searching my brain for the memory. "Um, no. I'm pretty sure I never modeled for a book cover." However, I'm not at all opposed to this idea. Perhaps I need an agent to handle things like that for me. I turn the book over, scrutinizing it. Sure enough there's a character—a matchmaker, from the couple of sentences I force myself to read—named Venus. Huh.

"Look!" Haydee flips the book so I can read the title. "It's called *The Gift of Venus*. And it was written by Maxine Miller, my *mom*. It was the first book she had published and she wrote it about what you did for her and my dad."

Huh. A book outing my shame and humiliation as a fairy godmother? Not sure how I feel about that.

"Is this what you saw when you were holding the statue?" I ask.

Haydee nods, then frowns. "You didn't know about this? Then how did you—"

I flip my hand at her and hand her back the book before she

suggests I read the thing. I'll take her word for it. "I just imbued the statue with the ability to show you whatever you'd need to know to believe I am who I am. If you needed to remember the book, then that's what you got."

The grin she flashes is positively infectious, and I can't help but preen a little. She totally digs me. And unlike my previous, Doubting Thomas godchild, she believes in me and actually *wants* my help. Closing my eyes I envision the glistening golden skies of Mount Olympus, smell the perfume of jasmine and freesia blowing in the breeze, hear the laughter of gods and goddesses at play. I can feel home again, closer than it's been in two millennia. And this godchild is going to get me there. I just know it!

"Shall I leave you alone?"

My eyes snap open again. "No!" If she leaves, I might wake up and find it's all a dream. "Sit."

With a bounce of excitement, Haydee parks herself back in the chair by the window. Knowing her even as little as I do, I'd have to guess that chair's for reading. The stack of books on the table beside the chair might give it away. And there are more books on a bookshelf in one corner, as well as tucked into a cubby beneath the bedside table.

"So."

"So?"

"Did you really introduce my parents? I mean, that wasn't all my imagination? My mom told me that story a thousand times . . . and wrote the book about it . . . so it could just be my subconscious. And I've touched that statue"—she gestures toward its new place of honor on my nightstand—"a thousand times, and it's never done that before. I—"

"Slow down!" I suggest. It nice that she's enthusiastic, but *seriously*. I start to explain as I hang up the rest of the clothes from my suitcase. (Yay! I even have my own closet.) "I didn't really introduce them. I was just there when they met and nudged them in the right direction. Happens a lot. It's a thing with me."

"You've done this before?"

I nod, slipping a hanger into the neckline of my favorite Prada top. I go over the basics, that I'm the Goddess of Love, completely unfairly demoted to fairy godmother servitude, through no fault of my own, and now I have a quota of Love Life Makeovers to complete before I can go home, blah, blah, blah. I can tell her MBA-enhanced brain is struggling to just accept it all as fact. She *wants* to believe. "You're my, oh, upon Zeus, I'm not even sure . . . 510th, 511th . . . match? Something like that. I'm a pro. You're in very good, well-manicured hands." I wiggle my pearly painted nails at her.

Okay, yes, I'm laying it on a little thick. But after last time, I'm taking adoration where I can get it.

"Anyway, your parents were easy. I was only around a few days. When I told your mom who I was, she took me to the museum to see the statue . . . and your dad showed up. I just pointed him out so she wouldn't miss him." I settle a few hangers on the rod in the closet and space them out for maximum wrinkle prevention. "How *are* your parents?"

It's not often I get the opportunity to follow up on the fruits of my labor. See, I can hook them up, but then they're on their own. Which is kind of a downer actually. It's hard to keep up the façade of being the positive, you'll-make-it-forever kind of fairy godmother, when you know there's the possibility they might crash and burn. But I don't dwell on that when I can help it. It's probably a good thing I only occasionally see what happens to them years down the road. If I knew the real statistics of my Love Life Makeover successes to failures, I'd probably be suicidal. Unless it's a high-profile couple who end up in tabloids I eventually hit the right spot in time to read, I just have to take it that they make it. Unfortunately, if they are high-profile enough to be in the rag sheets, they're not generally in it because their future was rosy and happy.

Nothing like having it announced when all *my* good work goes to shit.

When Haydee doesn't answer right away, I turn to check her out.

She's slumped in her chair, staring at her hands clasped in her lap. "Mom died when I was sixteen," she finally tells me.

"I'm sorry." It's not like I've never lost anyone. When goddesses mingle with humans, well, let's just say not everyone is immortal.

"Thanks." She pulls her knees up and snugs her arms around them. "Dad never remarried. I don't think he has it in him to fall in love again."

Ah, a good match. One of my successes. Made successful, not by me, but by the sometimes hard work of the "Cinderella" and "Prince Charming" themselves. "They were good parents?"

"They were." Haydee rests her chin on the top of her knees. "I don't see much of my dad anymore. He bought a bait shop a few years after my mother died so we wouldn't starve. He hates everything about it. But if he hadn't bought it, he'd probably have died of a broken heart long ago."

There's more to this story, I can tell. "He doesn't live around here?"

"On the other side of town, actually."

Interesting. Daddy disapproval maybe? Her relationship with her father sounds as bad as mine. I eye her curiously. "He must be proud of you and your accomplishments, though. Your store." Some dads are proud of their kids. Speak to them for things other than criticism.

She drops her feet to the floor and stands up to adjust the

curtains. "He doesn't get out much. At all. Actually. Not much of a reader anymore, either."

"He's never been to your store?" Upon Zeus, my father couldn't stay *out* of my life.

"Can we change the subject?" Haydee asks, turning around and hugging her arms tightly around her middle. "You know I have a thousand questions to ask. Not that I want to pry, but it's not every day you get to meet a real-live goddess."

"That's because not many of us spend a great deal of time hanging out with humans." Thank Zeus. Or in my case, *don't* thank Zeus because that's exactly what I'm stuck doing.

For the next ten minutes, Haydee peppers me with questions while I cart toiletries back and forth to the bathroom and get everything arranged just so. I pause to tell her about my marriage to Hephaestus (using my most descriptive words like "boring" and "predictable," which scares her, I can tell). So I reassure her by mentioning I am better known for my own personal match with my hot God of War, Ares. Which may reassure her that I'm not going to stick her with some lame guy with perma-dirt under his nails as her Prince Charming, but makes me all sad for home.

Finally, my suitcase is empty, and I tuck it into the back of the closet, before turning to my Gucci tote bag. I almost just slip the whole thing in the closet also, but then I remember the rule book. The one I'm going to study faithfully until I find the key to being the perfect fairy godmother. I'll put it on my bedside table so I don't forget.

"What's that?"

Ever the book bug, Haydee's up from her chair and across the room before I can shove the thing back in its hiding place.

She holds out her hand and I huff out a breath before handing it to her. She won't be able to read it anyway. It's in Greek.

"This would be the chain that binds me to this primitive planet."

"They're rules."

"You can read it?" I peer over her shoulder at the Ancient Greek symbols. "In *English*?"

"Sure," she mutters distractedly.

Huh. Guess it's just Greek to me. "Fairy godmother rules," I tell her. "Courtesy of Daddy Dearest."

Haydee pages through the book for a few minutes while I ponder my pedicure. She's all but vibrating with excitement, which isn't such a bad mental massage if you ask me. I bask in the enthusiasm for a few minutes. If only I could just let Ms. Bookish read the damn thing for me. It's obviously something she'd enjoy. I've only read a hundred or so of the thousand rules . . . out of boredom, or when I feel guilty.

"What do the starred rules mean? Are they more important or something?"

Starred rules? "Let me see that." I pull the book from her hand. She leaves her finger on the page she's referring to.

" 'Rule #471,' " I read, then shove her finger out of my way, at which point I notice the barely discernible star marking this particular rule, something I don't recall seeing before. Or I did and just thought it was Zeus's scribe's lame attempt to pretty up the book so that I wouldn't heave it across the room. " 'To truly match with skill, a Fairy Godmother worth her weight will refrain from using her mental powers to in any way influence the match.' "

Surely he jests!

"You have mental powers?" Haydee asks.

"Of course I do." I slam the ridiculous book closed and cross the room to toss it in the top drawer of the dresser, sending it crashing into the box that holds another useless reminder of my previous status, the Golden Girdle. Good, I hope it crushes the thing. It caused a lot of trouble during my last Love Life Makeover, so I'm not all that eager to have anything to do with it again anytime soon.

"You're not using mental powers on me, are you?" Haydee looks worried. *Pfff*. I'm the one with reasons to worry!

"Apparently, I'm not using them on *any*one," I pout.

I can do this, right? I can keep myself in sensory silence? For a second, I'm a little shaky, then I remember that I'm going to be the best freaking fairy godmother Zeus ever made. Much as it pains me to do anything he thinks he can force me to do, I'll do it. Because I am not staying here one minute longer than I have to. If that means I follow starred rules . . .

I turn back to the dresser and stare at the closed drawer. If there's one starred rule, there are probably more, right? Perhaps if I find *all* the starred rules, they'll fit together like a puzzle, showing me the way home!

Ha! Thought he was tricking me, did he? Well, I'll show him.

I turn back to what I hope will be my very last godchild ever, my smile, I'm sure, giving away my confidence. I'll rock this makeover like I've never rocked one before. "Anything else?" I offer Haydee pleasantly.

"One last question," Haydee says, standing in the doorway, "Then I'll leave you to your beauty sleep."

Shocked, I can't help squeal in horror before dashing over to the mirror in the bathroom and peering into it. "Is it that bad? Do I need beauty sleep?" I turn my head side to side, then glare in my new godchild's direction. "What do you see that I don't? 'Cause I look pretty damn hot to me."

She laughs. "It's just an expression. Seriously. I didn't mean to scare you."

Right. Like I was really scared. I know there's nothing wrong with me. "Fine. Go on."

"So, what's the real story behind your birth? Is it true you rose from the sea foam as a full-grown adult?"

My upper lip curls on its own. I choose not to examine that particular look in the mirror. "I was not born of *anyone's* nasty old severed genitals. My father is Zeus. My mother is Dione. I was conceived the old-fashioned way." Though how my mother stood my father's domination long enough to get it on with him—

"So where'd the sea foam story come from?" Haydee questions, thankfully interrupting the disgusting direction of my thoughts. "It's pretty popular."

"Oh, puh-lease!" I wave my hand dismissively. "You think humans have the monopoly on tabloid journalism? Not a chance. It was a slow news day on Mount Olympus when somebody decided to make up 'amazing new facts about the birth of the Goddess of Love.' Everybody ate it up like it was fact, and pretty soon it was being written in history books. Sheesh."

Haydee laughs. "Well, it may not make interesting storytelling, but it's nice to know the truth." She pats the door frame. "I'll let you sleep now. 'Night."

She's barely out the door before she turns back, a worried look on her face. "Can you really do this? Find me a husband in six weeks?" She waves toward the dresser. "Even without whatever mental powers you have?"

"Don't worry," I tell her, conjuring up my most confident, serious voice. "Now that I'm here, your True Love will show up in no time. It's a gift. Well, it's mostly skill. Mostly, I *slave* to come up with the right guy. But I'm always right. Trust me. True Love is winging its way here right this very second."

Haydee laughs, relaxing a bit, and clearly dismissing the extremely serious tone of my voice. Then she shrugs. "I have no delusions that I'll find my soul mate. Besides"—she glances down at her bare toenails—"it's too messy. I'm okay not going through all that again."

She doesn't elaborate, and nothing in her expression gives away her meaning. If I could read her—

Nope! Not gonna do it. I've officially begun the Mental Powers Diet. Lose pesky pounds of emotion overnight! Free yourself from the bondage of fatty feelings and aggravating attachments to human soul-sucks. Follow the fairy godmother rules to the letter. So *there,* King Kranky Pants.

I set Haydee straight. " 'Fraid I only do True Love."

Her smile is indulgent at best, dismissive at worst. "It doesn't need to be nearly as difficult as finding true love, trust me. I mean, I want the *right* guy. Someone who wants to be a father in a couple of years. Someone I'm compatible with . . . and won't want to kick out of bed."

I rearrange a couple of perfume bottles on the lacy runner atop the bureau. "Like Patrick?" I taunt.

"Well, no . . ." She sets her mouth firmly and then nods, though she looks as if she's trying to convince herself I'm right. Which I am, so she better get used to it. "Maybe I just have to create another plan, you know. A Man Plan."

I try not to cringe at her obvious attempt at a joke. She's new at this and must be taught. And what better teacher of all things Love than me?

"Men cannot be planned," I tell her in a stern teacherlike voice. "Men are like glorious gifts to pamper and pleasure us. They come as spontaneous surprises, not because you plan for them."

"But I plan for everything in my life," Haydee protests. "I don't know how to do it any other way."

I flash her my most dynamic grin. "That's why you have me now."

↢ 6 ↣

Venus

"That's Walt Kramer," Haydee whispers into my ear. Though she's done this approximately ten times already this morning—and frequently over the past two days as she showed me the town—she scares the crap out of me anyway, and the huge coffee table book of Oregon Coast ocean views I'm holding slips out of my fingers and barely misses Zeus, the freaky furball. He's been hanging out under my feet all morning. Watching me. Staring. Almost like he's spying on me. Surely my father wouldn't . . .

No, that's just too paranoid.

Zeus the Cat doesn't appreciate the near miss. He hisses and darts out from under my feet glaring at me, as if I need his approval. He finally settles under the table with the coffee by the front desk, which I've now determined is for the customers who need caffeine in order to remain awake while browsing the boringness that is books.

I may need some of that coffee to make it through the rest of this already very long day. Why again did I agree to help her out instead of just shopping my days away until Prince Charming shows up? Oh, yeah, because I can't read her mind, so I need to spend the time getting to know her, so I hopefully won't miss Prince Charming when he arrives.

That and I must just be a glutton for punishment.

I stick my tongue out at Furball Zeus before following my god-child's gaze toward the man in question, a few rows of books away.

What I see earns her an eye roll. Also approximately the tenth of the day. "Have you been to an optometrist any time in the last decade?"

"What's wrong with *him*?" She stands on her tiptoes and waves over the top of the chest-high shelves toward the male in question. "Be with you in a few minutes, Walt." When he acknowledges her, she turns back to me and lowers her voice again. "He's a really nice guy. Owns a couple of espresso stands around town. And he has great taste in books. Loves mythology. In fact . . . can I tell him who you—"

"No!" I hiss. "You may not reveal my identity to anyone. Can you imagine the media circus if this boring town figures out I'm here? And what's wrong with him is that he's a hundred years old."

"No way! He's fifty at the most."

"Fifty. Fifty *thousand*. There's barely a difference."

I shove the book onto the shelf, not really caring whether it's in alphabetical order or not. I'm not too sure how this whole Working Girl thing is going to, uh, *work* for me.

I've spent the day learning the routine, which basically consists of vacuuming, dusting, and lugging obscenely heavy boxes around the store (quite the feat in stilettos, let me just say, but sensible shoes are not my style) to shove books on shelves in an obsessively organized manner . . . and listening to Haydee recite the pros of all the men who come into the store. (Did I mention the lack of "hot" guys in this town? Apparently they all migrated inland.) Since none of them are "it," I simply tell her what the cons are. She accuses me of being too picky. I tell her she's not appreciating the matchmaking process.

"Isn't a fairy godmother supposed to take the guy I choose and make him fall for me?" Haydee questions.

I snort and reach for the next book. "You're kidding, right?" When a glance in her direction indicates that, no, she isn't kidding at all, I treat her to another eye roll. "True Love is much more complex and scientific."

"I told you I don't need true love." Haydee pulls off the shelf the book I just filed, and refiles it three books over . . . sheesh, like a customer looking in that general spot wouldn't have noticed it three books away. Surely if they're smart enough to read, they're smart enough to open up their eyes and do a little searching to find the book they want. "I need a guy with intelligence. Business skills are good. Did I mention Walt owns coffee shops?"

"If you want a coffee shop so badly, put one in here."

Filing a stack of three books at a time (showing off, I call it), Haydee looks startled, then contemplates the store thoughtfully. "Huh. I wrote in The Plan that I'd expand the bookstore someday . . ."

"What are you waiting for?" I interrupt. "An engraved invitation?"

"No. I just . . . there are other things on the list first."

So she puts her entire life on hold while she waits for the next item on the list to come due?

"Speaking of *The Plan*," she swings the conversation back around very pointedly, "we've been at this for two days already, and I haven't even had one single date. We let a whole weekend get away from us."

"Dates don't matter. Dates don't make matches. *I* make matches. You can't treat this frivolously," I insist, when I notice she doesn't believe me. "And you sure as Hades can't just pick any old guy off the street." I catch a glimpse of Mr. Wrong the Tenth, as he moves on to another aisle. When he catches my eye over the top of the shelves, he winks. Geez. "And seriously, couldn't you at least offer suggestions that don't threaten to burn my retinas? I may as well at least enjoy the view while I'm telling you you're wrong."

Haydee looks frustrated, but she can't be half as frustrated as I am. We're barely two days into this, and she's putting far too much effort into being difficult. All she has to do is let me do my job and follow my instructions exactly. Without arguing. And quickly. Then everyone will get along just fine. But no, she's gotta remind me every five minutes of her stupid deadline, just in case I've forgotten the urgency here. However, she isn't nearly as eager to get married as I am to go home.

"It's kind of like displaying books," I say, taking a break to dig into the M&M's I made her buy me this weekend. I wave toward the window display, still gorgeously filled with depictions of *moi*. "You don't display the boring and blah . . . you display the eye-catching and ogle-worthy. Same with men. You have to at least make an attempt at the hot ones . . . unless it's for duty instead of True Love, then it really doesn't make a difference one way or another. I mean, Prince Charles wasn't exactly Mr. Hunky Prince. But he and Di hooked up for duty, not True Love."

Haydee stares. "You matched *them*?" At my nod, her jaw drops. "They divorced! What kind of dysfunctional fairy godmother are you? I may not be holding out for true love, but I certainly don't want to become one of Nita's clients."

I have no idea who Nita is, but it doesn't really matter. "Well, I can't hang with my godchildren forever. Even True Love has its limits. Once I'm gone, it's up to them to put some effort into it."

"Well, see, that makes it even less important to find true love, right? I mean, all I really need is a guy who's committed to marriage, not necessarily looking for his soul mate," Haydee says. "It's more about dedication than attraction or emotion. The guy just needs to be willing to commit to a family, have good hygiene, and be kind to children and animals."

"Sounds like you're trying to convince yourself Patrick's the right guy."

"I'm not," she protests. "I know Patrick's not Mr. Right, which is why I need to find the right guy, not stand around waiting for 'true love' to waltz in the door."

Sigh. She just doesn't get it. Haydee is a True Love-r whether she wants to believe it or not. Most normal people are. But she's not going to get it until it shows up and bites her in the ass . . . or grabs her in the heart, as the case may be.

"Just stick to what you do best," I recommend, dismissing her to deal with her customer. "Books. Go play with your books and leave the matchmaking to me."

Usually I'm all about patience. Okay, not *always,* but most of the time I have the utmost confidence, if not enthusiasm, in the process of Extreme Love Life Makeovers. I show up, dazzle my godchild with my fairy godmotheriness (or at least browbeat them until they accept I am who I am), and then the Prince shows up and we get the show on the road.

However, by the middle of my third day in town, I feel that patience is overrated. Maybe because I've never actually had to hold a job while waiting for the process to work. Here I am, busting my bodacious booty, and the only males who have walked in the door have been candidates for the reject list. Not that Haydee hasn't done her darnedest to convince me that each one of them is sure to be The One.

My stomach lets out a very un-goddesslike growl. The clock on the wall only says eleven a.m., and I just had the package of M&M's, but I would never have been expected to endure hunger pangs as the Goddess of Love, and I have no intention of doing so as a volunteer bookstore employee.

Unfortunately, Haydee's trying to catch the eye of Walt the Coffee Guy and obviously can't be left alone. Without thinking, I send a little mental nudge across the room to Waltie Boy. Suddenly the hots he feels for the cute blonde he works with are irresistible. Once I see his expression change from paying attention to Haydee to thinking about someone else entirely, I know I'm good to go.

"I'm taking lunch," I call out to Haydee, after making sure she's still keeping a respectable distance from Mr. No-Way-In-Hades, though the chances of him paying her the slightest romantic attention are now slim to none.

She glares over at me like I've interrupted something important, and I return the glare right back, before suddenly remembering I wasn't supposed to use my mental powers.

Blast!

Does that rule apply only to using the powers to read my godchild or any mental powers . . . even if they affect the makeover only indirectly? I mean, Prince Charming can't change—he is who he is. Right? It's not like I choose based on my personal preferences or anything. It's preordained. So I didn't screw up anything.

It's a little late to worry about that now, says that little voice in the back of my brain. I think she's called a conscience, and I wish she'd shut up.

I practically hit the sidewalk running, half wanting to leave the scene of the possible crime and half from hunger. There was nothing in Haydee's damn house to eat this morning. Her nutritional habits are atrocious, as far as I'm concerned. TV dinners, Pop-Tarts, Cheetos, and Snapple seem to be her four major food groups. At the rate I'm going, I'll have to resort to panhandling to fend off starvation. Thankfully, I have a few dollars left over from the last makeover, when a very generous dot-com millionaire showered me with cash.

A few doors down from the bookstore is a small café. Pretending I'm not so hungry I'd actually be willing to eat the paper the menu is printed on, I peruse the offerings taped to the inside of the front door. There's a picture of some kind of pasta with cream sauce. It doesn't appear exactly five-star, but it's probably palatable. Bander is sadly lacking in classy restaurants, so beggars can't be choosers.

While I wait for the flirty waiter to bring me the plate o' carbs that will get me through the rest of the day, I pull out the Fairy Godmother Rule Book and open it on the table. I told you I would read it. However, after reading myself to sleep for the last two nights—finding most of the rules just a bunch of blah, blah, blah baloney, with no more starred rules in sight—it's hard to work up the enthusiasm to trudge through this crap again. Zeus—the god, not the cat—had to have been high when he wrote this trash, and so far I've found no magic formula for bringing this all to a glorious conclusion, ending with my triumphant return to Mount Olympus.

Rule #284, for instance, "Soliciting help from visiting deities is strictly forbidden and will result in starting the sentence over again."

I'm convinced this rule is just to tease, giving me false hope that one of my old pals might show up and break up the monotony of Earth life. That has *so* never happened in all these years. I've gone from the clear favorite goddess to social suicide apparently, considering I haven't seen a soul from Mount Olympus in two millennia. Not that I'd have broken the rule if someone did show up here to bail me out right this very second. No way was I taking the risk of starting this shit all over again.

The waiter arrives and plops down a steaming plate of noodles, creamy sauce, and knobs of mushrooms, with a side of crispy garlic bread.

"Can I get you anything else, pretty lady?"

He's a cutie I wouldn't mind having for dessert, but I'm on a mission. Food. Then study.

"No, thank you," I tell him, even as he's shoving a piece of paper into my hand. There's a phone number on it. By the time I look up from it, he's moving away, throwing a wink over his shoulder at me.

Well, maybe later. I tuck the slip of paper into my handbag then turn to my lunch, which reminds me how starving I am. My mouth waters a little when I poke at the plate with my fork. The noodles slither around the dish without enthusiasm. I know exactly how they feel. But they just have to buck up and accept their sentence. I have to. Learning this rule book isn't exactly my idea of fun, but I'm doing it. No thanks to my godchild, who seems to think she can do a better job than I can at finding a man. As if!

You know, if there was such a thing as a *godchild* rule book, one that starts off with "A godchild must listen and obey their Fairy Godmother without question," I wouldn't have half the trouble I have getting the job done.

In an attempt to make the pasta more palatable, I sprinkle it with a handful of M&M's, which immediately start melting on the hot noodles, creating tiny rainbow rivers flowing through the cream sauce. Forking up a mouthful, I close my eyes and let the flavors have their way with my tongue. Pretty dang good. Not that it makes up for my plight in life, but at least my stomach lining will stop eating itself in an attempt to ward off starvation.

A half hour later, I've eaten all I can and believe I might make it through the day without passing out. No thanks to my slave-driving hostess/boss. And I have dedicated my lunchtime to pretending to be the best fairy godmother I can be. Maybe if it looks like I'm making an effort, Zeus will have mercy on me.

Probably not. I was a fabulous *goddess* and he didn't give a flying fig. Why would he start now?

I read until my eyes lose focus and learn nothing. I slam the book closed crankily, only to have the cover flop back open, its leather binding flimsy from two thousand years of being lugged around. Rule #1 catches my eye, and I snort out loud. "Zeus is the ruler of all gods and goddesses, all powerful, supreme being, and don't you forget it."

Ha! The Titans should have remained in power. Surely they'd not have tried to stifle my growth and creativity just because I no longer continued to naïvely believe Daddy knows best. Perhaps a campaign will be in order when I return to Mount Olympus . . .

But right now I have other more important things to obsess about. I have to make sure Haydee doesn't do something stupid. I actually had to tackle her once yesterday to keep her from asking one of her customers out on a date! Just my luck, her perfect match will show up while she's flirting with Mr.-Wrong-in-More-Ways-Than-One.

Which reminds me of my possible rule breakage. Crap.

Still, I made it through my lunch without choking to death. If I was wrong to give Walt the gift of my innumerable charms, then Zeus would have let me know, right? Broken the heel on my Choos? Chipped a nail? Struck me with lightning?

Something feels off when I get back to the store.

When I turn around from stashing my purse and tote bag in the closet, Haydee's waiting for me . . . grinning mischievously.

"What?"

"You might just be good luck after all."

I move past her out into the store, refraining from rolling my emerald eyes. "Of course, I am. I believe I've mentioned that."

"Well, your fairy godmother charm is working. I have a date tonight."

Aaaannnnd . . . the lightning strikes.

7

Haydee

My frustration level was building. Okay, I admit that Walt Kramer probably wasn't the right guy for me. Something about dating a guy almost as old as my dad did kind of give me the creeps. In the last three days we'd crossed paths with plenty of men who would have been just fine. But, oh *no*. Venus found flaws in every one of them.

How was I supposed to make any progress if she wouldn't let me go out with any of them? If things didn't change, I supposed I'd have to take matters into my own hands, Goddess of Love or no.

Which was why I made a date with Conner Edstrom. He was a sheriff's deputy I'd known for years. Tall and athletic, I'd actually always thought he was pretty cute.

Venus took all of this with about as much enthusiasm as I'd expected. "That's not fair!" she'd shouted, though it seemed she was addressing God (Zeus?) or someone, shaking her fists in the air.

Then she'd forbidden me to go through with it. Then she'd threatened to cancel our agreement, which I pointed out wouldn't matter, if Conner and I were a match made in heaven. So then she'd gotten all smug and said, fine, I could do as I pleased, but she would uphold her end of the deal and we'd just see who came out the victor.

"Who *is* that?" My friend Joan appeared at the bottom of the stairs and stabbed a thumb back up toward the main part of the store, where I'd left Venus with strict instructions to call me if she needed me.

Considering there couldn't be that many people up there, since the chimes had only gone off a few times in the last half hour, she had to be talking about Venus. "My new *temporary* employee." I emphasized the part of the description I thought would most make up for whatever transgressions Venus had managed to commit. "Why? What'd she do?"

"Other than trying to sell me a copy of every single book on Aphrodite that you probably have in the store, not much."

"Hey, at least she tried to sell something," I joked. "This morning all she wanted to do was nap."

"You're not keeping her, right? She's going to mess up the chi in here. You know what she was doing when I got here? Tossing pennies from the cash register into the water element!"

A feng shui expert, Joan Forza took her water elements very seriously. As well as her earth, wind, and fire elements. I indulged her, letting her hang spirit-banishing mirrors and install water elements because she was my friend, and her design ideas were as attractive as she was in her own bohemian, free-spirit kind of way.

"Where'd you find her? Off the street?" she continued.

Kind of. "Of course not. She came into the store and was . . . very interested in mythology." Not really a lie.

Joan closed her eyes and took a cleansing breath. Realigning her chakras or whatever it was she did. She was an odd duck, but we somehow meshed. Though she'd lived in Bander her whole life, as I had, Joan was several years older, so we hadn't really known each other until I came back to town to open the store seven years ago. After a few friendly chats, we'd progressed to meeting for coffee. And our friendship took off from there.

A moment later Joan opened her eyes again, appearing calmer. "I sent good thoughts into the Universe."

"I can use all the help I can get." I slid a couple more books into their proper places on the shelves, turning a few others face-out to see if I could get them moving out the door, and then decided to just take the leap. My friends had to find out soon enough. Hopefully Joan would take my new life-direction better than Nita would. "So," I started, digging in the box for the next few books to shelve. "Venus is also a, uh, matchmaker."

Joan's eyes grew wide. "Really? You're going to start dating?"

I shrugged. "You know, biological clock and all." Not really, but now wasn't the time to give her the real explanation.

"It's about time!" Joan grabbed my arm. "Have you told Nita? She's going to be so furious."

"You don't have to be so happy about that," I laughingly scolded. "She's going to complain to you as much as to me." And complain she would. Nita Yang, my college roommate and the third of our Three Musketeers–like trio, had every reason to be discouraged about men, seeing as how she'd had the marriage from hell, followed by a divorce marked by a stalker ex and restraining orders. She'd moved to Bander to leave her ex behind in Portland . . . and for the support, though she'd be the last to admit she was "weak" enough to need support.

"What made you finally get on the ball?" Joan plopped down on the bottom step, settling in for a lunch-hour gossip session. "Not that you need a reason. It's about time."

"Frankly?" Or as frankly as I planned on getting. I'd just stick to what convinced me, not what brought it up in the first place. Nita knew about The Plan, having been around in college to pick up the pieces when I'd suffered a brief lapse in judgment and deviated from the path of The Plan. But it had never come up with Joan. I wasn't sure how she'd take it, being all about going with the flow and everything. "You and Hoop changed my mind. And Bull and Rose. My dad. Nita."

She raised her eyebrows. "I follow the reasoning behind the first two since we're pretty adorable couples. But your dad and *Nita* as arguments for dating? I don't follow."

"I don't want to turn out like them. The rest of you are all happy." Bull and Rose owned The Gull, our favorite bar. They'd been married a thousand years and still glowed when they looked at each other. "I don't want to be sad my whole life like my dad. Or angry my whole life like Nita. I want to be happy. Like you and Hoop are."

"Don't blame you there." She flashed the grin of a well-kept wife, and we both laughed.

"The problem is, I have no idea in the world how to go about it. Bander isn't exactly a hotbed of eligible bachelors." At least not that I apparently had the skill to pick out, according to Venus.

Joan pressed her lips together a minute, then took the plunge. "What about Patrick? Really, you know hurting Bear was an accident."

"Of course I know that." I shelved a few more books with my back to my friend, not wanting her to read too much into whatever she saw in my face, as was her tendency. "I just—" I turned around to face her. "Did you settle for Hoop? Or did you know that he was The One?" I knew the answer to this question. I saw it in their eyes every time they looked at one another.

Joan raised her hands in surrender. "Point taken." Then her gaze softened. "I just want you to be sure. Patrick's a great guy. I just thought maybe giving him another chance—"

"Won't work. Trust me." Maybe if Joan trusted me I'd be able to more easily trust myself. "Anyway, Venus has a . . . matchmaking business. We sorta bartered." Which I really hoped I wasn't going to regret, since, even though she'd apparently hooked my parents up, I wasn't seeing a lot of promise in Venus's matchmaking skills. At the rate her pessimistic side had her rejecting whatever prospects I put in front of her, I'd be out of Bander men to choose from by nightfall. Which left me only strangers who happened through town or vacationers who showed up in the next few weeks as tourist season heated up. I wanted someone local. Someone who'd stick around the town I loved. It could take years for someone to show up that Venus approved of.

And I had six weeks, two days . . . and some-odd hours.

Though if Conner worked out . . .

Joan reached out and snatched the book out of my fingers as one of the covers creased under my tense grip. "How's the southwest corner of your house?"

"What?" Abrupt subject changes were Joan's specialty.

"I'll come over and check out your house's energy and see what we can do to attract love. The southwest corner is your love corner. And how about your bed . . . your feet don't point to the door do they?"

Torn between laughing off Joan's crazy ideas and accepting all the help I could get, I finally decided to go for the latter. "No, my feet do not point to the door. Should they?"

"No." She thought a minute. "I'll come over tomorrow night. You call Nita and order pizza, and I'll bring everything you need. We'll get your house ready for your new man. And Hoop and I can wrack our brains for potential husbands. There's got to be someone in this town."

I didn't even have a second to comment before she was up off the step with a glance at her watch. "Lunch hour's over. The mayor has a meeting in forty-five minutes, and if I'm not there to remind him, he'll blow it off to practice his putting."

With barely a wave, she was up the stairs, only to turn around once more at the top. "Plan on seven, okay? That'll give me time to throw mac 'n cheese in for the kids and Hoop. And I want anchovies on my half of the pizza!"

Shaking my head at my crazy friend as she left the store, I followed her upstairs with my empty box. Where my *new* friend, who was really a whole different kind of crazy, was staring at the ceiling.

I followed her gaze but saw nothing. Just the same old ceiling that had always been there.

"What're you looking at?"

Venus held up one finger and then tilted her head this way and that, eyes narrowed like she was listening for something.

Finally she relaxed and nodded. "He's coming."

Okay. "Who?"

"Him."

With no further explanation, she wandered back over to the mirror and began rearranging curls, which really didn't look any different after rearranging than they had before. But she appeared to be satisfied with whatever adjustment she'd made, since she then grinned broadly at her reflection and blew it a kiss.

"You'll really have to be more specific," I called over my shoulder to her as I went to the backroom to break down the box and put it in the recycling bin. " 'Him' covers a lot of territory."

"Him," she insisted, following me. "Prince Charming. The *One*."

I laughed. "You can sense him coming? The way animals sense earthquakes or birds sense when it's time to migrate?"

"Are you insulting me?"

"No." I deposited the flattened box in the proper receptacle and turned to face her. "It's just a little implausible, isn't it? That you can just tell when the man of my dreams is going to show up?"

"Who's the professional here? You or me?"

Did I have to answer that honestly? The more I got to know Venus, with her cynical dismissal of every man I might have chosen to get to know better in the past few days, the more I wondered if whatever Venus may have done to get my parents together was more of a coincidence of proximity and timing than true supernatural matchmaking skills. Maybe they would have met and my dad would have asked my mom out without Venus's influence.

Suddenly it occurred to me. "You're just saying this because I made a date with Conner, aren't you?"

"*Pfff!* I canceled that a half hour ago."

"*What?*"

"Don't worry about it," she dismissed my outrage. "In ten minutes it won't matter anyway." She grabbed my arm and pulled me out of the chair, yanking me around to face away from her. "Make use of the bathroom mirror, and fix your face. And your hair while you're at it. Sex up, girl!"

Still sputtering, I slammed the bathroom door between us, if only to give myself a few minutes to calm down. She'd canceled my date! How could someone be so infuriating? And how did she manage to match anyone at all, let alone five-hundred-some couples?

It took all of five minutes to pretend to follow Venus's directions to "sex up." She might be disappointed at the results, or lack thereof, but I'd managed to get a date with Conner without a complete makeover, so surely if "The One" really did show up today, I'd be just fine.

Giving myself one last look-over, I sighed, feeling a little calmer, not so ready to murder my fairy godmother, and left the bathroom. I'd just call Conner back and apologize for my employee's prank phone call and we'd go out as planned. There was nothing a little explaining couldn't repair.

"It's about time," she snapped impatiently from her perch on the corner of the office desk, dangling a spiky sandal from one perfectly pedicured toe, and giving it what was probably considered a sexy little flip. "The doorbells chimed five minutes ago."

"Why aren't *you* out there?" Good thing she wasn't a permanent employee.

"It's for you."

Narrowing my eyes I stared at her suspiciously. It was probably Mrs. McMurtrey, my next-door neighbor, again. She'd come in Friday afternoon to buy the latest Rachael Ray book, because she needed some new recipes. Instead, since I was busy with another customer, Venus tried to sell her a book on tantric sex, after which very religious Mrs. M had smacked Venus with her purse and threatened to call the police. Venus haughtily informed me that she refused to wait on the "old biddy" again and that she smelled like cabbage. I'd sent Venus to the backroom, because I don't do anything to anger Mrs. M. She feeds me with all that Rachael Ray–inspired food, and I wanted to keep it that way.

"You didn't piss her off again, did you?" I guessed now, pushing past Venus into the store, praying I could repair the damage. I had enough worries right now without the fear that I'd starve to death without Mrs. McMurtrey's home cooking.

The store appeared empty at first glance. Typical of this time of day. Lunch hour was over and midafternoon was beach time for most tourists. I was just about to turn back to scold Venus for losing a customer when I spotted him.

He stood on the deck outside the open French doors, his head tilted back as if sniffing the air. His hair was shorter, a little bit spikier, like his world-traveler life had netted him some style. I knew when he turned around his jaw would still be square, his cheeks just a little rough, and his eyes the color of the Pacific Ocean on a sunny day. And he'd smell like pine-scented soap or wintergreen gum.

He wore a dark T-shirt, his bare arms more muscular than before, probably from climbing mountains or hanging from the wings of planes flying over herds of elephants in Botswana to get that illusive shot no one else had ever scored. He braced his hands at the waistband of his cargo pants, the pockets of which would be filled with cameras and spare lenses, his wallet, his cell phone, the lucky silver sand dollar I'd—

No. He wouldn't carry that anymore. Just like I didn't carry the bit of luck he'd once unknowingly given me.

My hand went to my side, remembering, but only briefly.

I couldn't believe it was him. Standing in *my* store. Thinking it was okay to waltz back into *my* life.

Wait a minute.

My head snapped around toward the door to the backroom, where Venus was obviously hiding out. Making sure *I* was the one to greet this customer.

Oh. *Hell*. No.

This was who Venus meant by *him*? Prince Charming? *The One*?

Her matchmaker—and Goddess of Love—license should be revoked immediately.

Derek Reed couldn't be *anything* for me.

Except maybe a target should I take up archery.

It didn't matter what kind of fate or goddess stepped in to say otherwise. It was simply not going to happen.

I started to turn away, to go back to the stockroom to tell Venus to take it back. To tell her that her goddess sense was short-circuiting or something. But just as I did, the front door opened, its chimes going off as a customer entered.

Derek turned toward the sound just before I did, our eyes meeting briefly before I yanked mine away and turned my back on him.

"Patrick!" I greeted my contingency plan with far more enthusiasm than I'd ever shown before, forgetting to hold my breath in the process. As a whiff of doggy disinfectant punched me in the nose, I accepted Patrick's usual casual embrace, but this time didn't turn my head when he kissed me.

It was a toss-up which of us was more startled when our lips met.

Before either of us could react, though, and before I could see whether Patrick's affection had had any effect on Derek Reed, the door opened again, and a group of local high schoolers burst in, laughing and chatting, and carrying frosty Frappuccinos. I stepped away like I'd been caught doing something I shouldn't.

Which I had been, though not for the expected reason.

Before I had barely a second to acknowledge that the latest graphic novels they wanted were on the back wall, another group of customers came in. Tourists, who just wanted to browse. After distractedly advising them to ask if they had questions, I located Patrick, with every intention of using him as my lifeline to keep me far away from Derek.

But Venus had already snagged him. *Now* she decided to be a model employee?

"What may I help you find?" she asked Patrick, leaning over the front counter to use her cleavage to optimal advantage. I'd have to mention to her later that we weren't *that* kind of bookstore.

Pointedly ignoring the elephant I could see from the corner of my eye, now standing near the French doors, I intervened. "I've got this one, Venus." Turning to Patrick I oozed charm like I'd never oozed it before, well aware that I'd probably scare the guy to death since I'd made it clear I thought of him only as a friend for most of the last year. "What can I help you with? Cesar's latest is in now. Or maybe this great joke book I found about cats yesterday. Venus doesn't think it's so amusing but—"

"But don't you have *another* customer?" Venus butted in, twitching her head forcefully in Derek's direction.

"Not at all," I stated pleasantly but firmly, maintaining eye contact with Patrick. "Patrick's a very loyal customer."

"We met the other day, didn't we?" Patrick stuck a hand out to Venus, looking a little awestruck. Well, she wasn't Bander's typical woman. She practically sparkled. Who could blame him?

Dragging his eyes away from her with what seemed like some effort, he turned back to me and flashed a smile. "What was that all about?" he asked, leaning toward me, until I was forced to stop breathing after all.

Why was this so hard? In two seconds I could solve all my problems, including the one who'd just walked in the door after almost thirteen years. All I had to do was tell Patrick I was ready. That I'd marry him. That I'd get used to the smell, and the memory of him running over my dog and then ultimately administering the fatal injection would fade.

I returned what I hoped looked like a sincere smile, while my heart tried to leap out of my chest to get at Derek Reed.

Who was. *So*. Not. The One.

"It's not really a good time to talk right now." I couldn't meet his eyes.

"Okay, we don't have to talk now." Patrick leaned in even closer. "Though maybe we could try it again when things are a bit more private." He straightened and nodded over my shoulder, then raised a friendly hand in greeting at Derek. "And he was here before me."

Yes, he was. In more ways than one.

Venus pranced around the counter, fluffing her hair as she came. "Do you want to show me your favorite book?" she cooed, making it sound like a sordid invitation.

"You don't even like books," I hissed, getting edgier by the moment. I could feel Derek's eyes on me, and I tugged my shirt over my waistband. The last thing I needed was for him to notice the tattoo I'd used to preserve the memory of that last disastrous summer.

Venus's gaze darted over my shoulder, and I could tell Derek must be coming closer. I didn't know why he was here, and I didn't care.

I really didn't.

But there was no way I could remove Venus and reclaim Patrick without making a fool of myself.

"Haydee?"

Giving myself up to my fate, I turned very slowly, drawing as much air into my lungs as I could without it being obvious that I might pass out.

Wishing I was a better actress, I feigned surprise that probably fooled no one. "Derek. When did you get back in town?"

"Yesterday."

Yesterday? And I hadn't noticed? Felt a change in the atmospheric pressure? Experienced an allergic reaction?

His smile, so broad it crinkled the corners of his eyes, threatened to undo me, but I kept it together. I'd fallen for that once before. "How nice for you." Tossing a glare in Venus and Patrick's direction, I grasped for something to get me away from Derek. "The photography section is downstairs to the left, near the windows. Feel free to browse."

Before I could dismiss him by stepping away, Derek reached out and snagged my hand. "I didn't come for books, Hades."

I jerked my hand from his grasp. It felt like it was on fire. "Don't call me that." Pet names were for people you were close to. Derek no long fit that description.

And I had no desire to be reminded he'd once found me hot as Hades. For one summer anyway.

"I came back for you."

I laughed. "Right. After thirteen years of chasing down the world's most exciting wildlife, you suddenly thought Bander would give you a bigger thrill?"

"Not Bander." He stepped closer, surrounding me with the scent of pine, just liked I remembered. "You."

My laugh of disbelief was no more than a weak puff of air. "The last time you were here 'for me,' you pledged your undying love and then rode off into the sunset for a life more exciting." I stepped away from the heat of his body. "Forgive me if I don't put much stock in your devotion."

Giving him my back, I stalked across the room to where Venus was flirting outrageously with my contingency plan, who had just risen astronomically in my estimation. Anyone . . . *anyone* was a better choice than Derek Reed.

I snatched away the phone Venus was holding. "I'm going to call Conner back and uncancel our date."

I stalked back past Derek without making eye contact and slammed the stockroom door behind me.

8

Venus

"What kind of fairy godmother *are* you?"

She throws her hands into the air to make her point, and I spot some kind of tattoo along her left side just at her waistband. Ooh, the girl has a wild side. I'll have to ask about it.

She spins around, nearly knocking me out with her right hook. Maybe I'll ask when she's feeling less violent. Now probably isn't the time to discuss her wild side. She might ask it to come out to play, and frankly I'm a little scared of her at the moment.

"He is *not* the right guy for me," she continues depositing the day's loot in the safe and spinning the lock. "The gay butcher is more right for me than Derek is!"

"I think you need to calm down," I tell her, dropping onto the desk chair and crossing my slender ankles out in front of me. The rule book is open on the desk, where I've been studying it whenever I have the chance. I rock, don't I? "Tell me all about Prince Charming."

"He is *not* Prince Charming."

Rage looks good on her. I should tell her to use that to make her man hot.

Maybe later.

"I understand that you think that to be the case." I can give her that. "But right here"—I tap the appropriate page—"Rule #613, subheading 'Regarding Prince Charming,' says, 'Once Prince

Charming has been intuited, no pressure from Cinderella or any other outside force shall influence the Fairy Godmother to deviate from the match.' In other words, I'm right and you're wrong." I look up at her, so proud of myself I can hardly stand it. "I'm really glad I decided to read this thing. I feel myself becoming a better fairy godmother with every page."

Haydee closes her eyes and breathes in and out. In and out. In. And. Out.

Ah, she's finally coming around to my point of view. Facing her mistaken beliefs will help her understand how right I am.

"You are completely and utterly wrong."

Or maybe not. "*Why* am I wrong?" Any answers she gives I can shoot down with my goddess prowess.

She opens her eyes. "You just are."

When she turns to leave the room to close up for the night, I follow her. "Hey! You can't leave it at that! I can't argue without anything to argue against." I slam the book closed and scoop it into my handbag.

"There's nothing to argue about." Her voice is the definition of utter calm, as she removes the stupid cat from the counter and deposits him in his carrier for the trip home. I resist the urge to kick his smug little face as he stares at me from behind the bars. If I didn't know better, I'd think there was a Mount Olympus spy among us.

"Yes, there is something to argue about," I tell her, tripping down the stairs behind her on the balls of my feet to keep from falling on my face. Stilettos and stairs are a deadly combination. "That guy *is* your prince . . . what's his name anyway?" If she wasn't giving off emotions like a heat wave behind that mask she's wearing, I'd be tempted to peek to get the answer myself. But I'm not about to fall off the Mental Powers Diet and leave myself open to disaster again.

"Derek."

"Derek what?"

"Derek-it-ain't-going-to-happen-even-if-Hell-freezes-over-Reed." She emphasizes the finality of her words by letting go of the cord she holds, effectively slamming the room-darkening shade over the sliding door that opens out to a patio beneath the upper-floor deck. "You may as well give up now. Because I will never date him in a million years . . . let alone do anything else with him."

Using my super deductive powers, I try to figure out what she means by that. *Never* never? Or just-until-I-talk-her-into-it never?

"He's exactly what you need," I tell her, following her back up the stairs, though she tries to stop me by turning off the light before I make it to the bottom step, and I almost do a face plant tripping over a stack of books on the floor. "He clearly gets you hot and bothered . . . and that's a good thing." Kicking the stack to the side, I manage to make it most of the way up the steps before she turns off the stairwell light also. Stubborn little— "You need to trust me."

"Ha! I trust you less and less every minute I know you," she shoots back. "Anyway, didn't you say you matched up Britney and Kevin?"

"Yes."

"Well, wasn't *that* just a train wreck?"

"Sarcasm isn't very attractive."

"You should know."

That's fair. Sarcasm *is* one of my favorite traits. I just don't like it in my godchildren.

"Remember your parents?" I have to get her back on track to trusting me. "I told your mother he was The One, she believed me, and they were deliriously happy."

"Yes, they were," she admits, opening the front door and allowing me to leave before her while she collects the cat carrier. She works the key in the lock before turning back to me. "But Derek's not staying in Bander," she says, "whether you want him to be my Prince Charming or not. Not that I'd start anything with him, anyway, even if he planted himself and grew roots. He's a nationally celebrated photographer, who goes where the action is. He lives for spur-of-the-moment dashes across the world. Bander isn't exactly the action capital of the world."

I can't argue that point. This place is standing so still I'm surprised ivy hasn't overgrown everything in town by now. Haydee keeps telling me to wait a month until tourist season really gets going, but I have my doubts.

We begin the walk home. How in Zeus's name she talked me into walking to work today, I'll never know.

"The thing is," I steer her toward more relevant topics as we stroll down Main Street, where I keep an eye out for shopping ops, "even if Derek doesn't plan to stay, that doesn't mean he's not the right guy for you. You can leave, you know. Planes, trains, and automobiles have made it much more possible to move freely about the country, and even the world, these days."

My sarcasm earns me a sharp look. "I can't just leave. I have a store. I have The Plan. I don't need to wonder constantly when my husband is going to get antsy and take off to parts unknown. I won't be dragged around the world on someone else's whim."

"How'd you two meet anyway?" I'm getting nowhere with the debate about going or staying, so I may as well change the subject and gather some info that may help me in the future. See? *Totally* not breaking my diet. I rock in the willpower department!

After pausing for so long I'm beginning to think this will remain a forbidden topic, my godchild finally speaks again. "We met in high school."

Then silence.

During which we walk another block and a half.

"Wow. Riveting story, Haydee. I can hardly stand the suspense."

"Ha. Ha."

Momentarily distracted by a possible place for purchases, I dodged around some workmen hauling shelving units into a building and dart toward the door of the establishment next door. Only to be yanked back by the purse strap by Haydee.

She points at the items in the front window. "It's a souvenir shop. For tourists. That's all they carry." She indicates a neon green T-shirt that says "My family went to Bander and all I got was this crappy T-shirt."

"Warning noted and appreciated." I shudder at the thought of actually wearing some low-class piece of trash such as that.

Goddesses do not wear cheesy T-shirts bearing iron-ons.

"So, *anyway*." Any more pointed than that and I'll stab someone. "You were saying?"

Haydee sighs. "We met in high school. I was a junior, and my mom had recently died . . . and I wasn't doing very well. My dad was kind of . . . unavailable, so I didn't have anyone to talk to. My friends were uncomfortable, unsure what to say, I guess, so they chose not to say anything. Not that they could find me."

"You ran away?"

"I hid. In the school library mostly."

"Why not somewhere interesting?" I scold. "Like the boys' locker room."

"Are you going to listen to my story or try to change history?"

"Fine," I grouse. "Tell it your way. Oh! But hold that thought.

This is more my style." I tug her into a darling little boutique store with nary an iron-on in sight.

"What are you doing?" Haydee asks when I give a little squeal of delight and head across the store toward my prey, er, the man who's going to fund my shopping trip.

"Plumping up my wardrobe," I say over my shoulder, then sidle up next to a distinguished-looking gentleman who practically reeks of wealth. "What's a nice guy like you doing in a beach of a town like this?" I purr. I haven't had a shopping fix in days—much longer if you count the lost time before I finally got to leave Cameron Creek after my last Love Life Makeover fiasco. I wasn't in any condition for retail therapy at that point.

"Venus, you can't—"

"Why, aren't you just a sparkly young thing?" My new friend leans in toward me, as his eyes cut left and right, as if checking for the little woman. Seemingly satisfied she's not around to take his head off for flirting, he gives his eyebrows a couple flicks upward, the universal signal for lechers the world over, then strokes his finger along the bare skin above my V neckline, catching some flecks of glitter I don't remember applying. "You really don't need that glitter to shine in my eyes."

"Ah, I'm in love."

"*Venus.*" Haydee grabs my arm and tries to drag me away. "What do you think you're doing?"

"I told you," I reply with a frown, a little miffed at having my one-man admiration society interrupted. "Plumping up my wardrobe. You may have all the money *you* want, but us displaced goddesses don't exactly have a steady income."

"But you can't—"

I halt her with a raised hand. "No humans will be harmed in the acquiring of my wardrobe additions. In fact, the little mental 'boost' I bestow upon my benefactors is more than beneficial to them."

Haydee frowns, but gives up bitching, er, acquiesces and goes to stare out the store window, letting me do my thing.

Which at this moment will involve talking Mr. Man here into buying me this sharp new designer blouse—

"Will you honor me by allowing me to buy you something?" the guy asks, his eyes twinkling at me.

—which, wow, takes almost no effort on my part. I mean, the guy's all over me like petals on a flower. I didn't even have to do my typical mental nudge to make him forget his wife waiting for him at home. But who am I to question impeccable taste?

"Why, aren't you just the nicest thing?" I give him a wink and a flash of my superb cleavage, because I'm just a giver like that.

While my new friend hands over his AmEx card to the clerk, with a grin on his face, I cross the store to smack Haydee upside the head. She's just come back inside with a newspaper from the stand out on the sidewalk. Now, she's alternately staring at the front page and searching for something, or someone, outside.

"Are you trying to *see* him or *not* see him?" I snap. "Because in one breath you say you don't want to have anything to do with him—*biggest* mistake of your life, by the way—and yet you're searching for him."

"I'm not," she protests, then holds up a newspaper—*The Bander Tribune*—so I can read the headline.

"Local Boy Turned Celebrity Returns." I shrug. "So? Doesn't mean he's not The One."

"Except for the fact that, according to the article, he's planning gallery showings in New York, L.A., and Paris." She raises her eyebrows at me as if she's proved a point. "Really sounds like a guy home to settle down, doesn't it?"

I'm unswayed by her doubts. "Which is why you're standing here looking for him out the window every two seconds?"

"I am not. I'm trying to make sure I can avoid him if he's around," Haydee says. *Lies,* I mean. She's not fooling anyone.

"Whatever." I dismiss her with a wave of my hand and check on the progress of my blouse. The Man with the Fat Wallet is looking somewhat dazed—a little shocking, considering I didn't even mentally touch the guy. When I repay him for the blouse with a chaste, yet incredibly sexy, kiss to the cheek, he reacts like I goosed him, but it snaps him out of his stupor so he can sign the sales slip.

A moment later my blouse arrives on the arm of my wardrobe savior. Standing on tiptoes, I give him another little peck on the cheek to take home and dream about.

When I turn back to Haydee, she's shaking her head at him as he wanders out of the store. "He looks like he just had sex."

"He looks like he's had the best sex of his *life*." Without even trying. Which just goes to show how powerful the Goddess of Love really is. All along I've been doling out mental libido boosts to supplement my wardrobe, when really all I needed to be was Fabulous Me. I hold up my cute little shopping bag. "It's all worth it, believe me. His wife will think he's entered his second sexual peak."

"Guess there are some benefits to being a goddess."

We exit the store after Haydee scrutinizes the street for the boogeyman.

"I need to sit," I announce, pointing across the street at a couple of benches.

She hesitates, figuring out that our little detour did nothing to derail me from the previous topic of conversation. But she gives in and follows me anyway. On the way to our destination, I'm stopped by two different men and offered a cup of coffee and a night of "fun and frolicking" at the local no-tell motel, respectively. I turn them down gently, of course, though thoroughly enjoying the ego boost I get from all the attention. Haydee is not quite as amused, I can tell. But this really isn't about her, is it?

Once we park it on a convenient bench and she settles the cat in his cage to be taunted by seagulls, she continues with a sigh. "We met when Derek found me curled up beneath a study carrel. He took my picture."

Which apparently almost started a fistfight between them when Haydee didn't take too kindly to having her sorrow documented on film. I listen while she slowly doles out bits and pieces of her past.

Apparently their relationship consisted of mutual antagonism, with each thinking their pain was more important than the other's. Haydee whose mother had died and whose father had sunk into such a deep depression he'd forgotten he had a daughter, and Derek, the quarterback destined for an NFL career who had blown out his knee getting sacked, who felt the loss of career was far worse . . . at least Haydee still had her dreams.

"When Derek finally confessed that he'd lost his dad, too, who had wanted him to play football . . ." Haydee shrugs, her gaze focused far away, somewhere out over the ocean in the distance. "That's why it bothered him so much not to play. I understood that . . . the need to be connected to the missing parent."

She turns to look at me. "It's really silly, actually. One of the main reasons I dreamed of selling books, besides loving them, is that I can buy my mom's books and keep them in the store. As long as her books remain in print, every time I sell one, every time I get a new shipment of them, I kind of feel like she's coming back to me."

I'd say something, but the emotions are getting a bit sticky, and I need to keep my distance.

Eventually, the Derek and Haydee of the past stopped arguing and formed a support group of sorts. While Haydee floundered emotionally, Derek had been her rock, the only person who understood the silent tears that sometimes overflowed when she least expected it. He helped her realize that the plan her guidance school counselor had forced her to create to help her get her life on track would at least help her move forward instead of remaining attached to the pain of losing her mom. And she helped him turn his attention to what he *could* do with a bum knee, like seriously taking up photography, for which he showed a talent.

"Then what happened?" I'm waiting for the part where they're so grateful for each other's support and friendship that they fall into bed together, losing their virginity, something. Anything to indicate what Haydee's real hang-up about Derek is. Because so far it's not making a bit of sense.

"We were just friends. We went away to college. Then he ran off to become a world-famous photographer. End of story."

I remain on the bench even as she gets up and begins to walk toward home.

"That can't be all!" I protest, finally jumping up to follow when she seems far enough away to be serious about ending the story before she's even hit the climax.

"Of course that's all." She doesn't slow down, even as I obviously struggle to keep up with her. "He went to the University of Washington. A year later I went to the University of Portland. I graduated, got my MBA, moved back to Bander, opened the bookstore. He went off to photograph the world. That's all, folks."

It's not all. I can tell. There was much unaccounted-for time in this story. My Love Goddess instincts are honed and refined to pick up on every little nuance. And Haydee's nuance is saying she's agitated. Hiding something.

I automatically begin to send out little feelers into her mind to root out the info I need. In two seconds, I'll have all the answers.

Only I can't. If I want to be a fairy godmother "worth her weight," I can only get my answers the old-fashioned way. And I'm going to be worth my weight, believe Zeus me. But it doesn't mean I have to be happy about it. Stupid, *stupid* rules!

I take off after Haydee with determination. "I'll get you to tell me what I want to know yet, dammit!"

Upon Zeus, I am not paid enough to put up with this kind of crap. The fact that I'm not paid anything at all makes it all that much more ironic.

I will have to continue my sleuthing until I get to the bottom of the sordid tale.

~ 9 ~

Haydee

With the wind whipping up and the fog rolling in, the beach was practically deserted. Of tourists, at least. Full-time residents tended to choose just this kind of weather for their beachcombing, knowing there'd be fewer tourists cluttering up their space.

Low tide let me run far out in the sand, away from anyone who might want to stop and talk. I was in no mood for conversation.

I turned north and headed for the hardpacked sand at the water's edge.

Venus stayed home after dinner—I'd insisted. Frankly, I needed to get away for a while. Away from her questions about my past. Away from her insistence that Derek was the perfect guy for me.

As if.

As I ran, I breathed in the salty air, hoping it would clear my head. Clear my heart.

Derek showing up in Bander for the first time in almost thirteen years? What in the world was that about? Maybe I should have just asked him this afternoon before latching on to the phone as an excuse to hide in my office for thirty minutes. I'd neglected my other customers, and had left Patrick wondering about my surprise kiss—and probably even more about why I'd kissed him and then announced I was going to call Conner back to reschedule our date—just so I could be a coward and avoid

Derek. I should have just asked Derek why he was back. Any confident adult would have. Maybe his mother was ill or he craved her home cooking. Maybe that's all it was.

Even though he said he'd come back for me.

That *so* wasn't fair.

I picked up my speed, sprinting hell-bent into a flock of sandpipers, sending them scattering in a cloud of feathers and protests. I knew how they felt, having their safe little world disturbed by an intruder. I totally understood.

Frankly, I rarely thought about Derek. Life was easier that way. Leaving the past in the past wasn't completely possible, like when his mother and I crossed uncomfortable paths on the street, but it sure as hell was easier when Derek was in Nairobi or the outback of Australia than it was with him in my backyard.

He obviously felt the same since he hadn't been home since he left over a decade ago.

I pushed myself to keep moving, though the desire to drop to the sand and curl up in the fetal position for the waves to sweep me away was tempting. Shaking my head, I practically spat out a disgusted breath. What the hell was my problem? Grown women did not allow men—or anyone, for that matter—to have this much effect on them. To think that once upon a time Derek had been the one person who made my life seem easier. Seemed highly improbable, considering how my life suddenly felt extremely complicated, because he'd shown up on my doorstep.

In high school, Derek and I had become the unlikeliest of friends—the has-been jock and the sad little girl whose depression threatened to put her in an emotional coma. It had been our personal pain and anger that drew us together. I'd scolded him for whining when all he'd lost was a career because of his football injury. He'd shot back that, even with my mom dead, I, at least, had a future, while his was "destroyed." We'd butted heads, each trying to make our own pain seem more important than the other's. Self-pitying anger as a healing tool. Psychologists everywhere would've raised their eyebrows at our unorthodox technique.

But it had worked. Derek had pulled out of his pity party about the loss of an NFL career that had once been a sure thing. He'd talked about getting a teaching degree so he could come back to Bander and help coach the next generation of possible football stars. And me . . . I'd focused on The Plan. The roadmap I had followed because it forced me to look forward into the future, toward what I *could* have, instead of what I'd lost. Not only that, it was my security. It was the one thing I could count on. Even when Derek moved on with his own life.

Especially then.

My confidence, once nearly nonexistent, had grown back like new skin over an old wound. I shook my head as I ran, a bitter laugh escaping into the fog bank. How in the world did he expect me to believe he was back in town for *me*? How was I supposed to believe anything he ever said to me again?

He'd once told me he loved me.

He'd once promised me forever.

The summer between my sophomore and junior years of college, something had just clicked between us. We'd stayed in friendly contact up until that point. Hanging out during school breaks when we weren't busy. Sneaking up to Portland with our fake IDs to drink beer or beach partying with our friends.

And then . . . it hit us. I couldn't explain it if I tried. Our affair had been explosive . . . and then so solid, so sure, that I'd been willing to give up The Plan. I'd drop out of school, follow him back to Seattle to be with him while he finished his degree. Then we would come back to Bander together. We'd planned it all out, whispering under a starry summer sky, wrapped in each other's arms.

Apparently, though, given a few days of contemplation, the idea of commitment had scared Derek Reed into throwing it all away. Years of friendship? Gone. Confessions of love? Worthless. Apparently, becoming an intern to an internationally famous photographer—which I found out about years later, reading a magazine article on him—had been more important to Derek than me. He'd never mentioned the internship. He tried to give me some lame excuse about how *I* needed time. *I* needed space. But it was all crap. I tuned him out when he started with that. It was clear our "relationship" had just been a fling. Despite our plans for the future. Despite his assurances of love.

He dropped out of college during his senior year, waved good-bye to me and Bander, and ran as far and fast as he could.

Looking back, he was probably right. One of us *had* needed time and space. Him. He had an amazing career. I couldn't begrudge him that. And, if asked, I would maintain until my dying breath that it hadn't hurt when he walked away.

But it had.

When he left Bander, Derek made it very clear where I stood with him. Nowhere.

Which was why I couldn't understand why he'd come back now. Why was he here *now* looking for more? And he was definitely looking for more. Men didn't give off the kind of body heat he'd radiated all over me at the store this afternoon if they weren't looking for a hook up.

He probably thought I was dumb enough to fall for it. After all, I'd fallen for it that summer. All his lovey-dovey words had probably been a ploy to get into my pants. I'd been stupid enough to fall for it then, but I was far older and wiser now. He wouldn't fool me again.

I reached the limit of available beach and turned back toward home—or at least toward town, since I still didn't feel like going home and facing my so-called fairy godmother just yet. The fog finally drove me to higher ground, where the beach remained mostly empty, except for someone walking a pack of dogs in the distance. Sand flew where several dogs dug for China or dead seagulls to roll in, while their owner forked up beach trash with a skewer, depositing it in a plastic bag carried in the other hand. A local. Only locals picked up garbage.

As I closed the space between us, I recognized a few of the dogs. Wonderful. I needed this confrontation like a hole in the head.

Patrick had enough pets to fill a kennel all by himself, and there was nothing they loved more than their evening romp in the sand and surf. When a couple of the dogs noticed me and headed in my direction for a greeting, Patrick raised his hand to wave.

Maybe I should look on the bright side. What I really needed in this situation was progress. Forward movement toward meeting my goal of finding a guy I could settle down with. A guy *unlike* Derek, who, if I was stupid enough to hook up with, I'd always worry would bolt at the slightest hint of commitment. I needed a guy I knew would stay in Bander instead of needing something bigger and better to keep his attention. Someone solid and steady.

Maybe it was time to take Patrick up on our pact. Why wait? What difference would another few weeks make?

"Hi there, Rufus." I slowed to a stop and bent to pet the little mutt's damp head. In return I got a slobbery kiss on the cheek followed by three more dogs wanting equal attention.

When I stood up again, Patrick was headed toward me with a smile on his face. He wasn't what I'd call handsome. His thinning hair allowed patches of scalp to show through, and he was a tad bit on the skinny side, though he loved to run. Something we could do together. Bonding time. And he loved animals, which was a plus in my book. Even when he'd run over Bear and then put him to sleep, he'd done it out of love and caring and respect for the animal. And for me. I knew that.

There was so much good about Patrick. He'd lived in Bander his whole life, though I hadn't really known him when we were kids, since he was several years ahead of me in school. It wasn't until I'd moved back to town to open my store, along with a dog and newly acquired cat who needed vaccinations and worm medicine, that we'd become friends of sorts.

And then we'd gone further.

"I've been thinking about you this afternoon." Patrick's eyes were warm and more than a little friendly. "You really have to explain the kiss."

I tried to drive out the memory of the man who broke my heart by concentrating on the man I was pretty sure would do everything he needed to do *not* to ever break my heart. "I was just testing the waters," I replied lightly, noting that as long as we were outdoors, I couldn't smell Patrick's "vet smell." "Wasn't sure if the pact still stood."

Patrick reached across the head of an Irish setter and took my hand. "Just waiting for the word from you. I never needed a pact."

I left my hand there for as long as I could before extracting it and turning to walk along the path he'd apparently been taking with the dogs. "You probably also need an explanation about my making a date with another guy right after kissing you."

He chuckled. "That crossed my mind, too. As well as why you were so pointedly ignoring Derek Reed."

I stared at him. "You know Derek?"

"He was only behind me by two years in school, and a Bander High star quarterback even as a freshman."

I took a few steps, picked up a stick, and threw it for one of the dogs. This could be normal for us. Walking along the beach, playing with the dogs . . . or our kids. It wouldn't be so bad, would it?

But it really wasn't fair to Patrick, even if I could get past my feelings about his part in Bear's death, to take him up on the pact when I suddenly had this big unresolved thing show up from my past.

"I hate to admit this," I began, "but we kind of had a . . . thing. In college. The kiss was kind of meant to show Derek that I'd moved on." I looked at him apologetically. "Don't hate me. It wasn't at all fair, I know, but he took me by surprise showing up like that today."

Patrick looked pretty grim, and I waited for him to chew me out. I deserved it.

"He wants you back?"

Did he? I shrugged. "I really couldn't tell you. But I don't want him back."

He contemplated for a few minutes. "What are the chances I'd be able to beat him in a duel?" he finally asked.

Shocked, I laughed aloud. "Seriously?"

He really was good-looking when he smiled. He was no Derek Reed, but that was a good thing in my book. "If that's what it takes . . . I'm willing."

Grinning, I touched his shoulder. And felt nothing. Though I wished I had. It would have all been so much easier. But that didn't mean he wouldn't end up being the right guy. I just needed to exhaust all my other possibilities first.

"It means a lot to me to know you're willing to pull out the dueling pistols to fight for me. It's a tough thing to find in a guy these days." I let my hand slip away. "But there really is no need for the challenge. Derek has no hold on me whatsoever."

"That's a relief. So then what does have a hold on you?"

I glanced sideways at him. "Are you always so perceptive?"

He raised his hands in a gesture of "What can I say?"

"What has a hold on me is my fear of making a big mistake," I finally said. "I can't just marry you because you're here, because we made a pact to be each other's last resort."

He cleared his throat pointedly. "Confession time."

I flushed, which had to have been the too-fresh ocean air stinging my cheeks, not the fact that Patrick had somehow figured out my aversion to his occupation. "I—"

Patrick spun around and stopped abruptly in front of me. "I don't consider you my last resort, Haydee. That stupid pact was my lamebrained way of asking you to marry me a year ago, because I thought you might feel the same way."

He'd— "I—"

"Don't feel that way about me. I get that." He picked up my hands and held them between us. They were warm in the chill air, but that was all. "But I think it's distinctly possible you might change your mind, if you'd give us a chance."

"Do you really want someone who has to 'change her mind' to be your wife?"

"If it's you," he flashed a smile that might have melted anyone else's heart, "that's exactly who I want."

I opened my mouth to tell him okay. To tell him I'd work harder at it. To let feelings develop, even though they weren't present right this very minute.

And then I remembered The Plan. And the fact that I still had six weeks, two days, and three hours left to make any life-altering decisions.

I just wasn't ready to spend that time changing my mind about Patrick, when it was possible there was someone else out there if I just gave it—and Venus, I suppose—a chance to find him.

"There's still six weeks—" I started, then stopped to frown, to contemplate what I could say that wouldn't hurt his feelings or discourage him. Or *en*courage him.

"And you want to see if you can find someone better."

His face made me want to cry. Patrick was a good friend before I let a dying dog put space between us.

"That's not quite how I'd put it," I said. "I want to make sure I—we—wouldn't be making a big mistake. Because how much worse would it be to agree to marry you only to find out a few weeks from now that I was wrong. I don't want to hurt you."

Venus

"Why again is she living here?"

The Asian chick is really getting on my nerves. And she's not even the one who thinks she's working some kind of voodoo magic to bring Haydee luck in her search for love. She's apparently just a bitter divorce lawyer. I'd say we're on opposite sides of the relationship fence.

I roll my eyes and check my manicure while Haydee bounces Joan's baby in her arms and explains, for the third time, to the infamous Nita that I'm her new employee, needed a place to stay, blah, blah, blah. She leaves out the part about me being her fairy godmother, of course, which Nita, being the practical pessimist that she seems to be, would never believe anyway.

Not that it's any of her business. But seeing how it's not my house, I can't exactly throw out the party pooper. She's spent most of the last thirty minutes trying to talk Haydee out of dating again, and Haydee hasn't even told her that Derek "The One" Reed is in town. Which leads me to the useless waste of effort expended by her other friend.

"I can't believe your toilet is in the love zone of your house!" This is Joan, Haydee's friend, who is doing some redecorating that's supposed to change the energy flow of the house or something. Apparently having a toilet in the "love zone" can be a problem.

Apparently, she's unaware that Haydee has *me*.

"I should never have let you buy this place. This completely explains the lack of men in your life."

"Can't do much about it now, can I?" Haydee calls down the hall to Joan, who had arrived with a picnic basket full of supplies for her "fung shway" magic stuff, or whatever it's called, which apparently didn't have anything to do with shoes. So it was an obvious waste of time.

"I have a five-rod wind chime at home that I'll drop off for you." Joan comes out of the bathroom carrying her basket. "That'll help some. I also added the water feature with stones and hung a picture of peonies—the Chinese flower of love," she points out to Nita, who sighs dramatically.

"How many times do I have to tell you that feng shui is Chinese for bullshit?"

"Your ancestors are rolling over in their graves," Joan scolds, then turns to Haydee, taking the baby from her and depositing him in the cloth sling-thing strapped to her chest. "Let's go check out your bedroom."

The three of them head for the stairs without even a backward glance in my direction. "What about me?" I ask, feeling left out of their games of futility. Just because I think it's completely unnecessary to add a bunch of props around the house when there's a resident fairy godmother on the job, doesn't mean I want to be a third wheel. Or fourth wheel, or whatever number I am. Anything beats locking myself in my room for another evening of cramming more useless fairy godmother rules into my head. What a waste! Besides, even if all this nonsense won't actually help Haydee find a man—mostly because she's already found him and just hasn't accepted it yet—it can't hurt. Any encouragement should be . . . encouraged. "What should I do?"

"You can wait for the pizza guy," Nita tells me with an attempt at a pleasant smile as she tosses me some cash. "And if any men come riding in on the increased flow of chi Joan's got going . . . shoo them away."

Haydee smacks her on the arm, though that was the most agreeable thing I've heard out of Nita's mouth since she got here.

Fifteen minutes later, when I've finally finished reading the *In-Style* magazine Haydee let me "borrow" from her bookstore, the doorbell rings. On the stoop stands a pimply faced adolescent holding out the pizza without making eye contact. I really don't like being ignored, especially when I'm wearing my favorite halter top, the one that accentuates my assets so perfectly that even a small-town babe like him should appreciate it. I like being appreciated.

I dangle the money just out of his reach until he looks up.

As soon as he does, I have my point proven. As his jaw drops, his height increases by about four inches. He puffs out his bony little chest in an attempt to look more . . . buff. It doesn't work.

His voice actually squeaks when he speaks so he clears his throat and starts again. "Pizza. Beautiful . . . lady."

"Yes, I am a beautiful lady," I agree, slipping the pizza box from his hand, letting my fingers brush his as I take it from him.

He nearly has an instant orgasm at the same moment I register how fucking hot the bottom of the box is.

"Shit!" I dash around the couch like a greyhound and drop the box onto the coffee table.

When I turn back to hand over the cash to the pizza boy, fingers stuck in my mouth in an attempt to suck out the pain coursing through them, he's right behind me.

"What the fuck!"

When I back up a step, he follows. "I've never seen anyone so beautiful. Will you go with me to the prom?"

Prom? "Your school dance?"

"Yeah. God, all the guys would be so . . . jealous . . ." His voice trails off as he reaches out to touch my—

He gets a smack on the hand. "Back off!" I use my stern goddess voice to let him know I mean business. It doesn't work, because he's still coming at me. "You need to leave now, baby boy. You're not old enough to play with the big girls yet."

"I've never had a real girlfriend," he mumbles, a goofy, dreamy look on his face. "Just a blow-up doll named Sally Suck-Me that the guys bought me as a joke. Only Sally can't go with me to the prom. You'd be so much better."

"Of course I would," I tell him as I circle the coffee table, trying to guide him back toward the front door. "But I'm way out of your league, dude. You wouldn't know what to do with real breasts anyway."

He starts giggling as we round the couch into the foyer. "You said *breasts.*"

I roll my eyes. The last time I'd been subjected to this crap was when I used the Golden Girdle to seduce a Greek land tycoon, and his stable boy caught us in the act and wanted to make it a threesome. Apparently I'm hot enough to drive them wild even without the girdle these days.

I get as far as the front door, and he's still following like a dopey puppy after a steak. "Come on now. Almost there." I reach behind me to open the screen door. "We'll go sit on the porch for a while, 'kay?"

The grin on his face is so eager it's pathetic.

"Let's go over to the swing, and I'll give you something you've never had before." I point and he tears his eyes away long enough to race to the porch swing before I change my mind.

Before he's got his ass on the seat, I have the door closed and locked between us. Then I spy the twenty that had fluttered to the floor earlier when he was too stupefied by my beauty to take it from me.

I shove it through the mail slot and call it good.

Upstairs in Haydee's room, the girls are having a heated debate about where to place a framed photograph of a mountain—at the foot of the bed or on the wall opposite the door. As if that's going to make a damn bit of difference to Haydee's love life.

"Are all the Bander pizza boys so horny?" I ask, dropping the box onto the comforter.

Haydee moves it to the dresser. "Not that I've ever noticed."

"Well that one was." I throw myself into the inevitable comfy chair by the window after tossing aside the three books littering the seat.

When everyone's mouth is suitably full of pizza—except mine, of course—I move in for the kill.

"You know, Joan, I'm really not sure why Haydee's making you go through all this. She didn't tell you Derck Reed is back in Bander?"

Nita practically chokes on her pepperoni as Haydee lets out a squeak of protest around her own mouthful. Only Joan doesn't react in any way other than to look back and forth between her two friends with curiosity.

When Joan's mouth is empty, she asks the obvious, "Who's Derek Reed?"

"The better question is why is he back here, and why the hell didn't you *tell* me?" Nita asks Haydee, her sunny disposition shining through every snarled word.

"It's not important," Haydee finally answers, tossing the rest of her pizza slice back into the box and shooting eye daggers in my direction.

"He's a man from her past," I mention casually, "though I don't know the details."

"The details aren't important," Nita interjects. "What's important is that Haydee stays far, far away from him."

"Oh, I don't know about that."

Nita rounds on me like Medusa on a pissy day. "What do you know? You have no clue what he did to her."

"What did he do to you?" Joan's shock is evident. Apparently friendship doesn't include the sharing of confidences in this case.

I lean forward in my seat waiting for the dirt.

Haydee refuses to shovel. "It was really no big deal, you guys. *Really*. We were friends in high school."

I cough into my hand as delicately as possible.

"And we had a *thing* . . . later. During college."

Ah ha! A *thing*. I knew it!

"It was really no big deal." Haydee retrieves her abandoned slice of pizza from the box to use as a shield. "Venus heard me mention it and just can't get it through her *thick skull* that Derek Reed means absolutely less than nothing to me."

Huh. Sounds like someone needs a taste of the power of the Goddess of Love.

Joan sucks some cheese off her thumb and attempts to look less interested than I can tell she obviously is. Reverse psychology at its finest. "Well, if you change your mind, all the changes we've made around here should help things along."

"I'm not changing my mind about anything to do with Derek Reed. In fact," Haydee pauses and I watch her through narrowed eyes as she stands up and crosses the room to her dresser. She retrieves a piece of paper from the glossy top before turning to Nita. "I mentioned this to Joan the other day, kind of, but maybe you can help, too."

"If it's murdering Derek for you, I'm all over it," Nita volunteers with an almost cheery smile.

Haydee ignores her . . . and the now more curious looks from Joan. Not that Nita seems to be the type to need much excuse for murder, but her anger seems disproportionate to Haydee's feigned nonchalance about the situation. I'm guessing from her vehemence, she, being Haydee's college roommate, was privy to the fallout from whatever the Haydee-Derek disaster was.

"So, you know that list of goals I made when I was seventeen?" she continues. "When my mom died and I was having a tough time of it? The Plan has been really helpful, and I'm up to the next item on the list. Getting married."

"Oh, here we go!" Apparently losing her appetite, Nita dumps her own half-finished slice of pizza in the box. "Have I taught you nothing?"

"Yes, we've talked about this. 'No man means no tears,'" Haydee quotes. "'There's no such thing as *free* love.' 'Marriage is a mental institution.' You've made that abundantly clear. And for you, maybe that's a good philosophy. But I don't want to be *alone* forever."

"Get a parakeet!"

"I have a cat."

"Get another one." Nita throws her arms out toward Haydee. "I beg of you, just because I'm the best divorce lawyer on the Oregon coast, don't make me show you what a shark I am. Let it just be secondhand knowledge. Or something you only know about through my extensive bragging."

Haydee pauses as if she can't even think of what to say, so I step in. "Maybe it would help if you were supportive."

Haydee glances at me, her mouth open in surprise. "Thank you," she says softly. "That means a lot."

Whether or not she misunderstands my motives makes no difference in this situation. I simply want to look more supportive than Nita, to get on Haydee's good side so she'll be easier to bend to my will.

"We'll do what we can, Haydee," Joan offers, though she seems to be most pointedly talking to Nita, who frowns and turns away in a huff. "I'm sure if we put our heads together, we can come up with the right guy for you." She waves around at the props she's placed around the room. "We've got the energy flowing a little better now. The right guy is bound to turn up."

I open my mouth to mention that the right guy has already shown up, but Haydee notices and dives past me, nearly knocking me out of my seat, smacking the wall beside me. At my shocked look, she says very pointedly, "*Spider,*" which I *know* is a complete lie. But I'm willing to keep my thoughts to myself for now.

It doesn't really matter whether everyone understands that Derek is The One or not; it only matters that Haydee figures it out. If her friends throw guys at her in the meantime, I'll just make sure none of them get further than a dinner out, which might provide me with better meals to make up for the fact that Haydee's kitchen lacks even a rudimentary selection of food.

Speaking of which, I push past her to take a slice of pizza.

"What do you need from us, Haydee?" Joan asks.

"Dates would be nice. Anyone you can think of or that I might *not* think of."

"Don't stress yourselves about it, though," I add. "After all, I *am* a matchmaker."

"Yes, well, any help will still be appreciated," Haydee points out.

"You got it," Joan assures her, patting the baby's back as he starts to fuss.

"Not from me, you don't," Nita grumps, doing a little fussing of her own.

Nor from me, I think.

All I have to do now is figure out how to keep Haydee from getting too close to any of the dates her friends toss her and how to get her and Derek in the same room as frequently as possible. After all, fires, even cooled, can spark again if given the right fuel.

❧ 11 ❧

Haydee

"Conner took Venus's little joke okay," I told Zeus the next night, as I washed my hands and face.

Deciding to shower in the morning, I snapped off the bathroom light and crawled between the sheets in nothing but a tank and my boxers with the books on them that Nita had found me for Christmas last year. As soon as I stopped moving, Zeus leapt onto the bed beside me and tucked himself against my knees.

"I just . . ." I struggled to put into non-lame-sounding words what "I just." But there was no way not to sound like a complete idiot. I had asked Conner out, but after sitting next to him at the town zoning meeting for two hours and then grabbing a beer with him afterward at The Gull, to make up for the "prank" Venus had played of canceling our date, I really didn't want to go out with him again after all. There was nothing bad about him that I could pinpoint. I just couldn't imagine sitting through a meal or a movie with him and having anything at all to say worth saying.

Venus would be thrilled. And I would be mortifyingly embarrassed to turn him down when he called me to finalize our plans for the weekend, since I'd already asked him out, then apologized profusely and asked him out again after Venus canceled.

So, I'd just avoid the phone until it was too late to make weekend plans. Of course that might be hard to do since he was likely to call the store where I couldn't avoid the phone. *Arggggh.*

This really wasn't going to be this hard was it?

Sleep was a bitch, dancing just out of range for me, refusing to let me latch on and disappear into oblivion. I used the time to brainstorm ways to meet the right guy, while simultaneously trying to convince myself that Patrick was the right guy, which would solve all my problems at once. "Right?" I said aloud.

Zeus snorted in obvious protest at being woken up for the twelfth time by my indecision.

Sighing, I flopped over on my side, sending the disgruntled cat onto the floor. I watched as he slunk through the moonlight and hopped up onto the windowsill to sulk. Then I closed my eyes, determined to get some sleep.

It seemed like moments later something woke me up. Squinting in the moonlight now shining across my pillow, I noted Zeus pacing back and forth across the sill. When something *plinked* against the pane of glass, he batted at it briefly before resuming his pacing.

What the hell? I pushed myself upright, cursing. If some stupid teenagers thought it was funny to throw rocks at my window at— I checked the clock—*midnight,* they were going to find themselves pretty damn sorry when I sicced Sheriff Howie on them.

Standing to the side of the window, using the curtains as cover, I scanned the front yard for the culprits. It took another rock hitting the window before I noticed the familiar old Ford truck parked on the street. A few seconds more and I spotted him.

Son-of-a-!

Grrrr!

I stepped in front of the window to let Derek know I'd seen him, so he'd stop trying to break my window, though no doubt the darkness prevented him from reading my lips as I called him a few choice names.

Wake me up in the middle of the night, will you?

I grabbed the throw that I had tossed across the back of my reading chair, upsetting the paperback I'd left there the night before. I ignored it and pulled the blanket around my bare shoulders before heading into the hallway and down the stairs. He probably thought he was cute waking me up like that. Like he'd done that summer. That had been our signal. I'd been staying at home with my dad and, after connecting again, Derek had thrown rocks at my window many times to get me up and out of bed to sneak around with him.

It wasn't going to work like that this time.

"What the hell are you thinking?" I snapped at him, descending the front porch steps into the yard. The grass was damp and cold on my bare feet as I marched out to meet him underneath the old magnolia tree.

He was probably thinking he looked charming and irresistible staring at my bare legs below the hem of the throw. And I, apparently conditioned like Pavlov's dogs to salivate over something I hadn't even tasted yet, responded with my heart tripping all over itself to beat faster.

Bugger.

"Getting your attention." Derek grinned as he gestured in the direction of my bedroom window, where Zeus remained watchfully examining us. "You have a new bodyguard, I see."

"Don't change the subject." I yanked the blanket tighter around my shoulders to ward off the spring chill in the air. "Why are you here? And I mean in town at all, not just here on my front lawn, disturbing my peace. Why aren't you off chasing down your next *National Geographic* cover? Or giving celebrity interviews to the *Bander Tribune*?"

For a minute I figured I wasn't going to get an answer. Derek just stood there, examining me. Torturing me. His mind was a thousand miles away. Or thirteen years in the past.

When I shivered, he snapped out of it, his face breaking into a smile. "I needed to see you. I . . . missed you."

For just a second I faltered. I'd missed him, too. At first.

He took the edges of the blanket and drew them tighter around my neck, most likely trying to warm me up. But really, it just made me colder when his hands fell away. "You still game for romantic midnight walks?"

Right. At his ridiculous words, I shook off the spell I'd slipped under. "I'm too old for games," I told him. "I have a business, a life. A plan for the future." He, of all people, had to understand that. He'd convinced me of The Plan's validity, after all, back when The Plan had been the only thing that got me out of bed most mornings.

"Plans that include Patrick Butler?" Derek leaned back against the tree trunk folding his arms across a muscular chest that my fingers itched to touch. "I thought maybe you two had become an item when he kissed you in the bookstore the other day. But then tonight at the town meeting you barely acknowledged him and spent the evening sitting with the cop."

What did he do, watch me the whole night? And what was he doing hanging out at a town meeting when he hadn't even been in town for over a decade? "My relationship with Patrick is none of your business. In fact, my entire love life is off limits to you as far as I'm concerned. You lost that privilege a long time ago."

He didn't argue. Probably because there was no possible argument he could provide that would change my mind.

But it didn't mean he'd given up. "The past was a long time ago," he reminded me, as if I needed the reminder. "Lots of things have changed since then."

I took a step toward him, not to give in but to make the point that I wasn't afraid I'd be unable to resist him. "You're so right, Derek. *Lots* of things have changed since then. I'm not young.

I'm not naïve anymore. I'm not driven by hormones or . . . or whatever drove us together that summer. I have a future to think about, and my future doesn't include fly-by-night lovers."

So there.

I gave him my back and headed toward the house.

"What if I'm not fly-by-night?" His words stopped me in my tracks. Not because I believed them. More because I knew whatever lame story he'd make up to get me into his bed would provide me hours of amusement. "What if I plan to stay in Bander?"

I laughed as I turned to face him. "*Are* you staying in Bander? Because when the NFL career didn't pan out and you tired of me, you were pretty quick to grab the internationally acclaimed photographer gig to get you out of town. So forgive my skepticism."

The words hit their mark, I saw, as a shadow briefly passed over Derek's face. But he recovered quickly, moving toward where I'd stopped at the bottom of the front steps.

"A lot of what I do depends on you." When he reached for the blanket this time, it wasn't to cover me but to pull me closer. His breath caressed my face, sweet like mint leaves brushed across my skin. "On whether you remember what we had once . . . even before that summer. Our friendship. When we were all each other had. Maybe we could help each other out."

I snorted at his last remark, which served as a splash of cold water to wake me up again. I was nowhere near that desperate. Sure, I could probably serve as a safe way to scratch whatever manly itch he had, but in what way did he think that would help *me* out?

I tried to take a step back, but ran into the bottom step instead, just making Derek grip my shoulders tighter to keep me from landing on my ass. "I am not an option," I informed him. "There are a dozen other girls in Bander who don't know you well enough to know you'll just say what they want to hear to get them to 'help out.'" I tipped my chin up to show him who had control of this situation.

Which only served to bring my mouth in closer proximity to his.

Which he took prompt advantage of.

The kiss rocked me to the core. I admit it. There was no way to deny it. And Derek knew it, too. Before I could stop myself, I'd swayed into him, gulping him in like a thirsty man in a desert.

But then I came to my senses. At least that's what I told myself later.

In reality, it was Derek who broke it off, putting just a few inches between us, but enough that I felt bereft of something I didn't even remember craving.

"I should have taken you with me," he whispered.

Except that he hadn't asked.

"You should have stayed with me," I replied.

I hadn't asked, either. I shouldn't have needed to.

Then I yanked the blanket out of his hands and ran up the steps into the house. I didn't slam the door but shut it firmly enough that I knew he'd get the message.

Venus met me at the top of the stairs. Before I could apologize for waking her, she grinned.

"I told you so."

No, I thought, as I pushed past her and locked myself in my room. I told *you* so.

There would be nothing happening between me and Derek Reed. Feng shui, fairy godmother magic, or not.

❧ 12 ❧

Venus

Despite much protest on my part, Haydee is out on a date. With a dude named Steven Kozak, a banker.

She discovered him at the grocery store while I'd been otherwise occupied catching up on the latest news in the *Enquirer*. Apparently, when he reached for the same box of Pop-Tarts she did, she seized upon the idea that they must be, I don't know, *soul mates* or something. That their mutual taste for junk food makes them compatible.

I can't believe I've been thwarted again! Before I could throw myself in front of the train wreck that is Haydee's love life, she introduced herself and asked him out for drinks. Tonight. After she had lunch with Conner. Like, why didn't she just tattoo "Desperate Loser" on her forehead?

Since she deserted me at dinnertime, and since I couldn't afford a decent meal at a restaurant (if one even existed in this town) because I'd actually found a yummy cashmere shrug I just had to have, I'm eating all her Pop-Tarts. Every last fake strawberry-flavored one of them. When she finds herself without breakfast tomorrow morning, maybe she'll think twice about shoving me aside for her exercise in futile dating.

By the time I get to the last Pop-Tart, I'm feeling a little sick. Even breaking it in half and sandwiching M&M's between the pieces barely makes it edible.

I'm feeling mentally sick, too. A week ago, I was on top of the world. I was going to ace this Love Life Makeover and show Zeus how much I rocked. Only now? Now I can't even fathom where all that optimism came from. This is all just too hard! And why is it hard? I have no idea! I'm the Goddess of Love, for crying out loud. This is supposed to come naturally.

Finally, I can't stand it anymore. I'll not remain in this house one more minute being stared at by the feline who shares a name, as well as the personality, of my evil father.

I've got to put forth more effort. Reading this blasted rule book, which was clearly created just to feed Zeus's freakish ego (as evidenced by the rule that says, "Do as Zeus says, not as Zeus does"), is doing absolutely nothing to get my godchild hitched. I know there was something more between Haydee and Derek, but I don't know what. This puts me at a distinct disadvantage in doing my job. I've got to take the stubborn godchild by the horns—or the shoulders—and shake some sense into her before it's too late.

I race upstairs to change. So what if it's not me on the date? I have an excuse to get out of the house, so I may as well look my best, right?

I finally settle on a champagne-colored silk cami to wear with my new cashmere shrug. I shake off some of the bits of shiny dust that have accumulated in my lingerie drawer, then decide they actually brighten things up a bit and leave the rest. I pull the slip of fabric over my head. When I open my eyes again, I'm face-to-face with Zeus, who is sitting on my dresser like he owns the damn place.

"What's your problem?" I hiss. "Cat got your tongue?"

I spin around and head for the bathroom to touch up my makeup. I'm clearly losing it, but I seriously can't help but think it's just too much of a coincidence that that cat and my father share a name. I mean, really, what are the odds?

And if it is Zeus—the god, not the cat—why doesn't he just say what's on his mind and get it over with? I'm getting really sick and tired of him watching me like he's just waiting for me to screw things up. Not that that would be out of the norm for him, but still you'd think, after two thousand years, he'd be over it already.

With a last satisfied look in the mirror, I deem myself presentable enough to be seen in public. More than presentable, as a matter of fact.

Fabulous.

I just need to make my godchild realize my fabulousness extends beyond my beauty into my skill.

I march downtown with purpose, thanking Zeus that Haydee lives but a golden apple's throw from the heart of Bander. I'd be at a severe disadvantage if things were any more sprawling around here.

Main Street is pretty busy this evening. I'm beginning to be able to tell tourists from townies, based on how much attention they pay to their surroundings. Townies move with purpose. Tourists look in every storefront window as if it may hold treasures just waiting to be had. Which they'd know wasn't the case if they paid attention to the fact that they are in Bander frickin' Oregon, a town so sleepy it's practically comatose.

Seeing Mama Josie's, the restaurant where Haydee's having a drink with Mr. Waste of Time, I step out into the street to cross. Halfway there, I pause, noticing Derek, aka Prince Charming, heading down the sidewalk carrying what looks like wood.

At the honk of a car horn, I snap out of it and dash the rest of the way across the street. He's not moving too fast, so I follow him, glancing toward the restaurant when I pass, hoping Haydee doesn't make any wedding plans before I can return.

Of course she won't. The man I'm following is her destiny,

and just because she doesn't know it yet just means I have to make sure she figures it out. And perhaps having a little heart-to-heart with the object of her eventual affection will be the key.

"Can I buy you a drink, gorgeous?"

Spinning around, I notice a blond surfer-boy type, exiting the souped-up car he'd just pulled up to the curb.

"Well, aren't you just the cutest?" I take a step toward him, knowing he'll improve my mood. Only then I remember my job.

Derek turns into an alley between two buildings. Not wanting to lose him, I bid the pretty boy adieu. "Another time, maybe!" I call out, then turn and dart after Derek.

Curious, I follow him into the alley between the Department of Licensing and a bait shop. Rounding the back of the building, making sure I don't slip on any of the grassy patches growing up through the mostly gravel path, I see that the back door to the bait shop is open. The sound of stacking wood drifts from the archway.

"Anyone here?" I call into the dim back hallway of the shop. "Hello?"

Derek pokes his head out of a room off to the left of the hall-way. "Can I help you?"

I flash him my best and brightest. Smile, of course. "I think I'm lost." I move toward him, wanting to see what he's doing with the wood in the back of what is presumably Haydee's dad's store. She mentioned he owned a bait shop. "Can you help me?"

Planting a hand on his broad chest—noting the nicely toned muscles bunching beneath his black T-shirt—I push past him into the brightly lit room. He moves aside with little effort, probably shocked at my boldness.

"Uh, what are you looking for?" he asks.

But I don't bother to answer, because I've just hit the jackpot. The room smells like turpentine and sawdust, which is swept into drifts against the walls beneath the workbench. Some kind of electric saw or something sits on a table in the center of the room. And propped against the walls around the room are frames in various stages of completion—some bare wood, some stained. Some empty, some already filled.

"Quite the collection of photos you have here," I comment, smiling slyly over my shoulder toward him.

"I'm a photographer. Do I know you?"

I gesture around the room at the half *National Geographic* Photo Museum and half Memorial to a Lost Love he's creating. I point to one of the portraits that fit into the latter category. "She's my godchi— *boss*. I believe you were in Mount Olympus Books the other day?"

He doesn't answer right away, seemingly distracted by . . . my body? He's giving me a thorough once-over.

I snap my fingers in his direction. He shakes his head like he's confused and returns his look to my face.

"Haydee?" I remind him, just a little bit annoyed that he's checking me out when I'm here to put the girl of his dreams right in the palm of his hand. "Remember her?"

"Of course." He clears his throat, glancing around at the photographs leaning against the walls, a mixture of landscapes, wild animals, and portraits that tell me more about the photographer than the subject of the portraits. "This is Haydee's dad's shop. He loaned it to me temporarily as a workshop to get some of these framed."

Curiouser and curiouser.

"I remember you now," Derek continues. "What are you trying to find?"

It takes me a second to remember I used the "lost" excuse to speak to him. However, now it has all played very well into my hands. "I'm trying to find out how you feel about Haydee," I tell him, lifting my eyebrows and jerking my thumb over my shoulder toward his inventory of pictures. Most are clearly shots from years ago. High school maybe. When she'd been happy. Running on the beach, in the stands at a sporting event, flying a kite. "But I think I've had my question answered. Quite well, as a matter of fact."

Once again, Derek seems a little lost to the conversation and way too focused on me. But a second later, he blinks a few times and snaps out of it.

"I'm actually a matchmaker," I tell him, turning to walk about the room, more closely examining his handiwork. And to get away from him a bit, because I'm not quite sure why he can't stop checking me out. Of course I'm beautiful, and my pull on men is renowned, but usually the Prince Charming can resist because his focus is so clearly on the object of his affection. "It's probably a secret that Haydee's looking to find Mr. Right, but I feel like I can trust you with it. Can't I?"

Finally, it seems I've sparked his interest with the topic. "It was part of her plan. To get married when she turned thirty-three."

"Exactly! And she seems to think I can help her with that. Only she's . . . not being very cooperative."

His eyes flick to the largest photo against the wall, a stunning black-and-white portrait. When he looks back at me, his face reflects what he'd obviously seen in the subject of the photo. Profound heartbreak.

"I came back for her," he says.

"I figured as much. And I'd like to help you with that."

He laughs, and I see the spark of what, besides his very good looks, Haydee saw in him when they were younger. "I'll take all the help I can get. What can I do?"

What can he do? I'm not sure, after the very admirable try he made in Haydee's front yard Wednesday night, that words will work in this situation. I have a feeling that whatever happened between them in the past, Haydee's mistrust in anything Derek says to her will make it impossible for him to convince her of his true feelings for her.

Suddenly, I have a brilliant idea. "Don't do anything."

"Nothing?" He looks surprised and more than a little doubtful. "I'm not really the sit-around-and-wait kind of guy."

I scoff. "That's why it took you thirteen years to come back and claim her?"

He cringes, but recovers quickly. "I had my reasons."

"I'm sure you did. But time tends to burn bridges, and they have to be rebuilt."

He nods. "Point taken."

I head toward the door and feel him step toward me when I pass. Narrowing my eyes at him, I give him the silent message to back off. "*That's* certainly not going to help the situation, Don Juan."

He scrubs at his face until he's back to normal.

"I'll be in touch if there's anything you can do," I tell him. "Be ready."

❦ 13 ❦

Haydee

Okay, maybe picking up a guy in the breakfast foods aisle of the store wasn't such a bright idea.

"Teaching the future adults of the world about fiscal responsibility is the most important task of our generation."

Yeah, maybe we can stick that right behind world peace and stamping out starvation.

Really, the fact that this date turned into a complete disaster had come as a total surprise to me. I didn't really know Steven, as I used a different bank—something that happily hadn't clicked with him yet. But I'd seen him around town, and he'd been in the store a few times, so it seemed innocent enough to ask him out. Wasn't that what I was supposed to be doing? Finding a husband? And if I couldn't think of anyone I knew well who fit the bill, I had to give a chance to guys I didn't know well.

Like this one.

Steven Kozak, bore extraordinaire, continued his speech, so I just kept eating. Somehow, boring drinks had turned into boring dinner. I'd not had to say a thing for pretty much the last half hour, so content was he to hear himself talk.

Good thing my chicken was tasty.

By the time we'd reached the dessert-and-coffee portion of our date, I was ready to hang myself from the light fixtures. Steven had yet to ask one thing about me, except to question how many financial books I carried in my store to do my part toward helping the world achieve a more financially stable future. To shut him up, I promised to look into that first thing tomorrow morning.

Only that hadn't shut him up. He'd just moved on to the topic of the economic irresponsibility of our government.

Yay me.

There'd been absolutely no chance at all of finding out Steven's thoughts on marriage and family—my sole purpose for asking a virtual stranger out in the first place but, truthfully, by the time we'd been served the before-dinner drinks, I'd pretty much eliminated him as a prospect and quit trying.

Only without any reason to be contemplating my possible future relationship with Steven, my mind kept drifting to the other night on my front lawn. When Derek had kissed—

The door to Mama Josie's opened up and I practically cheered inside. A new customer meant a distraction. Hopefully one that would last until this endless date was over with and I could go home. Even Venus's nonstop insistence that Derek and I were meant to be was better than this. At least I felt like I could participate in that conversation.

It was Venus who breezed through Mama's door, waving off the hostess's offer to find her a seat, and making a beeline for my table.

Bugger.

I quickly focused on Steven, trying to catch up on the conversation. No way was I letting Venus know that he wasn't fascinating. I pasted a smile on my face while my date continued yammering on about the rise and fall of interest rates and their affect on the housing market.

When she stopped at our table, I feigned continued interest as long as I could before finally looking at her.

"Venus, what are you doing here?"

"Haydee, there's trouble back at home!" She dramatically clutched her hands to her breast and tried to look distraught.

"What kind of trouble?" I eyed her suspiciously.

"Big trouble," she assured me.

I knew she was lying, but it was a way to get out of this date. Maybe if I looked reluctant to leave, Venus wouldn't use it against me in our next Derek or not Derek argument.

I interrupted Steven to make my apologies. "I'm so very sorry, Steven." I rested my hand on his arm, though there was absolutely no chemistry on my part. "Apparently there's an emergency at home. We should definitely do this again some time, though." Maybe when the ocean turned to freshwater.

Finally noticing me gathering my purse and jacket, Steven stopped talking for half a second. Then his gaze fell upon Venus, and his entire demeanor changed.

"Oh, my God," he finally muttered when he'd regained consciousness.

Apparently, Venus was more attractive than the latest financial news flash. He rose from his seat as if buoyed by helium, patting at his hair (a toupee, now that I'd had a closer look) and sucking in his gut.

Nice to know he hadn't felt the need to do any of that to impress *me*.

Reaching out, he snatched Venus's hand from her side, pulling it up to meet his lips. "Oh, my God," he repeated after the prolonged and rather gross kiss he planted on her. "You're . . . you're divine!"

You'd have thought he presented her with diamonds the way she lit up. "Why, aren't you nice to notice?"

"*Venus*."

She dragged her grateful gaze away from the Banking Casanova and huffed at me. "What? Can't you see I have a fan?"

"Didn't you come here for a *reason*?" When she shrugged and looked confused, I continued, "You know, to tell me there's an *emergency* at home?" Okay, I'm pretty sure she hadn't actually come for that reason, but whatever worked.

But that didn't work, either. The minute Steven started spouting mushy praise for the Goddess of Love again, she was a goner.

Then I watched her face change. She glanced at me briefly but then turned her sharp attention back to my date.

"Say, Steven," Venus purred, dragging herself closer to him with the hand he still held. His face turned so red as his body pressed against hers, I feared there was a coronary in his very immediate future. "I'm so *thirsty*. Do you think we could go somewhere for a drink?"

"What the—?" I couldn't even finish my thought, because suddenly Steven had developed super speed.

Before I had time to blink the two of them were gone. My date and my alleged fairy godmother.

I waited in the living room until nearly midnight before Venus finally dragged her sorry self home.

From the sounds of it, she'd also brought Steven home with her, though she'd at least had the sense to lock him out of the house (though he remained on the porch for a good ten minutes, bellowing to be let in). I didn't comply, because I fully intended to kill her and didn't need a witness.

"I can't believe you stole my date."

Venus didn't even try to look remorseful, as she dropped her handbag in the middle of the foyer floor and slipped out of her coat. "I did you the biggest favor ever," she groaned. "The man was an octopus."

Funny, I hadn't noticed an abundance of hands on him. Of

course, I wasn't Venus. The Goddess of Beauty had a bit of an advantage with men. I'd probably have been engaged by now, if I'd had that identity working in my favor.

Which made it all the worse that she'd stolen my date!

"Don't do it again," I warned her. "Just because you're delusional about me getting together with Derek doesn't mean you have the right to interfere with my life."

Venus huffed dramatically. "You really can't tell me that you thought that boring banker would make a good husband?"

"It doesn't matter! It's my call, not yours." I scooped her coat and purse up off the floor where she'd dropped them, and followed her upstairs. "Why'd you come to the restaurant anyway?"

"Doesn't matter," she called out from the bathroom. "I accomplished enough."

Enough of what, I wasn't sure.

～ *14* ～

Haydee

"Tell me again where we're going?"

I wouldn't have gone anywhere at all with Venus tonight, since I was still so angry with her about stealing Steven the night before. However, she'd been so cryptic and convincing that I really, *really* would want to know what she'd found that I couldn't resist.

It was just about dusk, and the streetlamps were flickering to life all down Main Street. There were few people about, since most of the stores on this street closed by six on Saturdays—only the bars and restaurants stayed open late.

"I never told you in the first place," Venus replied, trying, with only minimal success, to walk and shove her mass of blond hair farther into the too-small black stocking cap she had on her head. In May.

"And what's with the all-black look?" She'd forced me into black jeans and a black long-sleeved turtleneck, the only solid-black items in my closet. The shirt was too small because it shrank the last time I'd washed it, so I'd spent most of the walk down here tugging the hem down over the bare skin that kept surfacing at my waistband. "Are we planning on breaking and entering? If we are, I'd better warn you that my date with Conner may not have been successful, but he's still on speed dial on my phone, and I can have him here arresting your butt pretty dang fast."

Venus spun around on her heels, flapping her arms. "Will you just come along for the ride instead of questioning my every move? We're in disguise, if you must know."

"Disguise."

I glanced around at the familiar front door of Maisie's Yarn Emporium. Next store down was Fancy Freeze, the ice cream parlor Joan's mom had owned forever, and where I'd spent much of my hard-earned money as a kid. Another block down was my dad's bait shop.

"I don't think wearing black is going to keep anyone in this town from recognizing me."

"Well, it's slimming, too!" Venus huffed.

I rolled my eyes, and Venus spun around and continued to stalk down the sidewalk, leaving me no choice but to follow. Our covert mission apparently was farther down the street. Closer to Dad's shop. I was tempted to just walk right on by.

When we reached the corner of my dad's store, Venus raised a hand to halt my progress. Then, motioning for me to follow, she stepped off the sidewalk into a gravel and weed-filled pathway that led around to the back of the shop, using the downspout strapped to the corner of the building as a shield when she leaned over to peer into the front window of the store. There were lights on, though I knew the shop had been closed for a while. Most likely my dad was busy with paperwork, or ordering supplies, or confirming reservations for fishing trips.

Or pretty much anything to avoid going home. Or visiting me.

"What are we doing?"

"Shh. Look."

I leaned over her shoulder as she peered around the corner of the building. Basically all I saw were fishing and bait posters stuck to windows that really needed cleaning. I'd mention that to my dad, who tended to forget the little things in life, but it usually took something more monumental than that for us to talk. Like a death in the family.

"What are we doing?" I whispered to Venus again.

"Watching."

"Are you a fairy godmother or a spy?"

"Spying is a whole lot more exciting," Venus shot back wryly.

"It would make it a lot easier on those of us who aren't really being helped by the whole fairy godmothering thing." This earned me a glare.

"Pay attention."

In an attempt to follow orders, I looked over my shoulder to scan the street to make sure I wasn't going to get caught looking like an idiot, then shifted my position so I could see between the posters into the bait shop.

My dad was inside, as expected, and he appeared to be stocking shelves or something. But he was talking to someone, or listening to them anyway, which was kind of unexpected. A late customer? Craning my neck I fought for a better view.

It was Derek.

"What . . . what's he doing?"

I didn't really expect an answer. I was too shocked to see the two of them together, I just had to say something.

Venus turned her head to look down at me. "They seem occupied. Did you know Derek is using the backroom in the bait shop?"

What? "Why would he do that?" I was pretty sure he was living with his mother, which was just proof that he was all about the temporary. This "moving back to Bander" thing was so not permanent.

"You'll see." Venus flashed a sly grin. "Come on."

Another glance showed Derek still talking. As I turned around, I noticed his truck next to the curb across the street.

Majorly curious now, I followed Venus down the graveled path
to the back of the building. There was a main back door, which
led into a hallway that branched off into my dad's office on one
side and a storeroom on the other. Odds and ends were usually
stored there, off-season stuff, as well as extra stock.

At Venus's silent insistence, I stood up on tiptoe to peer through
the dusty barred window of the storeroom. Some of the overhead
lights were on, though too dim to really illuminate all that much.
They mostly lit the far part of the room, but I could see that there
was still stuff stored there. A lot more stuff than normal, actually. Not that I'd had any reason to be in my dad's storage room
for many years to know how much was typically kept there, but
this was definitely more than I remembered.

"What are we looking for?"

Venus looked dramatically up and down the alleyway, apparently taking the "spy" gig to a more serious level. I suppose there
was a chance that Howie or Conner could arrest us for trespass-
ing or being Peeping Tinas.

Then she gestured toward the far corner of the storeroom.

With a shrug, I followed her direction. On closer inspection of
the room, there seemed to be a wood shop set up, with moldings
or other long narrow strips of wood in varying lengths, stacked
against the walls. A saw sat on sturdy table I don't remember being there in the past. Piles of sawdust mounded around the saw
and had been swept into piles along one wall.

My dad had taken up woodworking? It didn't seem like something he'd do, considering that running from my mother's memory had been his only hobby for as long as I could remember.

Looking closer for clues into this new development, I noticed
some finished picture frames stacked against another wall.

"Check those out."

I startled a bit at Venus's voice. I'd been concentrating so hard on figuring out what was going on, I'd forgotten she was even there.

Following her gesture, my gaze traveled to a side wall along which groupings of framed photos were stacked. I recognized some of them instantly: scenic landscapes, wildlife in action, a few slice-of-life shots of native villages from remote parts of the world. I'd seen several of them in major magazines—*National Geographic*, *Condé Nast Traveler*.

Yeah, of course I'd noticed Derek's photographs. I mean, it wasn't like I sought them out or anything, but when they were *right there*, when I stocked my magazine shelves at the store, I couldn't exactly ignore them.

"Those are Derek's pictures," I muttered to Venus, unnecessarily, since it was obvious she'd brought me here with the sole idea of showing them to me. "So what?"

"Keep going."

With a frown I turned back, feeling foolish for being here. Feeling like an idiot.

Feeling curious.

So sue me.

I stepped to the side a bit for a better view. A little further down the wall, there was a group of black-and-white portraits. Varying sizes. Tucked in a corner on some shelves.

It took a moment, but when the recognition struck, I gasped.

They were photographs of me. As a teenager, a young woman. Some I'd obviously posed for. Messing around on the beach. Hiking up in the hills.

But one . . .

I'd been staring off into the distance. Tears streaming down my cheeks.

"Oh, my God."

Pushing Venus out of the way, I kicked aside the rock beside the doorway that I knew concealed a key. Shoving it in the lock, I threw open the door and stalked inside, not caring who heard me.

Standing in the storage room, peering at the evidence of a blatant invasion of my privacy, I started shaking. My chest heaving. My entire body vibrating with indignation. Anger.

Horror at what these pictures meant.

"Haydee?"

I spun around to find Derek standing behind me in the storeroom doorway. Dad stood just behind him. It was all I could do not to lunge at Derek. Pummel my fists against his chest. Let out all the rage exploding inside of me.

He watched me expectantly. But at first I couldn't speak. Couldn't begin to articulate my feelings about what I'd just discovered.

"We're okay, Larry," Derek said, without taking his eyes from mine.

Dad disappeared down the hallway. God knew confrontations weren't his thing.

I swung back toward the photographs, the pain hitting me again like a fist to the stomach. "I can't believe . . . you came back."

The photo had been taken at Christmastime. Four months after he'd walked permanently out of my life.

The cemetery ground had been damp where I sat, as raw and bare as my heart and soul had been at that moment. I'd honestly thought then that it was possible to die of heartbreak. The cemetery had been the only private place I had to let it all go.

If I'd had any idea he was there—

"Only that once." Like that made it all right.

A laughing sob escaped my throat. "Once was enough."

It was like finding out he'd betrayed me all over again. He'd

left me as if I meant nothing to him, not even after years of friendship, let alone after the love affair that had taken us by surprise
that summer. And then . . . and then after talking marriage, family, being together forever, he'd stomped all over my heart, telling
me it wasn't the right time for getting serious. That he had better
things to do. Then he'd deserted me.

Only he'd come back. He'd come back, tracked me down, seen
me at my very lowest, at a point where I thought my life was over.
And he'd done nothing but take my photo before disappearing
again.

The fact that he'd caught me broken, in pain— beside *our
child's* grave marker—and hadn't been moved to speak to me . . .

I spun and shoved past the man I'd once thought might be The
One, but who, *clearly*, never was. I dove out into the empty alleyway, barely registering through my angry tears that Venus had
disappeared. I just needed to get away.

"Haydee, stop!"

I ignored him and kept moving, heading down the alley behind the buildings, stumbling on chunks of grass and stray rocks,
wishing the growing darkness would swallow me up.

"I understand you're mad." He followed me, despite the fact
that it was completely obvious I didn't want to carry on any sort
of discussion with him.

"I'm not mad." Mad did not even begin to cover the depth of
my rage. I was furious. I was hurt.

"I was only home for a few days," he continued. "To see my
mom before I left for Africa."

"Completely understandable," I snapped, not slowing my pace
at all, while I dashed with the back of my hand at the tears streaming down my face. If he caught me, I'd show him my anger but *not*
my pain.

"I didn't want to hurt you all over again," Derek called out.

I halted behind the yarn emporium's Dumpster—a truly appropriate place to carry on a conversation as filled with yesterday's garbage as this one. "So why didn't you just visit your mother and be done with it? Why were you following me? Taking my photograph . . . in what was obviously a very *private* moment?"

And why the hell didn't you ask me what I was doing in a cemetery crying my eyes out, you bastard?

Derek approached me cautiously, invading my space. Making me twitch with the need to just turn and run.

Or reach for him.

"I'm sorry. I wanted to see you once more. And . . . and you were so beautiful sitting there talking to your mom like that. I couldn't let the moment pass."

A strangled laugh escaped me before I could stop it. There was no need to correct his assumption that it was my mother's grave I was visiting. I'd spent my entire savings on the marker that had been placed that day *next* to my mother's resting place. "Forgive me if I don't believe you. See, most people who run away to avoid someone don't tend to return to the scene of the crime to stalk them."

"I'm sorry I hurt you."

For just a second, I thought his look was one of regret.

Then I remembered it was him who'd made the choice to leave. And it was him who'd come back . . .

And apparently made the choice to leave a second time.

I turned and kept walking. "What are you doing at my dad's shop anyway? What's with all the pictures and the frames?"

"My agent's been bugging me for years to get a website going, to sell some of my work. Now's as good a time as any."

Right. While he was in one place for five minutes. Get the photos framed, list them on the site, and his worldwide popularity would sell them for him. The perfect supplemental income for the on-the-go adventurer.

"Hard to pack that stuff in a suitcase, though, isn't it?" I questioned. Maybe he planned on hiring a Bander local to oversee the sales for him.

"I won't need to haul it around," Derek answered as he fell into step beside me. He shrugged, then studied me for a moment before answering. "I was thinking of buying the Constantine house."

I shot a look up the hill where I knew the old house stood in the dark, speechless for a moment. I loved that house. The only reason I hadn't bought it myself was because it was so far out of my price range when I was in the market for a house. But I'd always thought that maybe someday . . .

"Why would you do that?" Unless he knew I wanted it and if he had it, I couldn't.

Then I realized that buying a house in town did not mean he was staying. It was a tax write-off—a *huge* one—for someone who made the kind of money he did. It was a stopping-off place when he came to town . . . if he came to town. There was no guarantee. Just because he said it was so didn't make it so. After all, he'd once said he'd love me forever, too. Didn't make it so.

"I thought I might have a reason to stay."

I glanced sharply at him, nearly letting myself sink into his ocean blue eyes. "You expect me to believe you're really staying?"

He shrugged. "Do I have a reason to?"

I snapped out of it. He'd come home without a word to me after everything we'd been through—everything I'd been through because of him. "Don't use me as an excuse to do anything. You didn't do it in the past, so don't start now."

I was concentrating so hard on being furious with him, that I didn't notice what he was doing until he poked me in the left side.

"When did you get the tattoo?"

"None of your business." I jerk out of his reach, nearly shaking with fury again.

Derek caught my arm as I turned down my driveway. "What's really the matter? There's something more going on here than you being angry about a relationship I fully admit I ended badly."

I blinked, staring at him, searching his eyes for the man I'd once unwittingly fallen in love with. And was horrified to find that I could almost see him. Even after all I'd been through. Even after how much he'd hurt me.

Because he had once given me a glimpse at everything I ever wanted in life. Love.

A family.

I opened my mouth to just tell him. To explain about the baby I'd been carrying when he left me. The baby I'd lost five months later. How much I'd needed him.

But I couldn't do it. Because he could do it all over again to me. No matter what he said, his track record of loving and leaving spoke for itself.

I squared my shoulders. "There's nothing going on here. And there never will be."

Without waiting for a reply, I marched up the walkway toward the bright lights of home.

❧ 15 ❧

Venus

"I'm fine. I'm fine."

If I hear Haydee say that one more time, I'm going to shoot her. We'd been making such progress.

We are *still* making progress. I'm not admitting defeat, despite how she stomped into the house last night after our little foray into spying. I hadn't actually expected her home for hours, figuring Derek would be able to talk her into a little reconciliation action. So much for telling him to "be ready." He really didn't step up to the plate on this one.

"I'm fine," she'd said to my raised eyebrows. The slamming of the door behind her had turned that into a complete and utter lie, but I'd had no luck finding out what happened since she'd locked herself in her room after that, apparently not wanting to talk about it.

Much as I wanted to believe the discovery of Derek's devotion had led to hot monkey makeup sex in the alley behind the bait shop, I'm pretty sure she'd have been in a better mood if that was the case. After thirteen years of pent-up sexual frustration, one tended to be a little more *glad* when it got released.

This morning Haydee came downstairs and moved through her morning routine as if last night hadn't even happened. But I, being the fabulously observant fairy godmother I am, knew better.

She didn't yell at me for having eaten all her Pop-Tarts for starters. Then, she burned her toast. And ate it like she didn't even notice the charcoal taste.

"I'm fine," she assured me with a halfhearted smile when I pointed it out to her, even offering to toast her a new piece along with my bagel (since I felt a wee bit guilty for eating all the Pop-Tarts, which are clearly her comfort food of choice).

Then, she'd dumped a can of bean soup into Zeus-the-freakish-furball's breakfast bowl instead of Fancy Feast. I started to mention it, but the stupid feline actually seemed to like the bacon-flavored legumes, so I just shrugged and let it go. He completely deserved a raging case of gas after using my closet as a litter box the day before.

Now Haydee doesn't utter a word all the way to work, where we're covering for somebody named Curt. I practically chew a hole through my lower lip trying to distract myself from the overwhelming urge I have to just take a teensy tiny peek into her head to see what happened last night. But I tough it out. I said I'd go cold turkey and I will.

However, somebody needs to make a patch to curb the withdrawal symptoms.

Before we open the store, I try the direct approach once more, but before I even utter a word, she halts me with a raised finger, and the fakest grin I've ever seen plastered across her mouth. "I'm fine."

"Fine," I huff back.

I'm fine, too. I'm better than fine.

I'm using positive self-talk, which I accidentally read about in one of the books I was shelving the other day, after it fell open on my foot. It said something about the power of our words to create our own lives and how we need to make our words mean something by never stating anything but what we want the truth to be.

If Haydee can be "fine" when she's clearly not, then I can be "fine" when I clearly am. Even though she's set up another stupid date. With the town mortician or something. (At first I'd have thought it was completely ridiculous for a town this small to have its own mortician, but that's before I'd been here long enough to realize that a body really *could* die of boredom. Probably happened with astonishing regularity in Bander.)

Anywho, because I am so fine (for real, not for fake like somebody else I know), I'm moving things along. Because my sorry Cinderella has once again forgone her chance with the town prince and has instead sought out the local undertaker, I feel I must use my time wisely. Not that I think she's going to find any sort of love match with this bozo, but because she's likely to say yes to the first desperate dude who mentions the M word. I have to be proactive in detouring her in the right direction.

I just have to figure out how to do that.

Starting with dragging out the stupid rule book again. As soon as Haydee takes off to run an errand, I abandon the books I'm supposed to be shelving, and sit behind the front counter with the book propped up out of sight of any customers.

The answer has got to be here somewhere.

~ 16 ~

Haydee

I was only here to deliver a book to my dad. Really. Once in a while I came across a book I thought he might like, that might spark his interest, drag him from under his rock. So I'd bring it to him.

"Thought you might enjoy this," I told Dad, passing over the latest political nonfiction bestseller. "It's getting great reviews." Visiting my dad wasn't usually at the top of my list of things to do, so I put it off as long as possible. I rarely ventured into the bait shop, an in-my-face reminder that my dad had given up his passion for writing books and was now wasting away running a business he felt nothing for. Maybe I should feel more kinship to the emotionally neglected bait shop.

He indicated the desk in front of him without looking up from the fly he was tying. Not for the love of tying flies, but because it gave him something to do between customers and fishing trips that kept his keyboard-itchy fingers busy.

"So, how's the season so far?" I asked. The spring Chinook salmon were running in the river, I knew, so that's where he spent his time in April and May.

"'Bout the same as every year," Dad said. "Catch some fish and not others."

I turned to stare at him. That was the closest thing to a joke I'd heard from him in years. Was he coming out of his depression?

Clearly that was too much to ask for. He was right back to

concentrating on his stupid fly tying, giving no indication that he even realized I was in the same room with him. I could have stood there another half hour without him speaking to me again.

"Well, Haydee, my beloved daughter, how's life going for you?" That's what he might have once said to me . . . okay, not in such a sappy way, but at least he'd have shown some interest in my life.

Which was why I didn't venture much into his.

And why I was leaving now. Before my mood deteriorated any further.

Dad cleared his throat. "So, Derek Reed's back in town."

I froze, my brain making a quick one-eighty. A display of finished flies that were for sale suddenly became fascinating.

"Actually, I . . . I was curious why you rented him the bait shop storeroom. I hope you didn't make him sign a long lease or anything. He'll be bored of Bander in no time and run off to some rain forest or something." The bitterness in my voice was obvious to all but the most oblivious.

Which apparently included my father, who shrugged. "He asked for the space."

He didn't elaborate.

"*And?*" I prompted, getting more and more aggravated. After all, he'd brought the subject up in the first place.

"I remember that summer the two of you were an item."

I blinked. "You knew about that?" God, what else did he know about?

"You snuck out to meet him practically every night."

My face caught fire. "So then you know that he also dumped me and left town for thirteen years." Only my superb sense of self-control kept my voice at a polite volume. "It might have occurred to you that renting him space in your shop might feel a bit . . . uncomfortable to me."

He shrugged and completely ignored my concerns. "Derek's a good kid. You could have snuck around with worse."

I shouldn't have had to sneak around with anyone. I should have been able to talk to my dad. The man who had once been the only man in my life. Who had had all of my love. Until my mom died and he "walked out" on me mentally, emotionally . . .

Seemed that there was a pattern maintained by the men in my life.

"You know, I really need to get going," I finally said.

Dad didn't even say good-bye. Surprise, surprise.

On the sidewalk, I tried to breathe away the tension. Then I realized the implications of my dad's brief confession. He knew I had been sneaking out to meet Derek? And he'd done nothing about it?

Part of me was really pissed—the part who was stomping down the sidewalk back across town, barely watching where I was going. Who lets their twenty-year-old—?

Okay, I was twenty at the time. Most parents understand that children who have reached the two-decade mark probably don't need to be told what they can and can't do. I'd been at college for two years. I was used to being my own boss. I didn't need him to be a *dad*.

Only I *had* needed him to be a dad. Since I was sixteen, I'd needed him to be a dad and he hadn't been.

Had he known I was sneaking out of the house at *seventeen*? Sneaking out of school? Sneaky was my middle name in high school. Not because I was out doing anything wrong. I wasn't drinking or smoking or doing drugs. But I wasn't doing anything good, either. Like studying or making plans for my future. I was surviving. Barely.

It had been my dad's job to notice that and help me through it, but he hadn't. Grief had been far bigger than my dad could handle. It had been bigger than I could handle, too. Thankfully, I'd had someone to help me through it eventually.

Derek.

Only Derek had proven himself as unreliable as my dad. He hadn't been there for me, either. Not when it really counted.

And not anymore.

❧ *17* ❧

Venus

This is very, very wrong. Not only didn't my plan to get Haydee hooked up with Derek succeed (in no way a reflection on *my* efforts), but Haydee's clearly punishing me for trying. No longer "fine," she's moved on to payback.

Working under such abhorrent conditions shouldn't be allowed.

"What's the number for the Department of Appalling Labor Practices?" I shout across the store at Haydee. She doesn't take me at all seriously, but continues to yap on the phone. I turn back to my terrible task, sniffing quietly in my suffering, mumbling to myself like a crazy person. "I'm so sorry."

Smoothing my hand across the embossed cover of *Venus, Goddess Extraordinaire,* I try to convey my deep sorrow at being forced to remove the book from the front window. "What a bunch of crap! Readers so do *not* need variety." I set the book aside and lean back into the front window to retrieve *The Art of Aphrodite*. A tiny whimper escapes me. "She says we're going to put gardening books in the display now . . . like people give a shit about getting their hands all covered with dirt. As if!"

"Muttering to yourself again?"

I keep my back to the Boss Who Shall Be Evermore Despised. "I'm protesting the eviction of the window's current residents. It's unfair. And making *me* do it is even more unfair." It's like ripping my heart out. If it hadn't been for this glorious display of all things Aphrodite, I'd not have given this godchild the time of day.

And wouldn't she just be sorry then?

"We can't leave the same thing in the window all the time," Haydee argues, picking up the books I've already removed from the display, ignoring my squeak of protest and moving about the room to put them away in their appropriate places.

At least I can visit them.

When she returns a few minutes later, I've got the print of the *Birth of Venus* down from the wall inside the display, and there's nothing left to do but start the grieving process. What are the five steps again? (Hey! This place is boring as all hell. I have to keep myself busy doing something—like trying to understand humans by reading self-help books they apparently never use, or their lives would be a lot less screwed up.) I think I am already up to depression, step four, having pretty much zipped through denial, anger, and bargaining before I'd even *started* emptying out the display.

You can see how far bargaining got me, and I really gave it my all.

Haydee holds out the new books—an organic gardening encyclopedia, of all things, on top of the pile. "Wanna do the display yourself?"

Me?

I do have a fabulous sense of style, which, of course, I should be able to translate into books, shouldn't I?

"Fine." I roll my eyes pointedly, so she doesn't get any bright ideas about me actually *wanting* to do it. This is done completely under duress. "Whatever."

She barely disguises her grin, thinking she's so damn smart, so I make sure to yank the books from her hands.

Without comment, she turns back to peruse the store for other gardening books. I work in silent protest, until Haydee finally delivers to me a box from the backroom containing a few garden-related props, including a trowel, some flowered gloves, and a bunch of seed packets.

"Seriously?"

"Yes," she says, dropping the box beside me. "It'll keep you busy for a while. No time to meddle with my life if you're decorating a window."

Whipping my head around, I spear her with a glare. Of course, she has her back to me, straightening a table, so she misses my displeasure.

"I'm not meddling. I know what I'm doing."

"We're just going to have to agree to disagree," Haydee continues, maintaining that there's an option to whether she follows my wishes or not.

If only I could make her see the light. I fear it's going to take a bash upside the head for her to realize that she doesn't have a choice in the matter. Derek is her Prince Charming, and there's no way around it.

"I met a really nice guy at the dry cleaners this morning," Haydee says, as if I care. "Totally hot."

I arrange the gloves so they flop over the edge of one of the books, making sure they cover the title, which no one will care about anyway. "May I point out that Derek is pretty hot himself, so the need to look elsewhere for quality isn't necessary?"

"You can point it out all you want. But since it's not going to help your cause, you may as well not waste your breath."

Grrr. It's like trying to persuade a lion away from a gazelle carcass.

A movement outside the window catches my eye, and I lean into the display in time to see Derek pull up in a truck, parking it directly across the street.

Come on. Come on. You need a book. Right now.

Subliminal mental messages without the benefit of my real mental powers do absolutely nothing. With only a passing glance in the direction of the store, Derek crosses the street diagonally, heading away from Mount Olympus Books.

Damn it all to Hades. How are they supposed to start anything if they're never together?

I need a way to get him in the store.

Dropping the rest of the props inside the window display in a pile, I turn to look about the store for inspiration. There's got to be a way . . .

The doorbell tinkles and Haydee's friend Joan comes in. "Hey, Venus."

Wheels still turning in my brain, I nod my head at the backroom, where Haydee disappeared a moment ago. "Haydee's in the storeroom."

Without waiting for a reply, I go back to my perusal of books. When my eyes make the connection, I can't help but grin. Gardening schmardening. I've found the perfect thing to get Derek "Prince Charming" Reed into Mount Olympus Books.

18

Haydee

I didn't even try to disguise my eye roll.

"I gave her gardening books to fill the window." I pointed to the abandoned box of horticultural props Venus hadn't bothered to pick up before shouting at me that she was taking a coffee break. "Apparently she thinks she can bring true love knocking at my door by baiting him with photography manuals."

Joan shook her head, peering at the display, which was now full of titles like *The Complete Imbecile's Guide to Flash Photography* and *Focusing on Fabulous Family Photos,* as well as the latest issues of *National Geographic* and *Travel + Leisure,* sporting— surprise, surprise—photos courtesy of none other than Derek. "I don't follow. Does this have something to do with that Derek Reed guy? Nita says he's bad news."

I picked up the unused window decorations and carried them behind the counter. Let Venus keep her display. She'll just have to admit she's wrong when she discovers Derek won't set foot in the store anymore. I think I made it abundantly clear how I felt about him.

"For once, Nita is absolutely right," I tell Joan, dropping the box to the floor. "Derek is totally bad news. And he's an internationally famous photographer . . . the magazine covers are his work." I gestured at the issues in question. "Didn't you notice the *Bander Tribune*'s shrine to him the other day? Ridiculous really.

He's making a pit stop is all. I give him another month before Bander bores him and he leaves."

Joan adjusted little Braden in his sling across her chest and looked like she really didn't want to say whatever she wanted to say. But she finally spit it out. "Derek was in buying groceries at Hoop's store yesterday. He's pretty good-looking. I can actually . . . see you two together."

I sighed. "Joa—"

She held up her hand to stop me. "I'm not trying to convince you. I'm just saying. I don't know what happened, but obviously it was bad, so I respect that you have your reasons for not getting together with the guy. But he seriously may be the hottest thing Bander has seen in a decade."

I couldn't help myself. I laughed. "I'd be lying if I didn't agree with you, but there are just some things . . ."

I hesitated a second, then just did it. "When Derek dumped me, I was pregnant."

Joan gasped.

"I lost the baby at about five months. Derek was long gone."

I turned and lifted the left hem of my shirt a few inches, displaying the tattoo I kept hidden most of the time.

Joan gawked openly at the softly colored angel wings settled just above my hip bone. I had a spark of momentary guilt for not having told her before. Only Nita had ever been privy to this particular Haydee Miller secret, but only because she'd been my college roommate at the time. It would've been impossible to keep from her. It went a long way to explaining her profound dislike of a guy she'd never met.

I pulled my shirt back into place and sagged against the counter. "The tattoo is a . . . commemoration, I guess." I wasn't the first woman to lose a baby, and it had been so long ago, most of the wound had healed. Until Derek showed up in town ripping it wide open again.

Joan's hands automatically went around Braden protectively. "I had no idea, Haydee. I'm so sorry."

"Me, too. Because I really thought Derek and I had something special." I pushed away from the counter, needing to move. "Apparently, I was the only one who felt that way. I can't trust him no matter how hot he is."

I plucked Zeus off the counter and deposited him on the floor where he belonged. Now if only I could put Derek where he belonged—anywhere but in my head. Where he had firmly taken up residence, even in my sleep. Was I the only one who had erotic dreams about past loves? I ran my hand across the counter, brushing off the cat hair, and tried not to shiver. There'd been a lot of touching in the dream I'd had last night. Groping. Sweaty bodies in the sand.

Why was it always the dreams you didn't want to remember that remained so vivid the next day? Give me a lovely dream about making out with Colin Firth, and I'd forget it before I had my eyes open five minutes. But this stupid erotic dream about Derek would probably feel real for the next week. Or forever.

And if I even gave the slightest thought to making that dream come true, which I wouldn't of course, but if I did, it would swiftly become a nightmare I'd already lived through once, and had no intention of repeating.

I shook my head to clear it. "There should be a law against erotic dreams," I muttered.

Joan burst out laughing, looking a little relieved that I hadn't continued down the morbid path I'd been traveling.

Instead I was traveling down a completely different morbid path. The path of destroyed relationships.

All this remembering made me nauseous. The thing was, our affair hadn't been about sex. That summer, I had truly been the happiest I'd been since before my mother had gotten sick. I thought Derek had been, too.

Before that disastrous thought took any kind of solid hold, though, the door burst open. In poured the Forza clan: Joan's husband, Hoop, and three more of their five kids.

"Mama!"

"Auntie Hay!"

I braced for Madeline's attack, sweeping the little five-year-old up into my arms. As she buried her face in my neck, my heart clutched, thinking about all I'd missed. All I'd been robbed of. It wasn't just a *baby* I'd lost all those years ago. It had been a piece of a man I truly loved. It had been my chance to have what Joan and Hoop have. True love. Except, if it could be tossed away so easily, it was never true love.

"Thought you were only going to be 'five minutes'?" Hoop accused his wife good-naturedly, using air quotes, then winked in my direction. "Not that I believed her for a second. Talking to you never takes 'five minutes.'"

I laughed along with him, though my mind was already far away from the happy family filling my store with all that I'd ever wanted. I held up the slip of paper Joan had pressed into my hand while we'd been hanging out in the backroom. Barney Dracket. *Hoop's college roommate. Park ranger at a nearby national park. Enjoys the outdoors, reading, and kids.*

I would definitely call him. With any kind of luck, maybe I'd get from him all that Derek had taken from me when he left all those years ago.

. . .

"Isn't this soothing?"

"What?!" I shouted back over Bach being played at near eardrum-bursting decibels over Barney Dracket's car speakers.

"Soothing!" Barney turned from the road and shouted in my direction. "I love this stuff. When I've had a hard day it really calms me down and helps me relax."

The only thing it was helping me do was develop a migraine.

"Can we turn it down just a bit?" I gestured to my aching head.

"Oh, no problem." Barney reached for the volume control, and I could almost feel my tension ease.

Except the volume dropped only negligibly. He'd barely moved the knob. "Tell me when you want it back up again," he said.

I sighed and sank back in my seat. Why was this proving so difficult? I wasn't that hard to get along with. I didn't have any disgusting habits. And though I wasn't a stunning beauty—like Venus—most of the men who lived in Bander their whole lives didn't end up with beauty queens for wives anyway. They ended up with the girls next door, a category I fit pretty well. So why was it turning out to be so tough to find a man who was worth a second date?

George, the Sacred Heart Funeral Parlor's undertaker, for example, had been totally hot and polite, and took me to a nice restaurant for lunch yesterday (then insisted on paying, though I'd been the one to ask him out), and . . . did I mention totally hot? Because really that's all he had going for him.

All through the meal I'd appreciated the "view," because the conversation sucked. We were worlds apart in every way. I'd thought we might share a love of running, since he was long and lean, but no. George couldn't run because of his fallen arches. He watched only foreign films with subtitles, while I was all about the latest romantic comedy or the occasional action film. George was a strict vegetarian with allergies to more foods than I even had on my weekly menu and abhorred any type of junk food. I felt it better not to mention my Pop-Tart addiction.

My fallback topic of conversation, of course, was books, but George was pretty sure the last book he'd read had been foisted upon him by his high school English teacher. He'd only been in my store that day picking up something for his sister's birthday.

I'd discovered all this before our meal was even served.

Only the sound of him chewing his food broke the complete silence that reigned after that. When I finally couldn't stand it anymore, I decided to see if I could find common ground by working in reverse . . . starting with what interested him and seeing if I fit in with that. Aside from prepping the dead for their final viewing before being buried six feet under, it seemed George's life revolved around World of Warcraft. In fact, as the date progressed, he checked his watch more and more frequently. Apparently he had another hot Saturday night date with someone he'd met playing WoW, and he needed to get home.

So, even if I'd been looking to get lucky last night, I'd have been turned down in favor of a Night Elf named Nanya. It was obvious George wasn't my husband-to-be, either.

And now there was Barney Dracket, park ranger, nature enthusiast. He'd been expecting my call, having been prepped by Hoop. We'd arranged an all-day Sunday date, which I'd agreed to, figuring maybe if I spent more than two or three hours with a guy I'd have a better chance of getting to know him. And we'd had a wonderful hike through the national park. We'd seen deer, a raccoon cleaning his dinner in the river, and Barney had regaled me with park ranger stories that had me alternately laughing and cringing. We'd had a fantastic time. I was counting on being asked out for a second date, thinking maybe I'd finally hit pay dirt.

Except then we got into Barney's little green truck. Where the conversation ground to a complete halt because you could barely hear yourself think, let alone speak, over the symphonic shrieks of Mozart or Chopin or whoever it was that was making my ears bleed at the moment.

It was a ridiculous deal-breaker, but a deal-breaker nonetheless. I liked my silence. I wanted to read in peace and quiet, not be forced to wear ear protection 24/7.

When Barney turned off the truck in front of my house, my whole body relaxed as if released from a vice grip.

"Want some mood music?" Barney reached toward the radio.

I grabbed his hand. "No! I'm fine. Thanks."

He continued to hold my hand . . . and it felt good. Maybe I could just forget—

I turned my head too suddenly toward my date and my noise-scarred brain screeched in protest.

Guess not. If I had this bad of a headache after such a short time, I could only imagine how infirm I'd be after twenty years of marriage.

"Thanks for a nice day, Barney," I said, extracting my hand from his before I got so desperate to move forward with The Plan that I forgot there was a reason he wasn't The One. "I had a great time."

"Me, too." He smiled and I paused.

On the other hand—

Every day that passed was another day wasted. Every failed date had Venus crossing her arms and saying "I told you so. Now what about Derek?" To which I replied with a resounding, "No fricking way!"

And then I went on another date that completely stunk. I'd been through four different men in the past two weeks. All with various versions of the same result. Failure.

What was the use of having a fairy godmother if she wouldn't just get the show on the road? Offer me other choices, or at least listen to what I was looking for in a guy? Any good dating service did that!

I didn't understand. Did they leave that part out of Cinderella? The part where Cinderella really wanted the blacksmith down the road and *not* the prince with a taste for adventure and commitment issues, but the fairy godmother coerced her into going to the ball and hooking up with Prince Charming anyway?

Was it against the fairy godmother rule book Venus kept grumbling about to match Cinderella with a *normal* person?

I got out of the car and headed for the front door. Barney followed me. At the top of the steps, he pulled open the screen door for me like a gentleman. And I started to cave. Seriously? What was a little loud music?

I smiled up at him and noted his eyes were a nice shade of green, that his teeth were straight and in good repair, and he had pretty good taste in clothes, which were clean and pressed. During our hike, he'd expressed interest in trying hang gliding and already enjoyed rock climbing, promising to take me to a great spot he'd discovered last summer. He was fairly well-read, preferring political thrillers (though he'd mentioned how he loved good symphony music playing in the background while reading . . . *shudder*). He was perfect in almost every way.

If I just leaned in and kissed him, maybe all my problems would be solved. There'd be an attraction between us. We'd go out again. I'd teach him to tone down the music. We'd get married and have little park rangers and bookseller babies. The Plan would be fulfilled, and I could just get on with the rest of my life.

If I just gave him a chance . . .

I leaned a little closer, gauging his response. He smiled encouragingly, leaning in a little himself. If I felt anything from our kiss, I'd go for it. I'd forget all about the car ride and the painful ringing I still had in my ears and—

The front door flew open, the suction practically blowing Barney and me apart.

Venus stood in the doorway, one hand on her hip, looking all goddessy in a silky white robe with gold sparkles. "How long are you planning on standing out here?"

"As long as we want." I reached for the door handle to pull it closed again, but Barney stopped me.

"Who's this *vision*?"

He was through the doorway before I could stop him.

"Nobody," I told him, shooing Venus away as forcefully as I could, gesturing up the stairs, indicating it would be appreciated if she'd disappear.

She didn't take the hint until Barney practically threw his arms around her. "Hey! Hands off the merchandise!" She yanked her bathrobe closed around her before we got too much of a show.

Apparently it had been enough of a show to get Barney going. It was like Steven all over again.

"Uh, Barney?"

"Not now . . . I think . . . I think I've found my dream woman."

"Yeah, I don't think so." Venus shoved at him, but her two hands were no match for the seeming tentaclelike arms Barney had developed. "What's *with* this guy, Haydee?"

"How am I supposed to know? He was fine outside!"

"Of course he was. It was you. This is me!"

With a screech, Venus gave Barney Multihands a shove and then whirled and took off up the stairs.

As soon as he recovered, he went after her. "Don't leave me, beautiful lady! I want you to bear my children, suckle them at your breast—"

"Back off, perv!"

This time when she shoved, Barney lost his balance and rolled backward down the stairs, crashing and thudding all the way.

"Shit!" I dashed over to his side and checked for a pulse. He was still alive, which meant he could sue me for everything I had. "Barney?"

His eyelids fluttered open. "Where is the goddess?"

What? "Wait. You know she's a—"

"No!" Venus shouted from the top of the stairs. "It was a figure of speech."

"There she is!" Miraculously recovering from his tumble, he was on his feet and heading for the stairs before I had the forethought to tackle him.

"Not so fast," I corrected, as I heard Venus slam the bathroom door upstairs. At least she was out of sight. Now if I could just get her out of his mind. "Time to go, Barney Boy."

"But . . . but . . ." He gestured helplessly toward the stairs. "I need . . ."

"Two minutes ago you were ready to kiss me on the porch. And they call women fickle."

Herding him toward the door (not an easy feat when he continued to twist and crane his neck toward the stairway where Venus had disappeared), I finally got him out onto the porch. "Good *night*," I told him. "By the way, playing Bach at full volume? *So* not soothing."

I darted into the house and barely missed slamming his fingers in the front door as he tried to get back inside. I threw my weight against the door and locked the deadbolt before sagging against the back of the couch.

"The coast is clear," I called to Venus, though, truthfully, I should have left her upstairs longer.

"What kind of idiots are you dating?" she grumbled as she came downstairs.

I glared at her. "Well, my fairy godmother *sucks* in the match-making department, so I'm left with no choice but to fend for myself."

"I do not suck," she protested. "You . . . you're *difficult*."

I sighed. "None of this would be difficult if you'd just listen to me when I tell you I'm never going to get together with Derek and find me someone else."

She pursed her lips and put her hands on her hips. "You mean like one of the losers you've picked?"

"*You're* supposed to be the matchmaker, not me." I hung my jacket up in the closet, resting my hand on the door a minute. "I admit I haven't had much luck with my candidates—"

"Maybe you keep dating Mr. Completely Wrong for You because deep down you really *want* Derek to be The One."

I didn't even try to stifle my incredulous laugh. "Yeah, I don't think so."

"Well, I don't know what else I can do to convince you," Venus huffed. "This is going to be a complete disaster if you insist on ignoring me."

Without waiting for an answer, which she wouldn't have liked anyway, she spun around. "Go away!" she shouted toward the living room window, where Barney paced back and forth like a lost puppy all but slobbering on the windows at Venus.

She crossed the room and yanked the drapes closed before turning back to me. "I can't take much more of this. If you would just cooperate, we could end this right away."

19

Venus

She isn't cooperating.

"It took me forever to get him to go home last night," Haydee complains. "He hung out on the porch crying for you for an hour. And I really liked this guy."

Narrowing my eyes, I glare at her before depositing the plate of microwaved M&M's pancakes on the kitchen table. "You didn't like *everything* about him. I can tell these things." Even without peeking into her mind to see. She may have thought she was going to let him kiss her last night, but I could tell she didn't really *want* to.

I brushed some glitter off my cleavage before sitting down so I didn't get it in my food. Truthfully, the thing with Barney last night had me a little worried. What set him off? I mean, yes, obviously, I am beauty personified, but that type of insane reaction really wasn't normal. That little episode, on top of the guy who bought me the blouse with almost no effort on my part the other day, added to Steven the Banker's reaction when I showed up at the restaurant the other night . . . what was really going on here?

"Don't you get that time is of the essence here? My ovaries are not getting any younger." Haydee grabs the freshly toasted Pop-Tarts and drops them on the plate as they burn her fingers. She'd apparently restocked. "I have a deadline to meet. Four weeks, two days, and fifteen hours left. If you keep screwing things up and distracting every guy I try to date . . . I need to get things going, not be thwarted at every turn."

"You do realize that you're talking like this is a business project you have to complete?"

Haydee plops down at the table across from me. This is our morning routine now, like an old married couple. "You told me yourself that both parties have to work at marriage. It's—"

"But *love* should be spontaneous," I tell her. "A man. A woman. Sparks. Attraction. Like what you have with . . . what's his name again? Oh yeah, *Derek Reed.*"

"Fairy tales. Myths," she adds pointedly, in what is, I'm sure, meant to be a dig at my roots.

"What. Ever."

I've lost my appetite now. She's too stubborn, and I'm getting hives from worrying about it. This one was supposed to be easy. But everything's going wrong. I could have turned off that hormonal surge of Barney Dracket's last night, but I can't use my mental powers of persuasion, not after using them on that Walt guy and having Haydee start off this horrible pattern of dating anything wearing pants. On top of that, Derek's doing a lousy job at convincing Haydee they're meant to be, though surely that's what he came back to town for.

And now that I think about it, he gave me a tad more attention than he should have at the bait shop. It's like there's a conspiracy against me, something keeping me from accomplishing this Extreme Love Life Makeover.

I glance around the room for the stupid cat, but thankfully he's not hovering about gloating.

Okay, now I'm just being ridiculous.

Shaking off my paranoia, I shove the plug to Haydee's Seal-A-Meal in the wall to let it heat. This appliance is the coolest thing ever. You just fill a plastic bag with leftovers, stick it in the machine, and it sucks all the air out and seals it up tight. Voilà! Instant M&M's pancakes for tomorrow morning.

"It doesn't matter whether you call it a fairy tale or what," I tell her, while waiting for the Seal-A-Meal to heat. "Your guy is Derek. Nothing's going to work out with anyone else anyway."

"Derek is not my guy," Haydee replies around a mouthful of fruity preservatives. *Way* attractive. "By the way, if he comes into the store because of your window display, *you* wait on him."

Crap. I'd completely forgotten about the window display. If something's really going on that's setting me up for an epic failure, like unstoppable man attraction . . .

What if Derek comes into the store and sees *me*?

Visions of Barney attacking me in the foyer last night crash-land.

I shoot a glance at the rule book next to my placemat, chewing my lip. What if I'm missing something else? Not that I mind drawing these loser wastes of time away from Haydee. But what's to stop Derek from coming into the bookstore, taking one look at me, and forgetting Haydee even exists? I mean, he'd been eyeing my assets pretty thoroughly that night at the bait shop.

"Why don't *you* go for Derek?" Haydee startles me out of my frightening thoughts as she rises from the table and throws her balled-up napkin in the trash. "He'll be a great diversion for you, and while you keep him occupied, just maybe I'll have a chance to find the guy I'm really meant to be with."

I stare at Haydee's back as she leaves the room and heads upstairs to dress for work. What if I *did* accidentally keep Derek occupied? So occupied that Haydee found someone else?

I chew my lower lip as the Seal-A-Meal seals off the remains of my breakfast. When it finishes, I unplug it and throw the pancakes into the freezer. Maybe I should call in sick. If Haydee gets even a hint that he might think of me like these other guys have been, she'll use it as ammunition to convince me he's not The One.

Only he *is*.

Damn it all to Hades. I can't help it if I'm irresistible to men. Can I?

I glance in the hall mirror on my way past. It truly is out of my hands. I'm the Goddess of Beauty, for Zeus's sake. What can I do about that? It's never been a problem before. Well, okay, there had been times in the past where my beauty may have caused . . . *strife* in a marriage. Or allegedly been the cause of a breakup. Or two.

But that totally wasn't my fault! It just wasn't a problem, though there were a few who thought I focused too much on my beauty to the exclusion of more important things, which is completely ridiculous.

However, I admit that in this case, it may, however improbably, be working against me.

So, I need to figure out how to use it to my advantage. If I can manage to keep all the *non*-Princes away from Haydee until Derek makes the right move, maybe that would work.

In my room, I pull open the top dresser drawer, looking for my lavender cashmere sweater to ward off the effects of the air conditioner at the bookstore, while I contemplate my options.

"What's that?" Haydee's standing in the doorway, dressed for work.

She's pointing at the box containing the Golden Girdle. The lid has fallen off again due to its shabby condition, which is rivaled only by the nearly equally shabby condition of the girdle itself. Ah! And there's my sweater.

"My Golden Girdle," I tell her, pulling the box out and handing it to her, watching her eyes light up, her Mount Olympus addiction showing clearly. "The atmosphere here is hell on it, as you can tell."

Haydee handles it gingerly, though the gold flakes off anyway. Maybe I could have been a little more careful with it. In my frustration at not being able to figure out the key to success, I've thrown the rule book into the drawer on top of the girdle box a few too many times, which probably didn't help.

"Does it really work? Attracting men, I mean."

"Not for humans, so don't get your hopes up," I tell her slipping into my sweater and admiring myself in the full-length mirror. "*You* have to do it the old-fashioned way. Which would take no effort at all if you went for the right guy—"

"But why would *you* need to use it?" She ignores my pointed suggestion and glances up at me from where she's tracing with her fingertips the fraying gold threads and jewels that are starting to become loose. "You obviously don't need it to get all the men in Bander to fall at your feet."

She's right. I don't. Look at me . . . just glowing and glittery without even trying. Men do fall at my feet. Which, with the exception of one, isn't such a bad plan.

"I don't use it . . . anymore," I clarify. I don't even know why I keep the thing around. It's nothing but trouble. A temptation. Crack in the hands of an addict. "It was a gift from Hephaestus." A troublesome gift. "I don't use it. Maybe I'll give it to a museum."

Because I seem to be able to bring men to their knees all on my own, thank you very much.

Now I just have to put this particular gift to good use.

❧ 20 ❧

Haydee

Every man in Bander can*not* be so shallow that a beautiful woman makes them forget they have any intelligence at all!

Except that's the way it looks. Every man who came into the bookstore this morning hit on Venus.

Every. Single. One.

Oh, except for the gay butcher, who actually flirted more with me than with Venus. Great. The only man I even had a chance with was the last one I'd choose to marry.

Venus skulked out of the backroom, giving the store a quick once-over before she came all the way out. She'd even developed a method. Scope out the store. If the latest customer was female, she'd duck back into the storeroom until she heard the bell again. If the customer was male, she'd make sure she got to him before I did. Once the guy checked her out, it was as if I didn't exist.

"Thanks a lot," I told her, as she dropped off a stack of magazines on the desk that needed to be added to the racks. "I know exactly what you're trying to do."

Venus nodded. "Keep you from making the biggest mistake of your life? If that's what you mean, then you're welcome."

Apparently our little talk this morning had made no impression on her whatsoever.

"You need to knock it off," I told her, stomping off to file the magazines. "Just because you've got the looks doesn't mean you have to use them like a weapon."

Venus rolled her eyes. "Isn't that a tad dramatic? Think about it this way, if you were meant to be with any of the Romeos waltzing into this store, they wouldn't take a second look at me."

The only way they'd take a look at me over her is if she wasn't here. I glanced across the room where she was examining herself in Joan's feng shui mirror. Maybe I should just cut her loose. It's not like I really needed any help in the store. I had it covered, along with my evening and weekend help, Curt and Kim. Venus was here for her services as a matchmaker. Which, I'd already mentioned, were a little lacking.

Maybe Venus and I just needed to really sit down and develop a strategy. One that, of course, didn't involve Derek, so she had to be willing to compromise on that.

Before I could bring it up, though, a group of older women came into the store, and I got caught up helping them choose a book for their book club.

"Something romantic," said Ethel Bainbridge, former Bander librarian.

"But not too steamy," Reverend Josephson's wife, Marjorie, added. "And I have to be able to take it out in public, so none of those covers with the cleavage showing."

"I understand," I laughed, helping them go through the romance section, checking covers for propriety and trying to remember which had been labeled risqué by some of my regular romance readers.

So busy was I talking to the book club ladies that I completely forgot about Venus until the door chimes rang out. I looked up automatically and found Venus standing at the front counter. As the new customer came in, Venus's look transformed from boredom to sheer evil delight. The customer was Patrick.

Liz Benson had been presenting a Nora Roberts novel for

consideration and poked me in the arm to get my attention. "What about this one, Haydee?"

Venus slid from behind the counter and slithered toward Patrick. Dammit!

I tried to extricate myself from the group, but by this time they had me surrounded, reading aloud over my shoulder, trying to come to some sort of agreement.

As soon as Venus was within Patrick's line of sight, she put her considerable "charms" to work. Thank God he was too intelligent to fall for it.

Only apparently he wasn't.

Like a compass pointing true north, Patrick turned from me to Venus with magnetic purpose.

"Wow."

"Yes," Venus agreed with a smile that threatened to ignite my entire store. Or at least Patrick.

She had no shame at all! Just because she'd figured out that the men in this town were so unused to her type of beauty that they got a little stupid when presented with it, didn't mean she had to use it to make sure I had no one left to date *except* Derek Reed.

Grrrr.

Turning a strained smile back to the customers at hand, I tried to finish things up with them before Venus turned her not-so-innocent flirtation with Patrick into something more serious. I may not want to marry him, but he was my friend, and I didn't want him to fall victim to her manipulations.

"Ladies, I think this would be the perfect book for your group. Shall I ring up four of them for you?" I pulled the books off the shelf and headed for the front desk without waiting for any sort of real answer. Luckily, they were pretty easygoing and followed me.

"Hello, Dr. Butler," Ethel, who owned about five Pomeranians, called out.

When Patrick didn't even blink in her direction, I leveled Venus with a glare that should have melted the makeup off her face, but which actually had no affect at all. She just winked at me and wiggled her fingers before turning back to her prey.

"Don't forget our senior discount, dear," Ethel reminded me, her face looking a bit pinched at having not received any acknowledgment at all from Patrick.

I had to get Patrick out of the store, but didn't know how I was going to do it. I knew from the experience with Barney Dracket yesterday, that it was unlikely I'd be able to distract him. I was just no competition for the powers of persuasion apparently available to the Goddess of Love.

"I have a coupon, too, Haydee, dear." Marjorie slid the coupon she'd clipped from my ad in the *Bander Times* last weekend. "We have to save money wherever we can in this shaky economy, you know."

By this time Venus had Patrick looking nearly hypnotized, and desperation hit.

"I completely understand," I said, turning my full attention temporarily toward the frugal women at my counter, an idea forming, even as I spoke. "Did you know Dr. Butler's running a special on . . . pet grooming? A secret special?"

"Really?" Ethel glanced toward Patrick, where he looked about ready to collapse into Venus's cleavage any second. "What's the special?"

"Uh . . ." I slipped Marjorie's book into a bag, then turned quickly to ring up Mrs. Buck, the last and mostly silent member of the group. "It's . . . oh, yeah! Whoever takes Dr. Butler out to lunch, gets fifty percent off their next grooming." I looked pointedly at Ethel of the many dogs. "No matter *how* many pets you bring in."

Ethel puffed up, obviously pleased at being let in on such a secret special. "I'll buy him lunch for that."

"Me, too," added Liz. "My angora cat, Raphael, got outside the other day and came home a tangled mess of burrs and twigs."

"Then by all means, why don't you both take him out to lunch?" I suggested, looking meaningfully at my watch. "And look, it's just about lunchtime now."

Handing over the last of the purchases, I nodded in the direction of Venus and her admirer, who really had another think coming if he thought I'd be okay with him hanging all over her, even though we really hadn't made any sort of firm commitment to each other. After all, I may have been casually dating different men, but I'd certainly not have flaunted my attraction to them in front of Patrick.

"Go for it, ladies," I urged. "In fact, you'd better hurry. I think the special may expire tonight."

"Come on, Marjorie," Ethel urged. "Let's show the good doc a good time."

Within moments all four women—making saving a buck a team effort—had surrounded Patrick and were herding him toward the door quizzing him on his dining preferences.

Venus found herself shoved to the back of the pack. "Hey! I had him first."

"Actually, I had him first," I snapped, practically slamming the door behind them. "What is with you? Patrick? *Really?*"

"Well, you don't want him," she shot back. "You've made that very clear."

"So why were you hitting on him?"

Venus braced her hands on her hips. "I already told you, I'm making sure you don't make a huge mistake."

"*Arrgggh!*" My vision was practically white with frustration. "He's no threat to your plan. Which is going to fail miserably no matter what you try to do. But you really have to knock this off!"

"And how are you gonna make me?"

My eyes shot open wide. Was she kidding? "I thought you were supposed to be such a good fairy godmother. You said you were going to work really hard at doing everything right so you could get out of this quote/unquote hell hole. What does your stupid rule book have to say about seducing half the male population in order to get your way?"

When her only response was to lose half the color in her face, I wondered if I'd hit a nerve. "It says you can't do that, right?"

"Of course not," Venus scoffed, although a tad defensively if you ask me.

"I think we better find out."

Before she could stop me, I raced into the backroom; the rule book was open on the desk, where she'd been "studying" in between accosting all my male customers.

Holding it tightly against my stomach, I began furiously flipping pages. "It's the starred rules you're most worried about, right? Which means there's a good chance those are the rules that are going to keep you from doing just any old thing you want to get your way."

"Give me that this second," Venus demanded, stomping her foot. "You have no right."

I ignored her and kept turning pages until . . . bingo.

Turning my back on her when she lunged for the book, I quickly read the rule. Then laughed in triumph and spun around to read it again, aloud this time. "*Starred* Rule #545: 'A Fairy Godmother must not use her *feminine wiles* in any way to advance or otherwise influence the love life of her godchild.'"

"What?!" Venus made a grab for the book again, and this time I let her have it. "You've got to be kidding!"

"Nope." I couldn't wipe the smile off my face. She'd have gloated herself if the rule had been in her favor. "No more hitting on my dates. No more luring away the men that come into the store, because any one of them could be The One . . . you have no way of knowing."

"I do too know!" she snapped. "Derek Reed is your Prince Charming. I have never been wrong about it before."

I softened slightly, mostly because I'd won this round, and it was possible Venus *had* never been wrong before, which would make this all the more traumatic for her. "It's okay to be wrong about things. No one is a hundred percent right all the time."

"No *human* maybe!" Venus slumped into the desk chair, the book open in front of her. "He's sucking the life out of me," she moaned. "No mental powers. Now no . . . I have to completely stifle my natural instincts! I don't know if I can do that."

"Oh, I think you can," I offered, heading for the front of the store as the chimes announced a customer. Venus, in her distraught state, never even considered leaving the chair to beat me to any men who might want to take me out. "And if you have trouble, I'll be sure to remind you."

The only sound from behind me was the soft groaning of a goddess losing her touch.

❧ *21* ❧

Haydee

"*I'll* get the door." I gave Venus a shove toward the kitchen Friday evening, not wanting her anywhere near this date no matter whether she'd try to use her feminine wiles or not. She wasn't likely to try anything, as she'd been completely subdued about the whole thing for the past few days. Apparently her desire to prove to her father she could be a proper fairy godmother had dwindled when she'd found out the sacrifices she was going to have to make.

Anyway, there was a possibility this guy could be The One, and I wasn't taking any chances with Venus. "There're fresh M&M's cookies, courtesy of Mrs. McMurtrey, on the counter."

I thought she'd argue about it, try to convince me it was useless to even open the door since "Prince Derek" was my destiny anyway, but apparently the pull of her favorite food was enough to make her give up before she even started.

"Don't expect me to save you any." She flounced through the swinging door with a huff. She'd made it clear all week that she was behaving herself under protest. The fact that she'd followed the rule at all, literally not leaving the backroom of the store most days, and consequently getting a ton of work done, had impressed me. However, I'd still had no luck finding any more dates until Nita finally decided to be supportive and set me up with one of her coworkers. I could handle an attorney.

I answered the front door with a welcoming smile.

The guy on the other side was about five foot one and bald. And not the sexy kind of bald. His pasty white head had wispy white hairs sprouting from it, most notably from a few prominent moles that grew like small brown mini-mountains from the dome of his head.

"I'm Clyde Hanville." He stuck a wrinkled hand through the entryway. "Nita Yang told me you were desperate for a husband. I thought you might be uglier."

I yanked my hand away and wished Nita a thousand deaths by torture. I should have known her offer to set me up was just so she could convince me The Plan wouldn't work.

But I couldn't exactly tell the guy the date was over before it even started.

"Let me get my wrap." I didn't mean it to sound like a sigh.

Venus lounged against the kitchen doorjamb, just out of Clyde's line of sight. I fought the urge to slap the smirk off her face.

"You know, now would be a great time to use those man-attracting powers of yours."

"Oh, no. I wouldn't dream of *interfering.*"

"Fine." I flung the wrap around my neck and tossed one end over my left shoulder. "Maybe Clyde will be The One after all. He's got to be better than Love 'em and Leave 'em Derek."

Love 'em and Leave 'em Derek was looking mighty good right about now. Better yet, dog-killing Patrick. I think I could be completely over that little trauma if it meant I could dump Clyde and go home.

"I don't have all that much experience in the lovemaking department." Clyde's hands shook a bit as he tore his sourdough roll into tiny crumbs, none of which he ate. "But I'm certain everything functions properly."

Nita had said the guy was a shark in the courtroom. I'd have staked my life on him being a *guppy* in the bedroom.

"So what do you say, Hailey? *Hailey?*"

I jerked my attention back to my dinner companion. "Haydee," I corrected.

"Oh, sorry." He dropped the remains of his roll and stuck his hands in his lap like a contrite little boy. "I apologize. I hope that doesn't affect things."

"Things?"

"Our relationship."

We have a relationship?

"Nita said you were very eager to marry and start a family. And I . . ." He pulled a small planner from inside his jacket pocket. "I'm free next Friday at four or the following Wednesday from noon until three."

"Free?" My grip slipped on the condensation on my water glass, and I barely saved it from crashing back to the table. "For what . . . exactly?" If he asked me on another date I was going to have to let him down easy.

"For the ceremony, of course." He pulled a pen from the spine of the planner and clicked it open. "If you choose Friday, we'll have to postpone any sort of honeymoon, but if Wednesday works for you, I would probably have time to fit in the trip to the court-house *and* a quick coupling at my apartment before I return to the office."

When I dropped it, the glass shattered quite spectacularly, spraying water and ice cubes everywhere.

As two waiters descended on the table, I leapt from my seat. I'd make it up to them later.

"Thanks for dinner, Clyde. I'm afraid I've changed my mind."

Not about murdering my best friend though, I thought, stomping between the crowded tables toward the front door. I was done. So very, very done with this blind date thing. Even though the unblind dates had sucked, too.

Maybe I was just done.

Arrgggh! I couldn't do this anymore. I—

I didn't even pause when Patrick stepped up beside me, take-out bag in hand and a bit of an I-told-you-so smirk on his face that I'd have liked to slice off with a steak knife just because he was handier than Nita . . . and because I was still a bit miffed at him for his behavior with Venus earlier in the week. I hadn't seen him all week long. He'd probably thought back on what he'd done and realized I wouldn't be all that happy with him.

"You know, there are easier ways to go about this than taking desperation dates." He pushed the door open and let me out ahead of him.

"It wasn't desperation." I shoved my way out the door. "It was a blind date."

"Gone horribly wrong."

"God!" I threw my hands up. "I can't even disagree with you!" I couldn't help it, I sagged against the lightpole on the corner of Spring and Salty and looked a bit desperately at Patrick, who I was just going to think of as my old friend right now, because I really needed someone to talk to. "Am I really that horrible? That I can't date a single decent guy, I mean?"

"If by that you mean *I'm* not decent, I'll have to take offense. If you mean that you're just wasting your time dating everyone *but* me, I'll have to agree."

"Hey, you're not perfect, buster." He'd drooled all over Venus himself just a few days ago. But I couldn't even say it with as much vehemence as I wanted, so disheartened was I by this whole process.

"You're mad at me?" He even laughed like it was no big deal. "Don't lump me in with whoever that loser was."

Despite my foul mood, I smiled. Patrick deserved major credit. He was gracious even as I, the girl he'd basically proposed to, tried everything possible to avoid saying yes. Which basically meant I had no right to be angry with him for being attracted to Venus. I needed to remember that she was to blame. She'd only come on to him to keep him away from me so that I'd follow her game plan.

I was so stupid.

I glanced back toward where I'd left Clyde muttering about quickies and the viability of his sperm. I'd be done with dates like that if I'd just say yes to Patrick. Who clearly was a better choice than anyone else I'd run across since I'd started this whole thing.

He got my attention again with a nudge with his shoulder. "How about if you and I go out? Just the two of us having fun. No pressure. Like we used to."

That sounded nicer than it should. Just hanging out. Being friends. Just like Derek and I used to—

Shit.

"I think . . ." I closed my eyes and took a breath. "I just need to be . . . alone. I think." I didn't know anything, except that going on a date with Patrick would be anything but "no pressure." "I'm sorry."

"No need to apologize." Patrick leaned in, his cheek close to mine, and kissed me on the temple. His whisper brushed my ear. "Just remember, I'm ready when you are. Always."

✒ 22 ✒

Venus

The clock on the mantel says it's nearly nine p.m., and Haydee still isn't home. She said she was going to a Bander Business Association meeting—something about zoning regulations and protecting her business, which she'd made sound really boring. Almost as if she didn't want me to invite myself to go along with her.

If she's lied and done something stupid––like elope with the beast doctor—I'm going to shoot myself. Intuition may tell me who Prince Charming is for each of my godchildren, but free will means they can do as they please if they don't have the brains to take my word as gospel.

Yet another roadblock Zeus left in my way.

If only I knew for sure what she was really doing tonight . . .

I peer around the corner toward the dining room, searching for what, I don't know. Spies? I mean, how would Zeus even know if I used my powers to just locate my godchild? And even if I did, it would just be for her protection. I can't go letting her make a mistake that would affect the rest of her life, could I?

Maybe just a . . . peek.

Biting my lip, I close my eyes.

Grrrr.

My eyes snap back open. "Stop looking at me," I snap at my father's namesake, who is draped across the arm of the chair across the room from me and has spent much of the last several hours glaring at me lest I make a move he doesn't like. Or to be my reminder that I've given up use of my powers to prove myself the better fairy godmother. Crap! "Fine. I won't look. But if Haydee hooks up with that vet, I'm going to pay him off to euthanize you. Feel me?"

I go back to the Fairy Godmother Rule Book I've been poring over for hours. It's giving me a migraine, which is pretty hard to do to a goddess, Earth-bound or not. None of this stupid book seems remotely important, but I know there are keys in here. Keys to getting me home for real. I swear Zeus has disguised them, though. Haydee found a starred rule in under a minute, but I've looked and looked and can't locate any more than that.

I jerk the book straighter on my lap. " 'Rule #725,' " I read aloud, just to irritate the cat, since he is the only one around. " 'Bonus points for matches made with no expectation of credit toward quota.' What in Zeus's name does *that* mean? Why wouldn't I get credit for a match? That's the whole point, isn't it?"

Once again, I'd like to give Zeus, the father figure, a piece of my mind. At least make the rules *mean* something. That is *not* too much to ask. I continue thumbing through the book.

"This is about the only one that makes any sense," I tell the stupid cat. " 'Rule #79: Image is everything. Clothes make the Fairy Godmother.' " I gesture to my reclining body, clothed glamorously in Gucci. "The one thing about which my father knew what he was talking."

I turn the crinkled old parchment page, smelling dust and ancient ink. " 'Starred Rule #80,' " I read, figuring I may as well read the rules in order for a while. " 'However, if a Fairy Godmother's image becomes a . . . problem, she must be willing to sacrifice it without a second thought.' " I lurch out of my seat, flipping back to reread rule #79, the rule that makes complete and utter sense of the reason for my existence as a fairy godmother, because at least I can be fashionable about it, and then back to #80, which tells me I have to be willing to *sacrifice* it! "Are you eff-ing kidding me?! Why you pompous, evil, rat-faced—*Eeeek!*"

Beside me, the lightbulb in the table lamp explodes in a shower of sparks and shards of glass.

Unable to believe what I've just read, I slam the book closed with a thud. "You're taking everything away from me! What . . . what is left if I give this up?" I look down at the gloriousness that is my combination of impeccable figure, spot-on style, and undu-plicated beauty. "You're . . . you're making me . . . human!"

Across the room, Zeus the cat lets out a meow I'd swear is mocking. I stalk toward him, eyes narrowed. "Daddy? Is that you? Are you—?"

When I get too close, the cat completely freaks out, yowling and dashing between my legs to hide out in Haydee's office.

Taking a deep breath, I force down the paranoia. "I'm going to bed." My voice is calm. My chin high. My reason for living un-questionably . . . questioned.

I stomp up the stairs to show my displeasure at the turn of events, but this is very unsatisfactory in bare feet. I have every right to feel crabby. Everything should be going my way this time. I'm being a good little goddess, learning the rules (a bit belatedly, but still!) and I'm keeping my nose clean and my conscience clear. I'm remaining emotionally distanced and professional, have not fallen off the wagon of my Mental Powers Diet even once. Okay, once. When I nudged that Walt guy in the direction of his True Love. I should get bonus points for that freebie. (Wasn't that a rule I just read?) I should get a medal for good behavior.

And what have I received for my efforts instead?

The command to . . . dress down?

Like Hades, I will!

Shuddering, I slam the book onto the dresser. Hopefully, in

the morning, Haydee will have come to her senses and decided to be cooperative. Derek will magically know exactly what to say to change her mind. And everything will fall into place just as it's supposed to.

I retrieve a slinky nightgown from the top drawer—just to prove my *image* is no problem whatsoever—shoving aside the box containing my Golden Girdle in the process. The lid slips off, revealing the formerly beautiful jeweled belt nestled inside practically shredded tissue paper. Unable to resist, I slip it out of its resting place and hold it up, letting the loose threads of gold and chunks of diamonds, rubies, and emeralds—many of them hanging limply from their fastenings—catch the dim light from the bedside lamp.

There's probably a rule about the girdle in the stupid book, too. Like #975 or some number no fairy godmother would ever have the fortitude to get to even if she read the book every damn night of her confinement. It probably mentions clearly that a fairy godmother shouldn't even *think* about putting the thing on for a second . . . despite how beautiful it is. How wearing it would be kind of like sniffing glue. The high achieved might feel good, but the fact that it could kill you even the first time you tried it isn't worth the risk. Or that obviously something this tempting—because getting attention is like cocaine to goddesses like me—is bad for you.

Even in its shabby, deteriorating state, it almost makes me willing to sacrifice myself again just to get a taste of its power.

But no. Not this time. Not ever again.

I shove the girdle back into the box, sending up a poof of sparkly dust that catches the light and scatters around the room before settling. I don't even try to brush it off. I deserve to be sparkly tonight. I'm as close to depressed as I've ever been—shocker, considering how long I've been stuck here on this Zeus-forsaken planet. So, a bit of glitter upon my person is the least I deserve.

174   *Shannon McKelden*

It's time to go to bed, ending a rather trying day. A trying week.

Just as I'm climbing into bed to forget life for a while, the doorbell rings downstairs.

"Is there no *peace* around here?"

Flicking lights on as I descend the stairs, I fully expect to find Haydee on the front porch, having forgotten her key. "If she's brought that vet guy back here as her new hubby," I tell Zeus—the cat, not the god—who's perched now on the back of the couch staring at me again, "I will not be held responsible for my actions."

Instead, it's Prince Charming on the other side of the screen door . . . holding out a bouquet of spring flowers large enough to fill three vases. "I think we've been moving in the wrong direction," Derek says, holding out the mass of flora. Clearly the lighting behind me has made him unable to see I'm not Haydee.

Grinning, I realize this is the perfect time to prove to Zeus—the god, not the cat—that my image is in no way detrimental to this Love Life Makeover.

"Haydee's not here right now," I tell him, pushing open the screen door to accept the flowers from him. When she arrives home to find them, she'll melt. What woman wouldn't?

Derek holds out the flowers, which I accept with a deep appreciative inhalation of the heady fragrance of freesia, carnations, and tea roses—more varieties than I can count. "I'll tell her you were here."

When I look up, though, Derek's face gives me the chills. His jaw hangs slack. Only propriety keeps his tongue in his mouth. "Beautiful," he murmurs, leaning toward me as if to smell me like I'd been smelling the flowers. "A vision from the heavens."

"Knock it off," I command, dodging back inside and slamming and locking the screen door between us. "I'm not Haydee."

He looks at me blankly.

"You know, Haydee Miller. Love of your life?"

When he reaches a hand up to paw at the screen, stroking it, but looking at me, I freak out. "Snap out of it!! You aren't attracted to me. You're attracted to Haydee. Haydee, you hear me?"

"Let me hold you, sparkly lady. Let me—"

"*Arrggh!*" Slamming the front door, I sag against it. "What's going on here? I can't be . . . I can't be *too* beautiful." I look pleadingly at the cat, who just sits there blinking, as if this means nothing to him at all. "Can I?"

Because if I am, it's going to ruin everything.

23

Haydee

"Are you sure you really want to shop *here*?" I may not know Venus all that well, but one look at her when she first showed up in my store told me that she wasn't the type to shop at Bargain Clothes Mart, where the specialty appeared to be fourthhand clothes. Most of which appeared more suited to wiping your dipstick when checking the oil in your car.

"We can't always have what we want, can we?" Venus growled plowing purposefully through the rather musty-smelling building. Giving a cursory glance at the chaotic layout, she pinpointed the section she wanted and headed for the far wall, which was labeled "Women" in black stenciled block letters on a water-stained wall.

I didn't really have a choice but to follow. She insisted I call Kim in to work this morning. She insisted that she needed to shop for "less image-enhancing" clothes for some reason. She *insisted* she needed them now, before she went out in public again. Bargain Clothes Mart was the worst I could do.

"What is it you're looking for again?" I asked, as she pawed through clothes I was pretty sure I'd seen on some transients under a bridge the last time I visited the city.

"Something to make me less hot." She held up a bright pink-and-green-striped, off-the-shoulder shirt that may have been part of the Valley Girl look of the eighties. After a critical look, she shoved it back on the rack. "Too much skin. That would be counterproductive."

"Counterproductive to what?" I asked, following her as she rounded the rack to the other side, where, if possible, the tops were even less fashionable than those on the first side.

She'd been acting very strange since last night. I'd come home from my meeting to find that one of my living room lamp lightbulbs had exploded, which Venus blamed on Zeus. There was also an unexplained enormous bouquet of flowers wilting on my foyer floor. Venus remained closemouthed about their source.

"I can't have the Prince hitting on me," Venus muttered, seemingly to herself.

"The prin— You mean Derek?" She seriously had to quit talking like this Cinderella thing was for real. I was willing to admit she was Aphrodite, but bringing fairy tales to life was just too strange. "Did something happen with Derek?"

"Of course not," Venus snapped before dodging to the next aisle over. "It's just, well, it's obvious I'm far too beautiful for my own good. So I need to tone down my image."

"If you think you're doing that for my benefit, don't bother," I told her. "In fact, why don't you just go for him yourself?" Which would keep her away from anyone who had a snowball's chance in hell of actually becoming my future husband.

She turned to frown at me like I'd lost my mind.

"What? Don't you deserve a little fun?"

She didn't bother to answer, probably as tired of the "Who's the Real Prince Charming?" argument as I was. I perused the rack a bit on my own, ignoring that little piece of my heart—I mean, *mind*—that protested the idea of Derek and Venus hooking up. If I didn't want him—and I *didn't*—then wouldn't it make total sense to let Venus have him?

"I get where you wouldn't want anything permanent," I told her. "So Derek would be the perfect solution." God knew, no matter what he said, he wouldn't stick around in Bander long.

One just doesn't go from internationally famous travel photographer to hanging out in a little coastal tourist town. In fact, I'd heard buzz around the Bander Business Association meeting last night that Golden Boy Derek had accepted an assignment to photograph Bander, as well as other Oregon coastal towns, for a huge spread in a travel mag. See? I knew it wouldn't be long before retirement got old. Next it would be coastal towns of the Mediterranean . . . someplace far away and far more exotic than Bander. "I think you should go for it."

"No, I am not going for it," Venus scolded, tucking a few of the ugliest shirts I've ever laid eyes on over her arm and heading for the pants rack. "Derek Reed is yours, whether you know it yet or not. I just have to get out of the way so he realizes it."

While Venus's reason for needing to look less attractive—to take her off Derek's radar (had she ever been on it?)—was misguided to say the least, I had to admit I wouldn't be totally opposed to her looking a bit less . . . tempting, I guess is the word I'm looking for. Completely aside from Derek, who was welcome to Venus for all I cared, *every* guy I'd even come in contact with in the last three weeks had gone after Venus instead. And it seemed to be getting progressively worse. Not that they were all meant to be my one and only, but still, I wanted a chance at an even playing field. They started out looking at me, but inevitably, as soon as Venus walked into the room, I ceased to exist. It honestly would only help my whole situation if she wasn't turning their heads.

I hung up the blazer I'd been looking at without even registering what it looked like and removed another. It had only been a little over three weeks since Venus had appeared in my life. Half of my time until my deadline had passed, but I felt further away from my goal instead of closer. It was frustrating as hell.

I glanced over at her digging maniacally through the shirts, returning to the rack anything that didn't elicit a grimace from her. (If it got said grimace, she kept it.) She truly was gorgeous. It wasn't going to matter that she wore rags. Passing by a full-length mirror, I glanced around to see if anyone was watching me. The coast was clear, so I gave myself a good look.

I wasn't hard on the eyes, in my own humble opinion. My figure was trim from running and the occasional trip to the gym. My eyes were clear and green, my complexion good. I dressed casual trendy. I wasn't Venus hot, that was a given, but . . .

Well, there had been a time, long ago, when at least one person of the male persuasion made me feel attractive.

Hot.

Wanted.

Needed.

Before my thoughts deteriorated into an instant replay of my erotic dreams, I headed back for Venus. I had three weeks, one day, and twelve hours to meet my marriage deadline. I couldn't waste time fantasizing about days gone by.

"Oh, seriously?" I ripped the Grateful Dead T-shirt, circa 1970, from her hands. "No way. Even if your dressing down benefits mostly me, I cannot let you wear this in public."

Venus swallowed. "Then it's obviously perfect." She snatched it back and put it in her pile.

"You realize everyone's going to look at you, and not in a good way?"

The color drained from her face. "It doesn't matter. It has to be done. I have to get it right."

She began frantically throwing clothes on top of the pile she already had. Something was really fishy about this whole sudden change of heart. This was a woman who prided herself on looking the part of the Goddess of Beauty. And now she was giving that all up.

"Venus." When she didn't respond, I latched on to her shoulder and spun her around to face me. Panic shone in her eyes. "What. Happened?"

At first she just pressed her lips tighter together. Then the dam burst. "I found another starred rule last night! One that said if my image interfered with the Love Life Makeover, I had to change it. And then Derek . . ." She shook her head. "Never mind. Anyway, since I read that stupid rule, now I have to wear rags!"

"What did Derek do?"

"Nothing." Venus turned and stomped away, headed for the counter, apparently having gathered enough for her new and unimproved wardrobe. "He's your Prince Charming, and I'm going to be the perfect fairy godmother and not allow my image or my feminine wiles to affect your match."

Despite the fact that our goals for a final outcome were different, her changes could only benefit me. I just wouldn't remind her that not being a temptation to Derek would also mean she was no longer a temptation to anyone I actually chose to date.

Win-win, right?

"I have a brilliant idea." I took one of the bags of clothes. "You can try out your new look when we have girls' night out at The Gull tonight."

"In public?" She looked like she was ready to pass out. Had to give her props, though. A few seconds was all she needed to pull herself together. "Fine." She lifted her chin and tossed her curls over her shoulder. "No problem. Daddy will see that I can play by his stupid rules. There's no problem at all."

24

Venus

I'm hyperventilating.

This hellish planet has rendered me fashion-dependent.

When Haydee appears in my bedroom doorway she finds me with my head between my knees trying not to pass out.

"Venus!"

"I'm fine, I'm fine." I roll over on the bed, not fine at all. I can't breathe. And I certainly can't be seen in public like this. "I can't go."

"Are you sick?" Very mom-like, Haydee lays a cool hand across my forehead.

"I *look* sick. These . . . these . . ." I gesture at my rags, knowing they are self-explanatory. I'm BCBG. I'm Donna Karan. I'm Juicy Couture at the *very* least. I am not secondhand, threadbare Grateful Dead! "I look hideous! I . . . I can't go out like this." Putting my awful clothes into my drawer beside my beautiful clothes had been almost more than I could handle. Until I'd actually had to put them on my body. Now I was having a heart attack.

She doesn't laugh, but when I lift my lids to look at her, she has laughing eyes. "It's not that bad," she assures me with half-assed sincerity. "Look, your body glitter left little gold sparkles all over you. That's pretty."

With a glare, I throw myself out of the bed. "Laugh all you want," I snarl as I stalk past my so-not-funny godchild. "You may think this is all amusing, but it's just wrong. Wrong I tell you!"

The mirror in the bathroom tells the same story as the mirror in my bedroom. I'm hideous. "I'm the Goddess of Beauty for fuck's sake! How can I be ugly?"

"You're not ugly."

I throw her a look that says, *Right*. Tell me another story. Another glance in the Reflection of Horror shows me that even Haydee in her layered salmon and yellow tanks and jeans looks better than I do. She's left her hair loose, soft waves tickling her shoulders—something most men would be hard-pressed to resist—and even applied her makeup a bit more artfully than normal. It is almost as if, despite her insistence that this is girls' night out, she's made sure she'll attract at least some male attention. She'll probably succeed.

But I won't. Because, apparently, goddesses *do* wear cheesy T-shirts bearing iron-ons.

I feel my chest cave in again. All the air is sucked out of me, and I collapse to the floor. If I were male, this would be the equivalent of castration.

"You know, they say 'beauty is only skin deep' for a reason." Haydee's looking at me like she's humoring a child. "You could be stunning and still be ugly if your insides are ugly."

I try to tune her out to wallow in my misery, but she sinks to the bathroom floor beside me.

"You're a good person inside, Venus. That's what makes you beautiful. Your beauty isn't found in a pair of designer jeans or a tube of lipstick or in a mascara wand. Your beauty comes from your heart."

Taking a shuddering breath I turn to look at her. "Are you sure?"

"Of course I am!" Bumping my shoulder with hers, Haydee

gives me a smile that makes me feel the tiniest bit better. "You try to help people . . . that's what makes you beautiful."

I *do* try to help people. I mean, that's what's important, right?

If I just avoid full-length mirrors for the duration of my time here . . .

Haydee stands up and holds out her hand to help me up. I accept her offer and rise, avoiding my reflection as I follow her out of the room. It's not like I have to give up everything, anyway. Before donning my fit-for-a-criminal garb, I artfully applied my makeup as usual. I am not completely without my beauty.

With a few deep breaths, I try to summon my confidence. After all, maybe I just need to remember how beautiful I am, how big my generous heart is, and then I'll feel beautiful no matter that I have to dull myself down a bit to accomplish said generosity.

I feel the corners of my mouth begin to turn up again in my typical, cheerful fashion.

And then Haydee keeps talking.

"Just remember, no matter how misguided your techniques, you're doing the best you can, and that's all anyone can ask."

"Misguided?" I reach out and catch her shoulder, preventing her from going downstairs until she's clarified. "What do you mean 'misguided'?"

She shrugs and gives me an indulgent smile. "Well, you have to admit you're not a very good fairy godmother."

"I most certainly will not!"

"It's okay," Haydee continues, heading down the stairs, and I'm too pissed to stop her. "Not everyone can be tops at their chosen profession."

"I didn't choose this profession! It was thrust upon me unwillingly." Haydee appears not to be listening to my protests, so I run down the stairs after her, not for one moment admitting that it's much easier to descend stairs in hideous flat sneakers than it is in stilettos. It doesn't matter in the least, since I look shitty as I'm *not* tripping down the steps. "And I'll have you know I'm very damn good at my job."

Haydee crosses her arms. "Madonna and Guy Ritchie."

"Grace Kelly and Prince Rainier," I shoot back. They were one of my best.

"Elizabeth Taylor and Richard Burton."

"Reese Witherspoon and Ryan Phillipe." Oops, they divorced. "Never mind."

With a shake of her head, Haydee grins at me again. "Forget it anyway. Tonight is about forgetting men. Tonight's about having fun and just being girls. Come on. Let's go clubbing, Bander style."

Bander's idea of clubbing is hanging out in a dingy bar full of smelly fishermen and cheap tourists who can't afford to drink at the country club. Aghast, I realize my commoner's costume makes me blend right in.

I think I'm hyperventilating again. I can't blend in. I *won't*!

25

Haydee

This was exactly what I needed. The Gull wasn't high class, but it was comfortable. I didn't have to think about men and who might be interested in helping me fulfill the next step of The Plan. I didn't have to feel pressure from Patrick to choose him. I didn't have to feel pressure from Venus to give in to the temptation of Derek Reed. I could forget that I have three weeks, one day, and three hours to complete the next step of The Plan.

I just had to relax.

And shoot a killer game of darts.

While Nita went off to get drinks, I took aim at the board again, visualizing the point piercing the bright red bull's eye, quivering momentarily in its target, right next to the last dart I'd thrown. I'd learned to shoot darts with purpose years ago, mentally putting it right where I wanted it before it ever left my hand. Kind of like The Plan, but for dart throwing.

Mel Burns, Bander Elementary's janitor and the current reining dart champ, wasn't appreciative of my skill. "Have mercy, Haydee!"

"Ha! Beat you again, Mel." I high-fived my opponent, who only reluctantly held up his hand.

"Best three out of five?" He plucked the darts from the board and extended the red ones in my direction.

"'Fraid not. The rest of my friends are back at the table."

I headed for our table in the far corner, where Venus tried to be invisible and Nita and Joan lined up enough Jell-O shots to take down a fraternity.

I laughed as I slid into my seat, gesturing at the practically neon-colored shot glasses. "How old are we?"

"Old enough to have fun. You guys at least." Joan saluted with her soda glass, then checked her watch. "The funner the better. I estimate thirty more minutes before I can't ignore my lactating breasts anymore and have to go home."

Nita smacked her on the shoulder. "Absolutely no bodily function talk. I forbid it."

"How about sex talk? 'Cause I might be able to get that to-night, too," Joan piped up hopefully, putting her hands on her hips and doing a little shimmy. She was dressed for sex all right, in a filmy blouse with a barely there cami peeking out between the unfastened buttons, her breasts plump with motherhood. She'd tucked her curls loosely into pins so that they softly framed her face. It's a wonder Hoop had let her out of the house tonight. He couldn't keep his hands off her when she *didn't* put extra effort into her appearance. Lucky girl. "*If* I'm not too late, that is."

"Okay, okay! I get it." Laughing, I chose an orange shot. "Ready? Set. Go!"

I tossed it back, then put my empty glass down and found a guy who looked like he was in college standing between our chairs. His sick puppy dog look was all too familiar.

"I bought you a drink, beautiful lady." He held out a beer to Venus, whose eyes grew wide. "Will you dance with me? I have the moves." He gyrated his pelvis in a slow circle.

"Ick!" Nita commented, with no such thing as tact.

"No, thanks," I piped up, shooing the young man away from the table. "This is girls' night out." Nita was right. I knew from experience tact wouldn't work.

Looking disappointed, he set the beer down on the table in front of Venus anyway, then slunk away.

Venus stared at the beer like it might bite her. "I didn't do anything," she muttered to me, staring around the room with a panicky look on her face, probably half worried men would pay attention to her and half worried they wouldn't.

"Maybe a Jell-O shot would make you feel better?" I pushed one in her direction.

She just shook her head. "I don't do alcohol."

"Well that would explain a lot," Nita muttered.

I shot her a quelling look, and she frowned, but thankfully shut up. My relaxing evening would not be ruined by crankiness or bickering. This night was all about girlfriends and good times.

"So how's the great man search going?" Joan asked.

"We're not talking about that tonight," I singsonged, surveying the room for distractions.

"Why aren't we talking about that?" Venus piped up, deciding that now would be a good time to come out of her funk. Switch the focus off *her* man problems and onto *my* man problems. "Did Haydee mention that she's having absolutely no luck at *all* finding a husband? I personally think that all would be fixed by taking the advice of her matchmaker—"

"Did I mention that Venus stole my date from me the other night?" I interrupted. "Right from the dinner table. Stuck me with the check and everything. *Brilliant* strategy for a matchmaker."

Instead of joining me in my indignation, Nita stood and held her hand out to Venus for a high-five. "I will pay you to do that to every date she tries to go out on."

"Aren't we supposed to be supportive?" Joan scolded.

"Yes," I agreed. "Aren't we?"

Nita didn't even bother to look chagrined. "A true friend wouldn't ask me to support her in such a disastrous endeavor."

"It's not like I've asked you to be an accomplice to murder."

"May as well have."

I heaved out a sigh. Nita hadn't always been so cynical. In college, we'd had a blast. Back then she'd smiled and laughed as we practiced our flirting techniques in our dorm room before hitting the weekend parties. We'd shared our secrets and our dreams . . . back when she still had secrets and dreams. She had good reason to be leery of men and commitment, though. Her ex—a law school classmate who'd swept her off her feet—had turned out to be a complete asshole, a mentally abusive womanizer who, after just a couple years of marriage, dragged her through the swamp of ugly divorces. He'd left her scarred, that's for sure. But I'd seen too many good marriages to believe that every one would be as bad as hers. I glanced up at Joan, practically vibrating with her eagerness to get home to the man she loved. I'd had that once . . . the urgent need to be with someone as often as possible. The almost overwhelming desire to be touching, connecting, 24/7.

I'd been there. Done that. And I had my own scars.

Was there any reason to repeat it more than once in a lifetime? I didn't *need* true love again. It didn't have to be that completely insane feeling to be right between a man and a woman. It could be simpler. I knew it could.

I snapped out of it as another man sidled up to the table and started breathing down Venus's neck—where he had a good view of her chest. "Can you give me directions? To your heart?"

"Seriously?" I stared at him, thinking I might know him from somewhere in town but unsure where. "That's the best pickup line you have?"

He completely ignored me while Venus turned what could only be described as a grateful look on her face. "Aren't you the sweet—"

"No, he's not!" I leaned into her, pushing Romeo out of the way. "Aren't you supposed to be behaving yourself? Remember the rules."

Venus opened her mouth to protest, then clenched her jaw shut and turned away from her pursuer.

"No, thanks," I told him for her. "Girls' night, you know."

Once he was gone, I noticed there was a line behind him—more men waiting for their crack at the slovenly dressed beauty queen. "Are you kidding me?"

Venus followed my line of vision and brightened visibly.

"Snap out of it," I whispered in her ear.

After a moment's more indulgence, she did. The men continued to hang back, hopefully to remain there since I gave them a look that left no doubt they were unwelcome.

"All right, all right," Joan interrupted, clutching her chest in obvious discomfort. "I know I just got here, but I have to go now. Really. I'm sorry, Haydee, you know I'd stay if I could."

So much for girls' night.

I laughed, though, and made shooing motions at Joan. "I understand." She had a newborn at home. Plus a husband who adored her. Besides, my friends weren't my keepers. There were still two other people at the table, as well as a whole bar of distractions.

"Thank you! You're a goddess." With a peck on the cheek and a wave, Joan dashed toward the door.

"That was seriously disgusting." Nita snorted into her beer mug. "When's she going to wean the kid so she can go back to normal?"

"He's only six weeks old," I reminded her. "Just because your maternal gene is dysfunctional."

"It has nothing to do with that. I just don't feel the need to share in the *joy* of breastfeeding." Tipping her mug toward the pool table off in the corner, Nita grinned as much of a grin as her cynical self could manage. "Now if you want to share something about how great it would be to swap bodily fluids with *that,* then I'm all for it."

Venus and I followed her gaze to the back of the room where three pool tables stood, each bearing games at various stages of play, pool and darts being the staples of entertainment at The Gull. The guy under observation definitely fit the definition of hot. At least what I could see of the nice muscular butt bent over the table, lining up his next shot.

There were no less than a half dozen women crowded around the tables vying for the attention of the pool players.

"Look at all those women," Nita gestured. "They're panting all over those guys like lovesick dogs in heat."

"Don't be a spoil sport. Just because you don't believe in love . . ."

"I believe in it," she corrected. "I believe in it being doomed to end badly. I believe it causes a lot of strife. I believe it costs a shit-load of money—"

"Spoken like a devoted divorce attorney."

"You know," Venus butted in very pointedly, "if people just listened to their matchmakers, divorce lawyers might go out of business."

I rolled my eyes at her.

Nita gaped at Venus. "You're not still trying to convince her that Derek's the right guy for her, are you?"

"I've got it!" Venus ignored Nita and directed her outburst toward me, looking suddenly quite pleased with herself.

"What?"

"Something bad happened between you and Derek."

Nita snorted on my left. "What was your first clue?"

I sent her a warning look before burying my head in my beer. What had happened to my peaceful night? The night I wasn't going to think about men. Or dating. Or marriage. Or the fact that a man I never wanted to see again had moved back to town. Which, even on a temporary basis, was causing havoc in my life.

"Okay, so you're not going to answer." Venus didn't sound all that bent out of shape about it, which meant she had more tricks up her sleeves. "So, if you don't 'fess up, I have to assume the worst." She leaned toward me. "Did he cheat on you with Nita?"

With a howl of disbelief, Nita jerked back so quickly she practically tipped her chair over. "Are you kidding me?" She swiveled toward me. "Is she *kidding*?"

I dropped my head to the table. "What happened to my peaceful, man-free evening? Was it too much to ask?"

"See?" Venus continued. "If you don't tell me, I can only make up stories in my head about what happened. And believe you me, I can make up some pretty damn good stories."

I rotated my head toward her. "The details of what happened don't matter."

"What does?"

"The fact that she really shouldn't be having these ridiculous thoughts of marriage in the first place," Nita snapped. "You shouldn't encourage her. Friends don't let friends ruin their lives."

Venus puffed up a little, looking insulted. Since Nita had no idea she was really Aphrodite, Goddess of Love, only masquerading as a lousy matchmaker, the reason for the insult was a little lost on Nita.

"I do believe I'm not wanted here at this table." Venus shoved to her feet, her breasts looking fantastic even in a threadbare Grateful Dead T-shirt that would've made me look like a trashy hooker. "I'm going to . . . the bathroom."

I watched her tentatively step out into the room, completely unsure of herself in her dressed-down state. Within just a few steps, to the completely ironic tune of Maneater being played on the jukebox, three different men had glommed onto her. If she'd been the one looking for a husband, she'd have had no shortage of options.

Of course, if I dropped all expectations, I could probably have my choice of at least a couple of the men in the room. As long as Venus wasn't around.

Only I had to have a few expectations, didn't I? I mean, if I wanted this marriage to last forever.

The bar door opened with a rush of sea salt–tinged air. In walked tall, dark . . . and the bane of my existence. I nearly groaned aloud. The fact that my gaze shot around the room to find out how close Venus was to Derek was completely involuntary.

So was the fact that I noticeably relaxed when I saw her disappearing down the hall into the bathroom. Like I really cared if Derek, like all the other men in the bar, couldn't resist her. Life would be sooo much easier if that was the case.

"Stop thinking about Derek," Nita snapped, noticing what had caught my attention.

"I'm *not*."

She gave me that lawyer look. The one that said she should not be interrupted while posing her arguments.

"He's poison, you know. I was there while you recovered, remember? And I know it's not *him,* per se, that's got you going. It's . . . it's the idea of him. What he represented. You know. The fairy tale. Love." She kind of shuddered the word as if she'd said "pus" or "feces." "He deserted you. He chose his career over your 'love.' Just because your plan says—"

"Don't argue with me about The Plan. It's not about finding some fairy tale. It's about moving on with my life, meeting goals. And don't wreck my night with your gloom and doom," I told her, tossing back the last of the Jell-O shots. "Just have a good time for once."

Nita opened her mouth to protest that she was just trying to be the voice of reason, to prevent me from ruining my life, to—

Luckily for me, she got cut off. The guy from the pool game leaned his hands on the table next to her and cocked one side of his mouth up. "Care for a game?"

I almost laughed at the completely bored look Nita aimed at him. With her exotic Chinese-American looks, men were drawn to her like fish to bait. Little did they know that she was more like rat bait. Poisonous. She preferred to do the attracting, the luring—thus the bloodred lipstick that matched her low-cut wrap top that perfectly framed her "goods." But when men came to her first, she usually turned them down. It was a lesson taught her by her ex, who pursued her until she'd given in to his charm and male magnetism. And then stomped all over her when he thought he might have found greener pastures.

"Do I look like I want games?" Nita licked a spot of foam off the rim of her beer mug, twisting her tongue around the lip with agonizing precision, just to torture the guy. "I'm in the middle of a party."

He glanced at me, dismissing me quickly. Not unusual when I was in the company of Nita Yang. Or Venus, apparently, though thankfully, she wasn't here to add to my feelings of inadequacy at the moment. Truthfully, it was totally okay with me. Husband hunter or not, barfly out-of-towners weren't on my list of potentials. But that didn't mean Nita couldn't catch one.

"You can go if you want," I told her. "I'm fine."

"Puh-lease. If I'm going to desert you, it'll be for better than *him*."

Ouch.

The guy got the message and beat it with a shrug.

"Sheesh. What gave him the idea I was even remotely interested?"

"Uh, the fact that you've been staring at him for the last twenty minutes?"

"I was admiring the art, not writing out a check to buy it and take it home with me."

When her eyes cut across the room again to find his, I realized what she was doing. She was trying not to desert me like Joan had done. But she wanted to.

As her friend, I was all for her having what fun she could.

"Go," I said. "It's been five minutes. Now it can be your move."

She spared me a momentary look before she was right back at the guy.

"*Seriously*. Go. I plan on drinking the events of the past few weeks into oblivion." And watching Venus struggle to ignore all the admirers she had suddenly acquired as soon as she returned from the restroom.

"True." Nita took a swig of beer. "I haven't been laid in three weeks. Otherwise—"

Oh, the *agony* of three weeks. Try almost a year. Not since Patrick and I . . . and I'm not even sure that counted, considering the complete lack of fanfare accompanying our connection. "I understand." Because that's what friends did. They understood their friends' needs didn't revolve around them. That girlfriends and loyalty went both ways. Even on girls' night out.

"Only because you're forcing me, you understand?" She tossed a few bills on the table to cover our beers, then leaned over me. "Treat yourself for once. Forget about the plan and getting married and all that other nonsense. There's a bar full of out-of-towners you'll never have to see again."

I nodded. Like that was going to happen.

And then she was gone. Which was okay. Really it was.

～ 26 ～

Venus

I pull the bathroom door shut behind me and breathe deeply.
And again.

And once more.

It's not working. Men are still attracted to me, which makes
me feel marginally better about the state of my disarray. Only I'm
not supposed to.

I'm not supposed to flirt with Patrick to keep him from talking Haydee into making the biggest mistake of her life.

I'm not supposed to use my charm to convince Derek that, despite her protests, Haydee really is perfect for him.

And I'm not supposed to be a man magnet.

Which, unfortunately, is exactly what's happening tonight.
And I'm not even trying.

I'm *not*.

Not that I don't want to. Upon Zeus, I want to. I want to go
out there and dance to cheesy country music. I want to twirl and
laugh and flirt and fall in love. Just like I used to do at home. (Not
real love, of course. That's for human suckers.)

But I can't do any of that.

What else am I supposed to do to behave? I dulled down. I
gave up my designer clothes for a wardrobe more suited for the
rag bag. I kicked aside a closet full of shoes worth a fortune and
traded them in for canvas sneakers I paid ten dollars for. I skipped

my products and pulled my hair back in a—*shudder*—a scrunchy, for Zeus's sake! What's left to take from me?

There's nothing left I can do to stop being the fabulous goddess that I am!

Taking a deep breath, I venture a look in the mirror. And see the same goddess. Flawless makeup. Fabulous, perky breasts. Trim waistline. Rounded hips, tapering to endless legs (thank goodness for the natural perfection that leaves them undiminished by the lack of heels). My figure is still stunning. Without even trying.

And if every guy is still hot for my bod, that means Derek will still be hot for my bod. Which is going to foul this whole thing up!

I have to try harder. I will make a sacrifice for the good of the Love Life Makeover.

Trying not to swoon, I yank the hem of the oversized T-shirt from the waistband of my cheap jeans and watch my figure disappear beneath the folds of fabric as they settle over my hips. Tears actually prick at my eyelids. Upon Zeus! What have I been reduced to?

Before I can chicken out, I finish the job. I pull a wad of paper towels from the holder and dampen them under the faucet.

One.

Two.

Three.

I attack my face with as much zealousness as I can, wiping off the foundation and blush that even out the skin tones that have only begun going downhill since living on this Zeus-forsaken planet for the past two thousand plus years. But I'm not taking off my mascara. I may have naturally luscious lashes, but it's the principal of the thing. I must retain some of my mask . . . I mean, freedom.

As I scrub, I chant "I am beautiful *inside*" over and over in my head to block out what I'm doing to myself.

And to keep from sobbing uncontrollably.

When I'm finished, I'm left with nothing but soggy, soiled paper towels in my hands, my beauty bled all over them. I steady myself with the edge of the sink, trying not to cry out. Trying not to pass out.

Dragging my gaze up to my reflection, I feel like I've been stabbed in the gut. It's . . . it's . . . hideous. I look like Cerebus. Only with just one horrible head.

I can't do this!

I lunge for my purse, but force myself to stop.

What if Derek shows up here at the bar? I must be unattractive to him. I must not overshadow Haydee in any way. I *have* to do this. For the sake of the makeover. For the sake of True Love.

For the sake of ever getting home again.

Curses on Zeus for making me do this! For humiliating me like a common mortal. He's probably sitting on Mount Olympus laughing at me right now.

❧ 27 ❧

Haydee

Was it weird to feel totally alone in the middle of a bar full of people? It was one thing to feel that way at home, with no one but my cat to talk to, but here? In the middle of The Gull, packed with citizens of Bander and the trickling-in groups of spring tourists?

The hum of bar conversation, the eclectic tunes playing on the jukebox, and the punctuated cheers or groans from the various games in progress, continued as if nothing had changed. My friends hadn't all deserted me. Venus, as soon as she returned from the restroom, wouldn't be keeping every man in the room from giving me a second glance, even while looking like a hobo.

And Derek hadn't just walked into the bar, making me want to run home and hide.

"Thought you wanted a night alone?"

Patrick slid into the seat next to me, pushing a fresh beer in my direction. I hadn't seen him come in.

"Until you got here, I *was* alone, in case you hadn't noticed." I smiled to counteract my somewhat snippy tone. I really didn't mean to take out my bad mood on him. He wasn't the bad guy in this situation.

"Good point." He saluted with his mug. "Do you still want to be alone, or would you be interested in a dance?"

I glanced toward the restroom, where Venus was still holed up, probably afraid to tempt fate by making another appearance.

If I wanted to have any fun at all, I should probably do it while she was out of sight.

I turned back to Patrick, who didn't look very vetlike at the moment, in a light blue button-up and blue jeans. He likely wouldn't smell like his office, either. And if I tried real hard, I could probably forget why I didn't want to marry him.

"I'd love to."

I wasn't too interested in testing out Venus's magnetism, so I made sure we went to the opposite side of the dance floor from the restroom door and that Patrick's back was to it, in case my flirtatious fairy godmother came out.

Once we started dancing, I almost forgot it was Patrick. My whole body relaxed. His dancing skills were only fair, but I didn't really care. Even the little bit of alcohol I'd had helped me let go a few of my inhibitions, and I just allowed myself to have fun and forget about everything. It wasn't like I was agreeing to anything more serious by dancing and having a good time.

So I just let myself float on the fun beat of the music.

"We could do this every weekend if you want." Patrick raised his voice over the sound of a Big & Rich song about saving horses and riding cowboys. "If we were married, I mean."

I crashed to earth with a thud. "Patrick—"

"I'm not pressuring you. But we had fun together before, Haydee, and we're having fun now." The music quieted between songs, then began playing something slow. I took as subtle a step backward as I could, though Patrick continued to hold my hand. "We were good together. We could be good together again."

The thing was, we really *weren't* that good together. The simplicity of our relationship was tempting, but . . .

"How about if I cut in before you start begging, Butler?"

Before I could protest, Derek appeared from behind me and

moved in front of Patrick, edging him out of the way and taking my hand in his. As he spun me around and tugged me into his arms, Patrick shook his head and then turned to walk away to the bar.

"That was mean." Though I had to admit, I was a little disappointed Patrick hadn't put up even the tiniest argument. What happened to his offer to duel for me?

Derek slid his hands along my arms and pulled them up to drape around his neck, our bodies flush against each other. My breath caught on the vague scent of pine soap. Memories rushed back in. Us dancing just like this. Bodies pressed shoulder to thigh, moving as one. A time I'd felt so safe and secure. So lov—

I retreated a few inches. Us dancing like this at a beginning-of-summer beach party had led to us in bed together. And yes, it had been the best of my life. Before or since. Patrick hadn't even compared to Derek.

"He's not right for you," Derek said, close to my ear, as if he could read my mind. "No matter how together you were before, it wasn't like it was with us, was it?"

I pulled back and met his eyes, to tell him he was delusional if he thought our . . . fling . . . had been anything special.

Instead I told him the honest truth. "No. What I had with Patrick wasn't like what I had with you. Patrick never told me he loved me. Patrick never led me to believe we'd spend the rest of our lives together. *Patrick* never broke my heart."

Before Derek could respond, I yanked out of his arms and headed for the door, swinging by the table to pick up my purse. Venus would find her own way home.

As I shoved open The Gull's heavy front door and stepped into the street, I heard Derek behind me. "If you even want a chance with her, Butler, let me talk to her."

Surprised, I actually paused and turned to meet Derek as he stepped outside The Gull. "You're giving up?"

He laughed. "Not a chance, but Butler doesn't know that. You do realize he's told practically the whole town that he's asked you to marry him?"

"Wha—"

My shock seemed to satisfy Derek. "Yeah, I didn't think you'd actually accept."

"*Arrgggh!* You are so arrogant, it's amazing." I'd deal with Patrick spreading rumors like that later. Maybe that was why the only dates I'd been able to get were the ones that ended in disaster. All the good men in Bander thought I was taken. But having Derek just assume I wouldn't accept Patrick's proposal because I'd been waiting for him all these years— "You're still as aggravating now as you were in college."

I turned and stomped down the dimly lit street, bypassing the smokers congregated on the corners. I don't even know where I was going, but I headed in the opposite direction of home. Maybe because I knew Derek would follow me and who knew what would happen if we were together in an empty house.

"You didn't think I was aggravating in college," Derek pointed out. "You loved me."

Yes. I had. "Past tense. Desertion dashes a huge wave of ice water on love."

He didn't respond. Hopefully completely consumed by guilt.

We passed his old beat-up Ford pickup a few blocks from the bar. "What? Can't afford a new ride, Mr. Bigshot Photographer?" More likely he just drove his old crap truck while he was in town. Why would he need a new one if he was headed out in the near future? I gestured at the fire hydrant next to his rear tire. "You should move it, by the way. Howie still has people arrested for that," I pointed out. As a teenager, Derek had gotten so many tickets for parking in front of fire hydrants that Howie finally made arrangements with Derek's mom to have him arrested and left in jail overnight. Apparently, it hadn't made much of an impression.

"It'd be worth it." He grinned, which didn't affect me in any way. "You could bail me out."

"The idea that you even think I want to have anything to do with you amazes me."

I expected a comeback. Something along the lines of, "Yeah, slipping me your tongue the other night really proved how much you don't want anything to do with me."

Instead he didn't answer, and we kept walking. Each step made me more painfully aware of Derek beside me. Of how we used to walk together that summer, just like this, along the beach, kicking up the sand, picking through tide pools to see who could catch more miniature crabs or find the tiniest unbroken sand dollar. How we'd drive up to Portland and wander for hours, just like this, side by side. Every moment in public a moment that we couldn't touch, couldn't wrap our arms around each other. We'd want to hurry, so we could be alone again. But we wouldn't. The anticipation added to the excitement.

I was so lost in my thoughts, I hadn't noticed Derek watching me, until he touched me. We'd rounded a corner, and down the street the bright stadium lights of the high school football field shone for blocks in every direction.

"Come on." Derek grabbed my hand and tugged me in the direction of the field.

I followed, telling myself Derek may have lied to Patrick, but he was right. If I had a chance to make things work with Patrick, I had to bury the past with Derek. We needed to talk. There were things I'd never tell him. But I did need to make sure he understood that I wasn't up for grabs. That he didn't have a chance with me. That I didn't trust him to stay in town, no matter how much he tried to convince me.

When we got to the edge of the fence that ran the perimeter of the field, Derek dropped my hand. "Wonder if they ever repaired the broken spot?"

In spite of myself, I laughed. The spot in the fence he referred to had been used for generations by Bander High students to sneak both in and out of school. "It's been that way for forty years. Of course they haven't repaired it."

"Bingo!" With a flourish, Derek leaned into the chain links, pushing them aside until a space appeared just big enough to squeeze through. "Apparently maintenance at Bander High hasn't improved." He gestured again for me to go through the hole.

"Are you serious?"

"Hey, you broke into your dad's store the other day. This should be nothing for you."

I opened my mouth to snap back at him, now that he'd reminded me of the photo he'd taken, which I still wanted destroyed, but he just persisted in directing me through the hole. Giving up, I ducked through, stepping onto the school grounds, which was a lot like stepping back in time.

"Remember the night we did this after my senior party?"

I laughed, as we made our way toward the stadium bleachers, where we'd be out of sight of the brightest lights. "How could I forget? You dragged me in here to steal the championship trophy. Thank God we didn't succeed. I could have gotten arrested."

"Hey, I needed something to remind me of what I almost had." The look on Derek's face told me he was far away in memory. Though his limp was barely discernible anymore, it was obvious his pain was still there.

"Don't you think your life turned out okay anyway?" I don't

know what compelled me to try to make him feel better. "You have an amazing career."

We'd reached the edge of the bleachers, and Derek started up, racing for the top, without answering. By the time I caught up, he was sitting on the topmost bench . . . the primo spot because here you could actually lean back against the walls of the stadium.

"There are more important things than wild and crazy careers that just serve to occupy your time until you can have what you really want," he told me when I stopped beside him.

He looked up at me, as if willing me to understand what he was trying to say. But I didn't know what to say. I mean, I did. I knew I needed to say that his excuses for leaving me were lame. Inexcusable. Unforgiveable.

No matter how my still-single status made it appear. I hadn't been waiting for him. I'd been fulfilling The Plan.

But when I couldn't force my mouth open to tell him what I thought, Derek continued. He waved toward the brightly lit field below us chuckling a little. "Remember when we talked about me getting my teaching degree, coaching football?"

The blood stilled in my veins. Of course I remembered. Clearly Derek didn't feel the same compulsion to follow through with plans that I did.

"Those were good dreams." Derek looked up at me, sliding his hands around my hips and pulling me gently to stand between his parted thighs, the intensity of his look making me shiver. "I missed you so much, Hades. Every day. Every minute."

My head moved slowly side to side even as my heart welled up, pushing outward at the tears that were too close to the surface. "Don't say that." His regrets didn't make anything better.

"It's true." When his hands touched the skin under the edge of my shirt, I nearly puddled at his feet. He'd been so right back at the bar. It had never been like this with Patrick.

Derek pushed up the edge of my shirt and pressed his lips to my stomach.

It would never be like this with Patrick. It couldn't possibly—

"Haydee, look at me."

I opened my eyes, forcing myself to look at Derek. I nearly gasped at everything his eyes revealed. Every bit of the pain and longing and . . . *loving,* that I kept tucked away in the recesses of my heart.

Without taking his eyes from mine, he brushed his fingers farther up under my shirt, smoothing his heated palms along my rib cage, pushing aside the fabric until he reached the edges of my bra. His look asked permission, but I couldn't bring myself to make the choice. I needed to say no. I wanted to say yes.

My body said yes.

I leaned into him, forcing his palms to slide up and over my breasts. My nipples hardened at his touch.

"I love you," Derek whispered, as he gently brushed my flesh, willing me to remember what it had once been like between us. "I always will."

God I wanted to believe him. I *needed* to believe him. To believe that everything we'd had hadn't been a lie.

When he flicked open the front clasp on my bra and shoved my shirt up, baring my chest to the chilly air, my head dropped back of its own volition. I couldn't have held it up if I'd tried. When Derek's lips closed over a nipple, I gasped and nearly cried out. He tightened his arms around me, pressing my belly into his chest as he took me into his mouth. Sensations I hadn't felt in so long shot through my nerve endings, driving everything else from my mind but this moment in time. This second.

Not wanting him to stop, I braced my hands on his shoulders, on his neck, on his cheeks.

"God, Haydee."

Derek dropped his hands to my waistband, fumbling with the button on my jeans until I almost lost it with impatience. My body knew what was coming. Where he'd next put his lips. How it felt to be loved thoroughly and completely by Derek Reed. And it wanted it.

I wanted it.

Finally, the button gave way, and Derek pushed the waist of my jeans down a few inches. Just enough to give him a glimpse of pink lace.

His face glowed as he looked back up at me, cocked the one-sided grin I'd once fallen completely in love with.

It would be so easy to do so again. To just let myself believe it had all been a horrible mistake. To let myself believe that we really were meant to be.

To fall.

Derek leaned in again, feathering his lips along the upper edge of my panties. Nibbling the skin along the thin barrier, toward the sensitive spot on my hip bone he obviously still remembered, he drove me nearly to insanity with the feelings rushing through me.

Maybe, my body chanted hopefully. Maybe this could be right again. Maybe this could be ours again. Maybe—

"Have I mentioned I find this tattoo a complete turn-on?"

My whole body stiffened.

Maybe . . . *not*.

Jerking away from Derek, I yanked up my jeans and fought with the clasp, needing to get out of here before my body completely betrayed me into forgetting that Derek Reed had abandoned me. Me and his *baby*.

"Don't touch me!" I snarled when he reached for me again.

"Haydee, what's wrong? What's the matter?"

As soon as my pants were buttoned, I snagged my purse while pulling my shirt into place again. It didn't matter that my bra hung loose under my shirt. I'd be moving too fast for anyone to see me before I got home anyway.

"Haydee, talk to me." Derek followed me down the steps and onto the field. "Come on. You used to be able to talk to me."

I whirled, barely avoiding being run down by him. Stepping to the side, I clenched my arms tightly across my chest. "All right, I'll talk. And I'll tell you to stay the hell away from me. Do not touch me again. Do not try to make me forget that you once walked away from me after telling me you'd love me forever." My breath came in humiliating pants. "If you had just been truthful that summer and just told me you were looking for a summer affair . . . if you'd just been honest about that, I'd probably have gone along with it. We'd have had fun in bed, and then we'd have gone our separate ways. But you weren't honest. You lied to me and made me believe it was more."

I turned and went to the hole in the fence, leaving Derek standing there looking like he wanted to say something. But he didn't.

I pulled the chain links inward, opening up my escape hatch before I turned back one last time. "I don't need this in my life, Derek. I need someone I can trust to stick around. Someone who won't take off for worldwide adventures when he gets bored. Someone . . . simple. And you're anything but simple."

Without waiting for an answer, I shoved through the hole in the fence once more, and headed for home without stopping to look back at what I was leaving behind for good.

Venus

For a moment at least, I forget my own troubles. The fact that Haydee just left the bar with Derek on her heels and Patrick the vet purchasing more beer at the bar just proves I haven't lost my touch.

Nita catches me pumping my fist in the air and gives me a once-over that makes my good mood plummet. "I'm not an expert, but I think matchmakers should have some sort of image to uphold."

At home on Mount Olympus I'd have been tempted to have her struck by lightning. "Do you want something?" I ask. "Besides a personality transplant?"

She ignores my jab. "I'm looking for Haydee. I decided to hook up with the guy from the pool game, and I wanted to let her know I was leaving."

"Haydee's gone." The satisfaction of telling her the good news improves my mood greatly. "She left with Derek Reed. Because she knows a good match when it's pointed out to her."

For a second Nita just stares with her mouth open. Her sigh is resigned. "I'm so not holding her hand when this turns out badly. You better stick around to pick up the pieces of the mess you caused."

Without another word, Nita heads back toward the bar. I follow. Since Haydee's gone, I won't be interfering if I happen to attract any sort of attention on the dance floor.

"Shit." Nita grinds to a halt at the end of the bar, and I nearly run into her.

"What?"

She nods her head toward a newcomer ordering a beer. "That's Haydee's dad. Good thing he didn't show up while she was still here. It would've ruined her whole evening . . . even more than leaving with Derek will."

In the thirty-five-plus years since I last saw Lawrence Miller, he's aged more like sixty years. And it's not just the gray hair and stooped posture. It's the sadness in his eyes. The way he observes the room without enthusiasm. Looking like he'd rather be anywhere else. This wasn't the same man who'd turned Maxie Johansen's head once upon a time.

"What's the deal between him and Haydee?" I ask.

"There is no deal between them," Nita says with a shrug. "He's pretty much ignored her since her mom died. Too depressed or something. Haydee tries to act like it doesn't bother her, but it does."

Hm, sounds familiar. I know a bit about disappointing daddies. Not that having a lousy role model for a father affected me in any way. I turned out fabulous without my father's help. I just know how it goes.

Nita turns from Haydee's dad. "He's the poster child for my argument against falling in love and thinking it's going to make life better. If you don't get hung up on someone, it won't ruin your life when they die. Or cheat. Or leave you."

As a fairy godmother, I am bound by duty to disagree with her. On the other hand—

She doesn't wait to hear my opinion, however. And as soon as she's gone, her place is taken by a group of men.

"She's mine, man!" A blond-haired, blue-eyed stud pushes his friend out of the way trying to get at me.

"I saw her first, dude. Back off."

Crap! Either they're blind as bats, or it's completely impossible for me to be ugly. Which rocks just a little, though you'll never catch me admitting it.

Flashing my most disarming grin, I push past them, heading for the end of the bar. "Sorry boys. You're going to have to settle for less than the best tonight, because I'm with him."

Haydee's dad glances up, startled someone has spoken to him. Before he can escape—because I can tell he's ready to bolt—I slip a hand through his arm and wiggle my fingers bye-bye at my admirers. "Maybe another time."

Once they move away, I turn back to the still-stunned man beside me. "You're Lawrence Miller." Though he probably knows this, I feel the need to tell him.

"I don't sign autographs," he grumbles, disengaging his arm and turning back to his beer.

It takes me a minute to remember he was a bestselling author once upon a time. "No problem. I don't read."

His look is almost comical. Startled. Unsure I'm telling the truth. Just a little pained when he decides I am. There's at least a spark of the real man left in there somewhere.

"You're Haydee's father." Perhaps a little reminder of whose parent he's supposed to be will help. After all, isn't it some psychological mumbo jumbo that women, mortal women anyway, can be affected for the rest of their lives by fathers who are absent emotionally from the relationship?

And okay, I read that in some self-help book, too. Wanna make something of it? I was bored and couldn't be held responsible for my actions.

"I'm working for her temporarily," I tell him.

He quickly turns back to his beer. But not before I see the flash of pain in his eyes. Waves of palpable sadness roll off him, which I quickly block.

But not before I feel them.

He suddenly turns back to me, scrutinizing my face carefully. "Don't I know—"

I shake my head. He shouldn't remember me. Only my godchildren are supposed to remember me afterward, according to the rule book (Fairy Godmother Rule #313: "Only a chosen godchild shall recall her Fairy Godmother. To all else, she shall be completely forgotten."), but I don't want to test it out and find out that in this one thing Zeus was mistaken. It could be a problem if Mr. Miller figures out he met me thirty-some years ago . . . and that I haven't aged a day.

Without thinking, I flash my sexiest smile. *Down boy,* I mentally tell him. *You've never seen me before in your life. I'm just another beautiful face.*

The mental nudge makes him shake his head a bit, but works its magic. He's just watching me now. Curiously. Not like men usually look at me, with admiration . . . or desire. He's the first guy in weeks who hasn't practically lost his mind trying to get my attention.

It makes me kind of twitchy, to tell you the truth. Sitting down was probably a mistake.

Back to the task at hand. "So, have you seen Haydee lately?"

He brings his beer mug to his lips while scrutinizing the array of liquor bottles behind the bar. "Been busy."

"Have you now?" I refrain from addressing him as "rat bastard," however appropriate. Though I don't know why I hold back. *He* can't strike me with lightning. "Shame to ignore your own daughter."

Instead of offering excuses or apologies, he pulls his wallet from his back pocket and drops a ten on the counter for his beer.

Not wanting him to leave until I'm done with him, I change the subject. "What do you do for a living?"

"Fish," he replies, then swallows the remainder of his drink, one foot on the floor ready to leave.

I wait for more, but it doesn't come.

Suddenly it occurs to me: What if there isn't any more? What if his sorrow has just been so much for him that he really and truly has nothing left to give?

Something nudges me in the chest region—in my heart, I guess—at the melancholy Mr. Miller wears like a dark shroud. It's unnatural. It makes me feel . . .

Is this how Haydee feels when she talks to him? This emptiness?

Ugh, it's those stupid human emotions again! I don't want to feel them. I really don't need them mucking up my life.

But the guy is so miserable even I can't help feeling a little sorry for him. And Zeus knows, I shouldn't feel sorry for a man who treats his own daughter like the plague, all but completely ignoring her, refusing to participate in her life, and yet wonders why she doesn't believe in—

But we're not talking about that right now.

Haydee's dad needs to realize that his treatment of his daughter may very likely end up causing her to be alone for the rest of her life. Or rather, it would if she didn't have me. But it's really making my job a whole lot harder than it needs to be.

"Another beer, Larry?" the bartender asks.

Haydee's dad just shakes his head and steps away from the stool, dismissing me like I haven't just been serving as his conscience for the last five minutes. Like he doesn't get it.

"Hey." I jump off my own stool to snag the back of his shirt, suddenly pissed all over again at being ignored. "I'm not done talking to you yet."

When he turns around, the blankness in his eyes takes me aback. Makes me suck in my breath.

I remember what he was like thirty-five years ago when he met the woman of his dreams. He was fun. A charmer, actually. Followed us all over the museum that day, practically doing cartwheels to get Maxie to notice him. I remember laughing that day. Really laughing for the first time after a long streak of . . . dutiful-type matches. Lawrence had been so in love with Maxie. There was a good chance he'd loved his daughter once with the same kind of abandon. But all of that's gone now.

It makes absolutely no sense that I get all mushy and sad about it. But I do. She misses it. What she once had with her dad. Is that why she's willing to settle for uninspiring Patrick? Because he doesn't make her feel much, so if, like her father, he cuts her out of his life emotionally, she won't feel such a loss?

My mind does a little mental eye rolling. It's stupid, really. Women are strong on their own. Fathers aren't necessary for our mental well-being. Seriously, who thinks this shit up?

However, to be thorough, I must accept that on this less than enlightened planet, it is possible that Haydee's daddy issues are affecting her life. Not that it's logical, but it's possible. Just because we goddesses aren't susceptible to things like that—

Which means, if something isn't done about Haydee's problem, it's going to continue to fuck up my life, even if she did leave the bar with Derek, and that just can't happen.

Huffing out a breath I give in to what I know I have to do. It's giving away a freebie, but there are sacrifices to be made in the name of love, I guess. If *my* father wants to punish me for it, so be it. Wouldn't be a great big surprise.

"May I walk you to your car?" I don't know who's more shocked, me or Mr. Miller. I tug on his arm before he can protest (if he could actually have worked up that much emotional effort) and guide him toward the door.

It only takes a jiffy to get things on the road to recovery for

Haydee's dad. By the time we reach the corner, I've delivered enough of a boost to get him on track. Maybe it'll even help him find what he once had with Maxie again.

It's not till I'm halfway home to Haydee's house that I remember the starred rule in the rule book. Crap. "To truly match with skill, a Fairy Godmother worth her weight will refrain from using her mental powers to in any way influence the match," it says. But what does that *really* mean? If it's talking about matches, then that should mean I just can't use my mental powers to force love onto my godchildren, right? Meaning I can't use my powers on Haydee.

Giving my services away for free should be my choice.

So I'm golden. Free from guilt.

I think.

❧ 29 ❧

Haydee

The heavy mist lay on my bare arms like an icy blanket I just couldn't shake off. Nita's words from the bar a few nights ago replayed over and over in my mind.

"He's poison."

She was right, I knew. Just being around Derek made me twitchy and uncomfortable. And that was only if I didn't give it a lot of thought. Any deep contemplation threatened to force me into a fetal position. Especially after what happened in the bleachers.

God, it was just like it used to be. Passionate. Fiery. He'd been gorgeous and charming . . . the person who understood me and supported me, even when others didn't. And then my hormones got the better of me and made me forget everything that had gone wrong with us. I'd forgotten the pain he'd caused. I'd forgotten that I'd nearly been left to raise a baby on my own because he was too damn selfish.

Derek was *not* the right guy for me. Not anymore. Passion was overrated.

And I'd been trying to find an alternative to Patrick for four weeks. Four weeks with a fairy godmother, for crying out loud! And I wasn't any closer to finding someone than I'd been in the first place. My birthday was in two and a half weeks. Even if I found a husband right away, our engagement would be brief at best.

When something caught my eye, I bent down to push the sand off the corner of a sand dollar. It was broken, though, not worth keeping, so I tossed it back into the surf and kept walking. It was a sign. No matter what Derek thought, what was broken couldn't be fixed.

So many things in my life felt broken right now. For so long everything seemed so easy. My life followed The Plan I'd created with so little effort. Now all of a sudden nothing was working. I couldn't seem to get anything right.

I stopped again, closing my eyes and letting the thick air press in around me. For fifteen-plus years, The Plan had been my light-house in the fog. Before The Plan, I'd crashed into the seawall over and over again. I didn't want to go back to being the girl who didn't know what she was doing. Who either ran blindly around smashing into walls or who stood frozen in place with no pur-pose. I liked myself the way I was now, dammit. I liked feeling confident and boldly moving through my life with purpose.

Only I hadn't been. For the last month I had not been moving boldly through life. I'd been tiptoeing. Avoiding the answers right in front of me. Refusing to make decisions again. I was that seventeen-year-old girl again. I was running from a life that felt empty and frightening. To move on, I had to exorcise my demons.

And what better way to exorcise them than to just make a choice? To take control.

To make The Plan work despite Derek reappearing in my life, I needed to make a decision. I *had* made a decision—a hard decision, yes, but any decision was better than the sense of noth-ing happening, of my life going nowhere. If I just kept going, I'd end up where I needed to be. One step at a time. Just like when I'd first started using The Plan. I'd woken up each morning and looked at the next thing on the list. And then I'd taken the step I'd needed to take that day to move in that direction.

And today's step was accepting that I already had someone who met all the criteria I had for a husband. A simple solution right in front of my face.

I stopped, listening to the surf's white noise and letting it drown out all my doubts. I pressed a hand to my side, to the tattoo that reminded me daily of how close I'd once come to loving someone with all my heart and soul. With a little nurturing, couldn't I have the same thing from someone I could trust? Someone steady and strong, someone I wouldn't worry every moment might walk away?

I had a life to live and things to do. It was time to forge ahead.

Turning back toward the path off the beach, I made my way through the fog, feeling the sand give way beneath my feet. Venus didn't know of my change of plans. But I didn't feel like arguing with her about it right now.

On the other hand, there *was* someone I had to share my decision with. Pulling out my cell phone, I called Nita and told her to meet me at the bookstore with a bottle of something strong.

She beat me there by five minutes, true to her word carrying a bottle of tequila and a curious look.

"Ah, perfect." I unlocked the front door and ushered her in. "Liquid lunch at its very best." I was not an alcoholic, but it had really been a stressful couple of days. And I was safe here with Nita. If I drank too much, there was no need to worry we'd start making out behind the bookshelves.

While I went to adjust the building's temperature to ward off the leftover chill I had from the beach, Nita dropped the bottle off on the front counter, and then headed into the back. She returned a minute later with two mini paper cups. "Not exactly fine china, but they hold liquid."

We headed downstairs in unspoken agreement. The row of shelves farthest away from the stairs ran parallel to a bank of windows opening onto the patio under the upper-floor deck. It was too cold for outside, so we settled on the floor, using the bookcases to lean against. On the floor between us, Nita splashed tequila into the cups and recapped the bottle. "What are we toasting? Or running away from?"

"Help me forget about Derek. Once I do, everything will be fine."

"Is this about you leaving the bar with him the other night? By the time I noticed, you were gone. What did you do?"

Nothing.

Almost nothing.

"It doesn't matter."

She raised her eyebrows and stared at me pointedly.

"It doesn't matter! Just help me forget."

"Well, that I can do. I'm all for forgetting about men." She raised her cup to mine. "Here's to pest removal!"

I laughed at the unsatisfying whisper of a clunk our cups made together, then tossed back the booze, shuddering as it went down. Nita quickly refilled. It would take more than an inch of tequila in a Dixie cup to eradicate Derek.

Derek, who once would have been the person I could share my troubles with. Derek, who had been my "Nita" back before Nita existed.

But I wasn't thinking about that now.

"So, how do I get rid of him?" I asked, pretending to contemplate. Except maybe I wasn't really pretending. I really had no idea how to evict him from my life.

"How about a spell?" Nita swiveled around until she could see the books at our backs. We just happened to be parked in the metaphysical section. She slid a thin hardcover from the shelf. "Here. There's a go-away spell somewhere in here."

"And you know this how?"

She shrugged. "Never know when you might need these things." When I gave her a look, she continued. "Okay, shoot me . . . the woman who wrote this book was my client once. I helped her divorce her husband."

"So the go-away spell didn't work for her, huh? She still had to hire a divorce attorney?" I poured another cupful. "I don't need a spell. I just need to remember all the reasons I don't want him in my life. Right?"

"You mean like listing his faults?"

"Sure! That would work." Making Derek unappealing would surely keep me from wanting him. And Nita had heard just about every one of my reasons for hating Derek Reed. She'd probably been more than glad when our junior year was over and I, mostly, stopped talking about him. "You go first."

She snorted. "Can't think of anything yourself?"

"I haven't had enough to drink." And every time I thought of Derek, I thought of his hands on me, and how good it felt and then I couldn't—

She topped me off again and settled back against the shelf. "Okay, you once called him arrogant."

Perfect! "Yes! He thinks he can waltz back into town and just jump into my pants like nothing ever happened."

Nita raised her perfectly arched black brows. "He tried to jump into your pants?"

I shrugged. "Had his tongue down my throat." As well as a few other places. "Same thing. He wanted it. I could tell. Where does he get off?"

"Good point. Oh, and he's been a nomad for the last decade,

hasn't he? And I hear he's living with his mommy right now. Not exactly the kind of stable, settled guy you want, right?"

"Definitely not," I agreed, sipping my tequila, which warmed me nicely and took the edge off. "He keeps telling me he's staying, but living with Mommy is make-believe permanency. He said he was thinking of buying the Constantine House."

Nita looked surprised for a moment. "The Constantine house? The one up on the hill? The one you love?"

"Yeah, but he didn't. I drove by and checked." Not that it would have made any difference if he had.

"It wouldn't mean anything if he did anyway," Nita said. "A tax write-off. A waypoint for places far and wide on his way to Belize or . . . or Paris."

"Exactly." I raised my cup in honor of her brilliant conclusion. One that I'd come to myself, but it was still nice to know I wasn't the only one skeptical of Derek's intention to buy a house.

"Oh, I know," Nita continued, "he can't face reality. You've told him you're *never* going to get back with him."

I forced my head to nod. "Never." I'd never feel his hands on me again. I would never kiss him or lay my head on his shoulder and feel his arms around me. We'd never laugh together over old memories . . . or make new ones.

We drank in silence a moment, while I wracked my brain for more cons for the list. Why was it so difficult?

"You can't trust him," Nita offered.

Bingo! "Now we're talking." I saluted with my cup. "I most definitely cannot trust him. He's a Walkaway Joe. At least I know Patrick's going to stay put."

Nita gaped at me. "Wait a minute. You tricked me. This isn't just a 'forget about Derek' thing. This is a 'talk you into Patrick' thing."

"No, it isn't—"

"It is! You have your heart set on fulfilling that plan of yours, and you just want a reason to pick Patrick, who might be a marginally better choice—though, you *know* what I think about the whole marriage thing, no matter who it is."

"Nita—"

"No." She leapt up from her seat on the floor, nearly knocking over the bottle. "I don't think you really want to get married at all. You're just looking for a sperm donor to help you re-create the family you lost when your mom died, and if that's all you're looking for, you *should* choose Derek, because he probably has really hot sperm and your babies would be gorgeous."

My hand froze with the paper cup almost to my lips.

"Oh, God," Nita muttered. "I'm sorry." She quickly set her half-full cup on the windowsill. "I've obviously had too much."

Releasing a deep breath through my lips, I forced a smile. "It's okay. I'm good. It was a long time ago." I downed the whole cup at once this time. "I'm going to accept Patrick's proposal."

I couldn't meet Nita's eyes at first, but finally I had to see what she was thinking. As if I didn't know.

Instead of looking shocked or disappointed, or even angry, she looked resigned.

"Why are you telling me this?" she asked, looking a little like it was hard for her to breathe.

"Because you're pretty much my oldest friend and I'm not going to do it behind your back." Even if she told me how stupid I was and how it'd never work. If she was my friend, I needed to treat her like a friend, through thick and thin.

There was really no question in my mind anymore who was the right guy for me. Patrick was a nice guy. He was stable, loved animals and reading. He owned a business, a home, and had roots here in Bander, where I wanted to stay the rest of my life. All things that Derek was not. He'd been trying to get out of Bander since we were kids, first with an NFL career, then his exciting life-on-the-edge photography career. He hadn't been compelled to return home for thirteen years. And now he'd been back in town over a month and showed no signs of sticking around. He lived with his mother, dropped hints to the press about his gallery showings around the world, was still accepting freelance assignments, and drove the same crappy truck he'd driven as a teenager. All signs his stay in Bander was as temporary now as it had been thirteen years ago.

So who did I choose? The one who represented everything I wanted or the one who'd managed to get under my skin and into my heart once upon a time, but who couldn't get out of my life fast enough? There was no question in my mind which of the two men was the better choice for me.

"Okay."

I glanced up at Nita. "Okay?" There had to be a catch. Perhaps I was missing it because of the tequila. "Why?"

She took a deep breath, then forced her mouth to open. I could practically see how much it took out of her to do so. "Because I'm your friend, and I need to be supportive. Because even if I think it . . . could be a mistake . . . it's your mistake to make, and I have to let you do it."

My chest tightened. "Thanks. That means a lot to me."

Nita nodded then turned to stare out the windows again, snatching up her cup and sipping. "So when are you going to do it?"

I stood up. "No time like the present."

Before I chickened out. Before the tequila wore off.

❧ 30 ❧

Haydee

Outside the Bander Veterinary Clinic, I read my wallet copy of
The Plan one more time.

It hadn't changed.

"Get married" was the next thing on my list. It always had
been, and it always would be. The rest of the list was just words
until I went through with this one. Once I'd moved forward, I
could do all the rest of the things I'd planned for my life. And
the rest of my life didn't need to be complex. The phrase "Keep
It Simple, Stupid" was classic for a reason. Because it made things
easier. The rest of my life, my love life, did not need to be difficult. It needed to be *simple*.

So that's what I was going to do. I was going to get married.
Plain and simple. To the right guy. The guy who wanted to make
me happy. Not the guy who just made me hot.

Taking my last fresh breath for a while, I pushed open the door
and stepped into the sterile, antiseptic waiting room. I ignored the
flashback I had of Patrick carrying Bear's lifeless body into this
very building less than a year ago, and focused on whether I'd be
able to pull this off or not.

Mrs. Riordan, my former seventh-grade English teacher, now
a somewhat crabby retiree, sat stiffly in one of the seats, a rather
ugly dog in her lap. I gave her a small wave, then looked around
for Patrick.

He stood near the back of the room at a small counter.

"Got a minute?" I stepped up beside him. It was now or never. I could barely breathe, and it was only partially because of the smell.

Patrick turned from the chart he was jotting notes in. His face broke into a grin when he saw me. "I think I can spare one." He leaned around me. "Can Pepper wait a few more minutes to get his claws clipped, Aggie?"

Mrs. Riordan grinned broadly and actually batted her eyelashes. "Take your time, Doctor. And don't do anything I wouldn't do."

Patrick laughed and placed his hand at the small of my back to guide me down the hall to his office. "Hold my calls," he instructed his receptionist, Bev, as we passed.

"I can't believe you call her Aggie," I said, grasping for small talk to calm my nerves. "I'd be afraid she'd give me lunch detention."

All the way down the hall to Patrick's office, which thankfully didn't lead past the room in which Bear had taken his last breath, I struggled to relax. Surely Patrick could feel how stiff I was, and I really didn't want him to think I didn't want this. Because I did. I wanted to marry Patrick Butler.

Once he'd closed the door behind us, he slipped off his lab coat and hung it on the back of the door. Which actually helped. Maybe if I just asked him to make sure he didn't look like a vet when he came home at night, maybe took a shower before he even said hello to me . . .

And watched really carefully before backing out of the driveway.

"Please tell me you're here with good news and not to break my heart." He smiled when he said it, but I could see the lack of confidence in his eyes.

It was time to put him out of his misery. And, as a result, I'd be put out of mine.

"I'd like to . . . accept your proposal."

Patrick's face lit up, and I relaxed just a fraction more. He really was a nice guy. Just because everything wasn't perfect didn't mean we wouldn't work. We'd get used to each other in bed, and things wouldn't always be awkward. I'd eventually forget about the past. We'd make new memories, and they'd be happy ones.

"You won't regret it, Haydee." He stepped forward to grip my shoulders, then stooped to look me in the eye. "I promise I'll be a good husband, and we'll have a family together, and we'll be happy."

Which was exactly what I wanted.

He pulled me toward him, and I slipped my arms around his waist, nestling my head against his chest. Ridiculously, my only thought was that I'd miss the scent of pine.

"When?" Patrick asked from somewhere above my head.

"When?"

"When can we get married?" Suddenly excited, Patrick stepped out of my arms. "I know just getting married in front of a judge would be quicker and easier, but I think we should do it right."

"How . . . how so?" God, it wasn't like I hadn't thought about this all week long. That I hadn't known Patrick would take the news and run with it.

"I want you to have a church wedding, with a gown, and flowers, and bridesmaids." His eyes crinkled at the corners when he smiled at me and told me all the things he thought I wanted to hear. "This will be our only wedding, and I don't want you to be disappointed. But it might take a bit longer to pull it together, so we'd have to extend your birthday deadline a bit. Would it be okay to just be engaged by then?"

"I—" I was too overwhelmed with the enormity of what I'd just committed to that I couldn't speak. Really, it would be okay to just be engaged by my birthday, wouldn't it? I mean, the spirit of The Plan would still be honored. And what was a few days give or take? "Whatever you want, Patrick. I just . . . let's do it as soon as possible."

"Perfect!" He grabbed my hand. "Let's go surprise Bev and Aggie."

Good. The sooner we told people, the sooner the entire population of Bander would know we were getting married, and the sooner my past would stop haunting me.

As we stepped through the door, Patrick stopped once more. Then he bent and kissed me. Thoroughly.

You couldn't say I didn't put effort into it. And the fact that I didn't melt into a puddle . . . I tried not to let that bother me.

"My wife. The best phrase in the English language."

I was happy . . . that Patrick was happy. Surely my own feelings would catch up with time.

As soon as we hit the lobby, Patrick slung his arm over my shoulder and announced to the room in general, "Haydee and I are getting married!"

Surprised faces turned in our direction. Bev, Mrs. Riordan . . . and Derek Reed. Who stood at the counter holding an open box and a shocked face.

When Patrick noticed Derek, he grinned even more broadly. Crossing the room, he clapped Derek on the shoulder, not in a mean way, but like a good sport. "Hey, whatever you said to her the other night, man, thanks. It worked. What have you got there?"

"Kittens born in the cab of my truck overnight," Derek muttered, pushing the box in Patrick's direction, all the while not taking his cold gaze off me.

I tipped my chin up slightly. He wasn't going to get to me. I'd made the right decision. He could just learn to live with it.

"I need to get back home, Patrick," I said, needing to get out of there. I'd done what needed to be done. No need to linger. "I'll call you later."

"Hey."

I paused and accepted Patrick's kiss. While not being able to take my eyes off Derek's glare. Tough. He'd just have to get used to this, too. At least as long as he was in town.

I'd almost made it to my car when I heard my name called. Not bothering to pause, I slid the key into the lock and pulled open the door.

Derek stopped me by shoving it closed again.

"Is this because of Tuesday night? To keep yourself from being tempted?"

"Of course not!" God. Like I was that shallow.

"Then why now? You've had years to marry the guy, if you're so sure he's the right one. Which I sincerely doubt, since you had half your clothes off for me in the stadium."

"You're an ass."

I flung open the door and put it between us, throwing my purse across to the passenger seat with such force it burst open and spilled all over the floor.

"Just because you can't forgive me," he growled, "don't make the mistake of marrying him."

"It's not a mistake," I corrected. "It's the most right thing I've done in my life. Following The Plan has *never* failed me."

If anything Derek looked even angrier as he leaned over the door and got in my face. "That plan has failed you more than you'll ever know."

For a second I didn't know what to say, his vehemence about The Plan was such a surprise.

Then I snapped out of it. It didn't matter what he thought about The Plan. Or anything else about my life.

"Good-bye, Derek."

❦ 31 ❧

Venus

"I can't believe you actually went through with it," I yell at Haydee's back, because she refuses to look at me because she knows I'm totally right about this. "It's a mistake, I tell you! Of astronomical proportions!"

She doesn't bother to answer me as she violently chops, then dices, then minces a pile of celery into watery slop. Apparently she only shops for groceries and cooks when she's highly agitated. We have an entire kitchen full of food to prove it, and I'm too sick about the whole situation to even enjoy it.

Though I'm not sure what she thinks she's making. Or that it'll be edible even if I could eat.

"Okay, fine." I shrug, though she can't see me. "Don't forget to invite your father to the wedding. He'll want to share in your joyous day."

There's only a brief pause in chopping. Then she goes at it again.

Arrgggh! What if this is somehow my fault? What if, by giving that Walt guy a little boost in the right direction, what if, by giving Haydee's dad what he needed to move on with his life and be happy, I set off some karmic retribution that's about to fall upon my head?

I broke a rule—not like I'd never broken one before, however inadvertently, but this time I was supposed to be the picture of fairy godmother perfection—and I was being paid back.

Only I'm not going to give up. I can't.

"Oh, and I'd suggest bouncers posted at all the church doors."

Haydee stops chopping, swiveling on her heels, waving the butcher knife back and forth. "What are you planning to do?"

"Not me." Though if I could think of something I might be tempted. "But I think it's highly likely Derek will have something to say when the minister asks if anyone has any objections."

"No, he won't." Haydee snatches another stalk of celery from the pile and begins to destroy it, too. "He's not invited to the wedding."

"Whatever you say. It's your funeral . . . I mean, *wedding.*"

I turn back to the book I stole—borrowed—from the bookstore. It's all about mistaken love. I was studying it to try to understand ridiculous humans with all their faults. "You know, it says here that rebound marriages have a ninety-nine point nine percent chance of failure. And since you're only marrying Patrick to get out of having to marry Derek, it's nearly impossible for it to work out between you. I'd put Nita on retainer now just in case, if I were you."

It's as if she doesn't even hear me speak. Upon Zeus! What do I have to say to the girl to get her to understand?

Fuzzy Zeus jumps onto the kitchen chair beside me and sits down to give me the evil eye.

I lean over and hiss in his face while Haydee has the water running and can't hear me. "What have you done, you old bastard? Haven't you screwed with me enough?"

"Are you carrying on a conversation with the cat?" Haydee asks from across the kitchen.

"Of course not. I was talking to you . . . haven't you screwed with me enough? Can't you see that I'm right? That I know whereof I speak? I'm the Goddess of Love, for Zeus's sake!"

Haydee turns and frowns briefly in my direction before turning back. But not before I see clearly the worry in her eyes. "You really need to give up trying to talk me out of this. It won't work."

"What will? Anything?" I throw my hands up. "Can't I say anything that will make you realize this is a horrible, horrible mistake? Like my marriage to Heph was a mistake—"

Haydee spins around looking surprised, and I almost bite my tongue off. "*You* married the wrong guy? You're the Goddess of Love!"

"Ah!" I vault from the chair pointing an accusing finger in my godchild's direction. I'll use this to my advantage. "But I didn't choose Heph to marry. My father was throwing his weight around in arranging that doomed union. If it had been up to me . . ." I'd have what? Married Ares? Married . . . who? Who had the Goddess of Love really *loved*?

It shouldn't be so difficult to answer that question. Should it?

"But it *was* up to you, though, wasn't it?" Haydee asks quietly. "You could have said no. You could have walked away. But you chose to marry Hephaestus. Didn't that mean you had some faith that it might work?"

"Of course not!" It meant that I had to marry him or I'd have become a fairy godmother long before I *actually* became a fairy godmother.

With a sigh, I sink into the kitchen chair again. I'd had a time limit to bow to my father's pressure. To accept his conditions of remaining on Mount Olympus.

To remember why I was the Goddess of Love.

I turn away from Haydee and stare out the kitchen window into the backyard, where a spring rain has washed everything clean and new. For a moment I wish I could just run outside and be washed clean and new again. New like when I was a young goddess. When being the Goddess of Love meant everything to me. When making matches had been a joy and bringing lovers together was my whole reason for being, and that was enough for me.

But I hadn't felt that way in a long, long time. Since being a fairy godmother, I'd recited the words, but hadn't felt the feelings in so long I wasn't sure I even knew what they were anymore.

Haydee goes back to chopping her probably nearly liquefied celery. In just a few days she's going to marry a guy she thinks will buy her some time. Appease the gods, so to speak. Make her forget about Derek once and for all.

What if I'd been given a choice by Zeus?

Oh, wait. I had.

I'd been given a choice: be sentenced to fairy godmother servitude (a desperate attempt on Zeus's part to remind me of my place in the scheme of things) . . .

to marry Heph . . .

or to fall in love . . . for real.

I bite my lip and survey Haydee from the corner of my eye, afraid if I move she'll notice and confront me again. She probably feels she has only a limited number of choices, too.

Give up on her belief that her plan is the only thing holding her together and try to move forward without it . . .

put her trust in a man whom she once loved with all her heart, but who had somehow lost her trust . . .

or marry Patrick.

Who am I to criticize her for taking the easy way out?

Oh, yeah. I am her fairy godmother. Whether she likes it or not. Whether I like it or not. My success in making her see the light of True Love is the only chance I have to ever go home again.

Besides the fact that I speak from experience when I say that marrying the wrong guy will be a disaster. After all, marrying Heph ultimately hadn't helped me avoid being sentenced to Earth. In fact, it probably hastened it.

But maybe, if I'd taken the last option, opening myself up to real love . . .

"You can't marry Patrick." I leap out of my seat, nearly knocking over the chair in which the feline Zeus had settled to glare at me. He darts through the partially open kitchen door and disappears. "I forbid it."

There's no pause in the chopping. "You can forbid it all you want, Venus, but that won't change things. We set the date for the beginning of July."

I grit my teeth. What I wouldn't give to use rule #419 right about now: "Mental influence may be used once and only once on the subject." I'd use my mental influence all right. I'd mentally smack Haydee upside the head and force her to see what a mistake she's making.

But no. I'm the best damn fairy godmother Zeus will ever see. I will remain calm and in control. I'm "worth my weight" no matter what he thinks about me. So I'll fix this without mental coercion of any sort.

I just have to figure out what will change things my way.

Wait! I jerk my head up to glare at Haydee. "July? What about your birthday . . . on *June* twenty-fifth? What about your plan?"

Haydee shrugs. "We can't plan a wedding that fast. I needed to compromise."

Arggh! "Compromise? But you told me how disastrous things turned out when you deviated from The Plan. You said—"

Haydee whirled around, fire in her eyes. "I know what I said, Venus. But some things can't be helped. I care about Patrick, and I'm marrying him. Get over it."

✎ 32 ✎

Venus

Getting over it? So not my thing.

I bide my time, waiting for the right moment to make my move. I've had four days to think and plot and plan. Since I've basically been magic-bound by my ever-so-supportive father, I have to do things the old-fashioned way. The—*shudder*—human way. So, I will halt this fiasco of an engagement with good old sabotage.

Haydee took the day off today, leaving Kim and me in the store to run things. She and Patrick have their first wedding prep meeting at one, when they meet at the flower shop to pick their arrangements for the ceremony.

"Thanks! Come again!" I parrot to the fifth customer I've helped in the last fifteen minutes. Since when is this place so busy?! We've probably made a bajillion dollars by now. I glance at the clock to see that it's nearly twelve-thirty, and I still have to get into costume.

The door chimes ring again, ushering in another customer. If I don't get out of here . . .

In an Oscar-worthy performance, I bend over double, clutching my stomach and groaning loudly enough to draw Kim's attention from where she's helping another customer across the room.

"Venus?" She dashes to my side. "Are you all right?"

"Food . . . poisoning," I gasp, throwing in a couple of gagging noises just to throw the fear of vomit into her so she doesn't try to make me stay.

It works, and I'm out the door with well wishes and a bit of a shove.

As soon as I'm out of sight of the store, I run. I've plotted out my plan of attack with a Bander Chamber of Commerce map. First stop: the McDonald's restroom to costume up.

Bander Clothes Mart proved to be very helpful in providing just the right look for following my godchild about town unobserved. Plus there was no need to find a rich man to fund my purchases when a poor man would do. Prices at Bargain Clothes Mart were as low-class as their attire. However, I've put together the most fabulous disguise, if I do say so myself. My new floral print housecoat (stuffed with a pillow from Haydee's couch to disguise my primo figure), saggy support hose, and scruffy slippers, all topped off with a curly gray wig and hideous fruited hat, turn me into old Mrs. Cronos.

I hobble into the floral shop mere minutes behind my godchild and her never-going-to-be bridegroom. Where Patrick is chattering away with the florist, and Haydee's feigning interest that probably has no one fooled.

"What do you think, honey? Rosebuds or carnations for your bouquet?"

While Haydee contemplates the ultra-tough decision of which flowers to put in the bouquet she has no desire to carry, I maneuver myself into place.

"I'll be with you in a moment, ma'am," the florist tells me with a smile.

I cringe inwardly at being addressed as ma'am, but just raise my eagle-headed cane—another prop—and grunt. With a few shuffling steps, bent over double to give the illusion of a dowager's hump, I manage to insinuate myself between the florist and the book she has splayed open on the table next to a giant metal bucket of calla lilies. She shifts around the table to stand beside the blushing bride-to-not-be.

"Haydee?" Patrick encourages.

She shakes her head to get back with the program, and moves closer to the table to peer into the book again.

Standing up on tiptoes (while maintaining my stooped posture, which is far harder than it looks!), I pretend to smell the lilies, while noting the bucket is plum full to the brim with water. Perfect.

"The rosebuds are nice," Haydee finally says, with so much enthusiasm, I almost believe her.

Not.

"Great!" Patrick says. "How about——"

Before he can place an order that will never need to be fulfilled, I give the lilies another sniff, and . . . *oops*!

With a tap of my cane, over goes the entire bucket. Water and leaves and fragments of flowers go flying, the majority a direct hit square in the middle of Haydee's chest.

"Oh!" She stumbles backward into Patrick's heroic arms, where he keeps her from landing on her ass on the slick floor.

"So sorry," I mutter in my little old lady voice. "My bad."

I'm nearly to the door, with the other three shaking off, and the florist offering profound apologies, when I turn back and wave my cane in their direction again. "Probly bad luck to get married now, you know. 'Cording to old country tales."

Haydee and Patrick are gaping at each other in astonishment as I turn and push the door open to the street.

I'm fully aware that Haydee's determination to go through with this sham of a marriage isn't likely to deter her just because she got a bit of a soaking and bad advice from an old crone. But I am prepared.

With any luck, their schedule is so tight, that Haydee won't bother to go change. Their next stop is Vincent's, Bander's premiere (and only) Italian restaurant, where the doomed couple will be taste-testing possible dishes for the reception. Really, I tried to convince Haydee not to bother, but she refused to listen to me.

Which means I'm up again in my next performance. For this one, I've donned a dark wig, serviceable black lace-up work shoes, and a slutty French maid's costume (the closest thing I could find to a waitress's uniform), which I've accented with one of my own black push-up bras with lace edging that shows above the scooped neckline of the costume. I'm counting on my natural charm to get into the restaurant as their "new waitress," Lucia.

To look the part, I've loaded up on the cosmetics—my first use in a week. And I mean loaded. I'm pretty sure I'm unrecognizable as anything but a clown at this point. I check myself out in my compact before knocking at the kitchen entrance to Vincent's and try not to cringe. This disaster is nearly as hard to take as the hideous clothes I've been forced to wear lately. Only the fact that I can't see my own face makes it bearable. In a last-minute stroke of genius, I use an eyebrow pencil to dab on a good-sized beauty mark to the left of my upper lip, just to help ensure Haydee doesn't pick up that it's me.

I knock at the rear entrance to Vincent's and find myself greeted by a middle-aged woman wearing a hairnet. Dammit. I was counting on lusty Italian stallions on which to work my considerable charms.

"I . . . I am Lucia," I stutter, working out the Italian accent I'd been practicing the past few days. "I am new waitress?"

The only thing she does is narrow her eyes, giving me the once over. "New waitress?"

"Yes, yes," I encourage. "Hired by . . . Vincent."

As her glower deepens, and I'm cursing myself for not coming in the front door where the men are likely hanging out, my savior appears in the form of a, well, if not a stallion, at least he's Italian.

"What's going on, Ma?"

"Lady says she's our new waitress, Sonny," Ma grumbles, like she isn't falling for my act.

But it doesn't seem to matter. Sonny Boy is in love. Or lust anyway.

"Lucia, Lucia!" He shoves his mother out of the way and drags me into the restaurant kitchen by the bodice of my dress.

"That is me. Lucia." I let him keep his finger tucked down the front of my dress, though if this had been anything but the most desperate of circumstances, I'd have cut the finger off at the knuckle with the closest butcher knife. "The new waitress."

"And my new wife!" Sonny announces.

At first I gulp, but apparently "wife" is the magic word. As soon as he says it, Ma transforms herself into my greatest ally.

"Welcome to the family, Lucia!" She embraces me to her ample bosom, pounding me on the back. "Make yourself at home."

Sonny's still breathing down my cleavage, so Mama cuffs him on the ear. "Don't just stand here, boy! Get the samples set up for our wedding couple. Show your bride what you're made of."

I find myself settled on a high stool close to where Sonny's working. Though he spends more time mooning over me, while Mama can't stop grinning and nodding across the room, scoping me out as daughter-in-law material, I'm sure. It's only when Mama is called out front to greet the wedding couple—who are

definitely Haydee and Patrick, I notice when I peek out the swinging kitchen door into the main part of the restaurant—that I have
the chance to do my ugly, but necessary, deed.

"Sonny? Sweetie?" I hop off my stool and sidle up next to him.
It takes barely a second for him to drop the ladle of sauce he's been
spooning over pasta in sample bowls. "I should probably practice
cooking . . . if I'm going to make you a proper Italian wife."

He's practically panting over me, so far gone it doesn't even
register that I've dropped my fake accent. While I promise him
untold bedroom adventures with my eyes and my lips, I work on
a little creative seasoning with my hands. I don't even know what
I'm throwing in the pot, but it can't be good. I do know I've added
enough salt to induce a hypertensive crisis. Which will serve my
purpose just fine.

By the time Mama comes back to the kitchen to take the
samples out to her potential catering customers, Sonny's a slobbering mess, and I'm taking it because it's the most action I've
had in a very long time.

"Sonny!" The cuff across his ear sends him reeling. "Work
now, make babies later!"

"Yes, Ma." A contrite Sonny nods obediently and hands the
tray of doctored samples to his mother for presentation.

The moment she's gone, he's slobbering all over my neck, and
I don't have anything better to do, so I stick around. A few minutes later I check my watch, just in time to hear the gasps and
groans from the main restaurant, as someone gets a good taste of
my vastly lacking culinary skills.

"Sonny!" Mama's voice bellows, as I hear another male voice
begin cursing in Italian. Real Italian, not the fake Italian I was
spouting a moment ago.

"Sorry to poison and run," I tell my potential paramour, "but
my work here is done."

I'm out the back door a bare second before Mama snatches Sonny off his feet behind me.

I'm starting to sympathize with actors and the hard work they put in day after day at their job, because I've only been at this acting gig for a few hours and I'm ready to throw in the towel. But I'm on my last performance of the day. When I'm done with this one, Haydee will have to say that her marriage to Patrick is doomed. Too much bad luck in one day.

After leaving Vincent's, I hightail it down the street to the county courthouse, where I duck into the bathroom and change back into my old lady costume.

Being Bander, the courthouse has only one window, which deals with everything from building permits, to complaints about the road conditions, to issuance of marriage licenses. That's what Haydee and Patrick stand in line for.

And that's what I stand in line for.

"I want my damn marriage license," I holler at the city hall clerk, who looks ready to flee any moment. We've already been at this for ten minutes, and according to the clock, the courthouse closes in just ten more. All I need to do is keep the clerk occupied until time is up, and then my godchild is out of luck for at least another day, during which time I can hopefully make her see the light.

"Ma'am, I'm terribly sorry, but I can't give you a marriage license. It's illegal to marry a . . . a dead man."

"I don't care if the groom is dead!" I shout, really getting into my show. I wave the photo of my "dead fiancé," which I picked up at an antiques store I'd discovered yesterday, in her face again. "He had his way with me, and I might be pregnant!"

The clerk pales, and I grin inwardly at her discomfiture. I'm so brilliant I want to break out in applause myself.

Behind me, I can hear Haydee and Patrick, as well as another man, grumbling to one another about the crazy lady.

"Let me just get my supervisor," the clerk finally says.

"Fine, but hurry up about it," I snarl. "I need to be made an honest woman."

Another five minutes tick by before the clerk comes back with her supervisor, a pinch-faced balding man with glasses resting so far down on the tip of his nose they look ready to fall off any moment. He looks ready for an argument, and I'm ready to give him one.

When they get to my window, the supervisor steps up to speak to me, but points over my shoulder to Haydee and Patrick behind me. "Please follow Daisy to the desk over there, and she'll take care of you before we close." He leans toward me over the counter. "Now what is it we can do for you, ma'am?"

"I . . . I . . ." I don't know what to do now. I hadn't planned to have my scheme foiled. I need a new scheme!

But while Mr. Supervisor gives me all the reasons why I can't marry a dead man legally in the United States, my brain ceases functioning. Haydee and Patrick fill out the paperwork that will allow them to get married, and I . . . I got nothing!

This isn't fair! This should have been easy. All I had to do was think like a human after all. Maybe that's impossible. Maybe I can only be a devious goddess. Maybe—

"Ma'am? We're closed now. I'll have to ask you to leave."

I snap out of it and turn to stare at the supervisor, who apparently talked his way to the end of the day while I was suffering my silent panic attack. "But—"

The only sound is that of the window slamming down, nearly taking my fingers off in the process.

"You don't have to be snippy about it," I snap.

When I turn to go, I see Patrick plant a big wet one on Haydee. Ugh!

"Get a room," I growl as they pass me, then hope they don't take me seriously. That would be a very bad thing.

"Oh, no," Patrick answers, his face glowing. He waves a sheet of paper at me as he walks backward toward the door, holding a far less excited Haydee by the hand. "We're on our way to see a minister about a wedding."

Holy Zeus! That wasn't on Haydee's itinerary for today!

I'm so screwed.

Haydee

To his credit, Pastor Haverly was doing everything possible to make us feel comfortable. Only I wasn't doing too well in that department. I was more on edge now than ever.

It was amazing we'd actually made it here. I had calla lily fragments dried to my shirt, and was still feeling a little damp in places, after some crazy old lady upended a bucket of flowers on us earlier today. Then Patrick and I were nearly poisoned by our potential caterer and will probably never be able to stomach Italian food again.

And finally, we almost didn't get our marriage license because of the same crazy old lady who'd tried to drown me with the flowers, who insisted on getting a marriage license to wed a dead man. At which point, I started to think maybe we were being given signs that our marriage was destined to be unlucky. If Patrick had expressed the slightest doubt, I'd probably have jumped at the chance to cancel. But no such luck.

Instead I just had hives. A nervous twitch.

And a serious conscience problem.

It's everything I want, I told myself for the thousandth time as we sat in Pastor Haverly's homey office going through the ceremony checklist one item at a time. Patrick sat beside me on the overstuffed couch, looking thrilled to be finalizing our wedding plans. But then he'd looked thrilled all day. Even with all the mysterious obstacles that kept popping up.

I had to get a grip. The next step of The Plan would be fulfilled by marrying Patrick. We'd start our family, and I'd come up with ways to expand my business. All parts of The Plan that were just waiting for their turn.

Besides, as soon as I was married, the pesky problem in my life would also disappear, probably literally, because he'd finally see that I was totally serious about not wanting anything to do with him. Patrick and I would get married and—

I swung around to face Patrick in the seat next to me. "Where will we live?"

Only the ticking clock on the wall responded for a few seconds, before I realized I'd interrupted Pastor Haverly. "Sorry, Pastor. It's just . . . I think we forgot to talk about this."

"It's okay, honey." Patrick took my hand and moved it to his lap where it sat uncomfortably waiting for its opportunity to return to my own lap. "We can live in my house. It's bigger."

It was also a modern monstrosity of steel and glass without warmth or personality. Mine was old and cozy, like a real home should be.

"But I like my house. It was my first big purchase," I told the pastor, to get him up to speed. "All part of The Plan, you know."

"It's okay. We can live in your house," Patrick replied easily. "It'll be a tight squeeze to get some of my stuff moved in. But we can add on once we have more than a couple kids."

Wait. More than— "How many kids were you thinking?"

Patrick grinned. "I'm the youngest of ten. I'd love a big family."

The youngest of— "Ten?" How did I not know this? It's not like Patrick hadn't lived in Bander his whole life. Just like I had. We'd been friends for several years now. How could I not know there were nine other Butler children?

"Perhaps you two have a few more things you need to discuss

before making any firm wedding plans," Pastor Haverly piped up. I must have looked panicked, because he quickly held up his hands in surrender. "I don't mean you have to call off the wedding, Haydee. Just maybe . . . postpone. Until you've had a chance to make a few more decisions about your life."

What decisions? There were no decisions, especially regarding family size. The Plan called for two kids. My uterus was not some baby factory assembly line.

But if I postponed this wedding, God knew what disasters could happen. If not with Venus and her nutso ideas, then with . . . the other disaster in my life.

"Haydee?"

I turned back to Patrick. "I'd rather not postpone. This is nothing that can't be talked about later." Or solved with a quickie tubal ligation after baby number two.

"I'm glad you agree." Patrick planted a kiss on me before turning back to the minister, completely ignoring my frown.

What had I just agreed to?

"Now the church has a standard set of vows we use," Pastor Haverly continued, seemingly unconcerned by the fact that Patrick and I had barely covered the basics of "Getting to Know You 101" if I didn't even know how many siblings he had, "but you're welcome to add to them, personalize them, if you wish."

"I'd love to write my own vows to Haydee," Patrick said, then turned to me, eyes shining, "as I'm sure she'd like to write her own to me?"

Fake smiles could look natural, right?

"That's a splendid idea," the pastor joined in enthusiastically, obviously completely fooled. "Personal vows are always special. Really from the heart."

Suddenly I had the urge to scratch. My entire body was turning into one big hive, I was sure of it.

What in the world would my vows to Patrick say? "I promise to like you, respect you, and try to forget you killed my dog? I promise to not hold it against you that you're really not that great in bed, if you promise not to hold it against me that I'm basically using you to get away from past mistakes I made and to be able to cross another item off The Plan?"

Bugger.

"Sure. Personalized vows are fine." I'd figure out what to say later. Joan was good with words. Maybe she'd write me vows that worked like an incantation to make things work for me and Patrick. "Do you happen to have an antihistamine on you?"

Both the pastor and my . . . fiancé . . . gaped at me. Until there was a knock at the door.

"I'm so sorry." Pastor Haverly stood from behind his desk and crossed to the door. "I've no idea who would be bothering us. I left strict instruct—"

Seriously the first thing that crossed my mind when the door opened was that my life was turning into a bad joke. And then it all became completely clear. The flying bucket of flowers, the nutty lady at the courthouse, and the over-salty sauce at Vincent's—though I wasn't sure how she worked that one—all the work of one Venus Cronos.

The moment my "fairy godmother" walked into the room Pastor Haverly was on his knees at her feet.

"Oh, heaven above, it's a vision sent from God!"

"I object to this wedding!" she shouted, using her foot to nudge Pastor Haverly out of her way.

She barely managed to get into the room, since the pastor, who was very happily married last time I'd checked, clutched at her calves in an effort to keep her from running away from him.

"Oh, vision of loveliness, I devote my life to you—"

"Silence!" Venus commanded. And he followed orders, staring

up at her from the floor, rubbing the hem of her ratty second-hand jeans against his cheek like they were silk and staring at her adoringly. "I bring news of this woman's unfaithfulness."

She thrust a finger in my direction, eliciting a gasp from the pastor, though he didn't seem all that concerned with anything but Venus.

"She has had impure thoughts about another man, who is not this man."

"I'm having impure thoughts about you, beloved," Pastor Haverly groaned from the floor. "Punish me?"

You're kidding me, right? Even the men of God in this town couldn't resist my fairy godmother?

Wait a minute. I glanced toward Patrick, who looked as if someone had drugged him . . . with adoration. "You, too?"

When he didn't answer, I waved a hand in front of his face. He merely smacked it out of the way. "Don't block my view of this angel."

"Never mind me," Venus commanded, looking a little panicky. "This woman must confess her sins of loving another man. And accept her punishment of not marrying you."

A silly grin transformed Patrick's face. "Would that mean I could marry you instead?"

"Never!" Pastor Haverly roused himself from the floor, and held up his fists in a boxer's stance. "She's mine!"

"As if!" Patrick shouted back, apparently deciding Venus was worth dueling for, though *I* hadn't been that night at the bar.

"I'm no one's, you fools!" Venus announced.

The pastor clearly didn't hear her, because he turned from Patrick and threw his arms around her. "I will prove to you my love, my love."

When I saw he intended to dip her and plant a lip lock on her, I'd had enough.

"Venus has been very, very bad," I told them, yanking her out of the pastor's grip and pulling her toward the door. "She's grounded."

"I will break you free, beautiful goddess," Patrick proclaimed, coming after us.

I stopped him with a hand on his chest, while shoving Venus out into the hallway with the other hand. "Sorry, boys. You're out of luck."

I barely had the door closed, when I heard a fist connecting with someone's cheek.

"She's mine!"

"Once she's had me, she won't remember you even exist!"

By the time Venus and I were out the back door into the church parking lot, I'm sure I was nearly purple with rage. "What are you trying to do? Of all the harebrained— And seducing a minister?!"

Venus calmly flicked her hair over her shoulder. "That wasn't what I set out to do, but it worked fabulously, if I do say so myself. And did you see the look on lover boy's face? You can't marry someone who'd stray so easily."

Arggghh! I punched the button on my keys to unlock the car doors. "You broke the rules." At her look of confusion, I continued, waving at her in explanation. "Not even counting all the other crap you've pulled today, you seduced Patrick and Pastor Haverly. You used your *feminine wiles* to . . . to influence my match."

"I told you it was an accident!"

When Venus ducked into the car to avoid me, I slid into the driver's seat and locked the doors purposefully. "You're sabotaging my marriage to Patrick. There's got to be a rule about that."

She rolled her eyes. "There's also got to be a rule about royally fucking up your life by marrying the wrong man in order to get back at the right man."

"I'm not—"

"There's *probably* a rule about not allowing your entire life to be dictated by a list—written when you were a child, and in pencil, which Can. Be. Erased."

"I can't—"

Venus smacked the dashboard with her palm. "There's *probably* a rule about not distrusting men just because your father let you down."

"My father?" Wait. "What does this have to do with him?"

Venus, looking a little wide-eyed, clamped her mouth shut and turned toward the front window, suddenly scratching at her arms. "Never mind. Just take me home. I think whoever had this T-shirt before me had fleas."

Or maybe someone else in this car had found herself allergic to her own conscience.

❧ *34* ❧

Venus

I can tell my pouting is going unnoticed. The sun is shining, but I don't feel any of it, because I can see the "finish line" up ahead. Loading bags of garbage into his truck.

Unfortunately, my godchild hasn't seen the light.

"Stop staring at him." Haydee tosses her trash bag into the growing pile to be hauled off to the dump, and turns away quickly before Derek notices her.

Bander Beach Clean Up Day is apparently a monthly tradition throughout the tourist season. Once a month, starting in May, most of the townies gather on the beach with plastic trash bags, gloves, and various sharp objects with which to stab garbage. I will admit it's actually rather fun, since I'm hardly attracting any attention at all for the first time in days. Apparently the trick is to wear ugly old work shirts borrowed from Haydee's closet. Anything from my drawer is apparently just too attractive, no matter how unattractive.

"It's just a matter of time," I tell her, taking a new bag from the pile and then jogging to catch up with her as she strides down the beach to our next garbage gathering destination. "You'll realize how wrong you are and how right I am."

"If I didn't realize it after your horrible attempt at manipulating the situation," Haydee says, "I'm not likely to come to that conclusion no matter how long you pester me about it."

I stab at an empty juice carton with a stick sharpened to a

point and then transfer it to my bag. "I'm right about Derek. You'll see."

"You're not, so I won't."

I am. And she will.

"I don't trust him," Haydee says.

Here we go again. "Who *do* you trust?"

"Myself. The Plan."

"Which could be fulfilled just as easily with Derek Reed as Patrick," I remind her. "I could still win. I have eleven days left in which to convince you that you don't have a man because you don't trust anyone."

"Of course I do," she protests.

Wait a minute. Suddenly, I get it. I narrow my eyes at her. "It wouldn't matter *who* I found, or who *you* found, would it? You don't trust anyone. Patrick's just the lesser of two evils."

When she doesn't bother to defend herself or contradict me, I stomp off down the beach needing some alone time.

Of course, she follows me, since we're trash buddies today.

For a while we just wander the beach, sticking to the edge of the grassy dunes, where it's less crowded, listening to the waves and the gulls and our own thoughts. Haydee's thoughts are practically loud enough for me to hear them. But I, being a good goddess, force them away. I have too much I need to think about. Like how to break up Haydee and Patrick and then teach her to trust her heart to someone who broke it once already . . . in eleven days.

"There is something I think you may have been right about," she finally says.

Only *everything*. "Really?" I flash her a brilliant smile. "Imagine that."

She laughs, then goes back to the serious business of trash

gathering. "The thing about not trusting men because my father let me down."

My grin disappears. "No. I was totally wrong about that."

"No, you weren't. At least partially. I mean, I'm completely justified in not trusting Derek."

Out of the corner of my eye, I see her stop and rest her weight on her stabbing stick. I, however, dutifully continue to work. I will have no part in this ridiculous conversation about fathers and men and—

"I've always said I didn't want to be like my dad. Or Nita. But I already *am* them."

"*Pfff!* I've met them, Haydee, and believe me, you're nothing like them."

"You've met my dad?"

Oops. "No. I meant just Nita. I've met Nita. And she's bitter and crabby and . . . so, no, I don't see the comparison."

She gives up her suspicious look and goes back to work. "But I'm just like both of them. Nita's husband cheated on her, and now she doesn't trust men not to be assholes and cheat on her as soon as they get serious. And my dad doesn't trust people not to die on him if he lets himself love them . . ."

She trails off for a minute, and I think maybe I've dodged this particular bullet.

"What about you? What's your relationship with your dad like? Don't you think it affects your life?"

And we have a direct hit—fairy godmother down.

"We're not talking about me," I remind her, suddenly noticing a used tissue thirty yards down the beach. I must get it right away.

"Doesn't it make sense, though?" she calls after me, then follows when I don't stop to listen. Upon Zeus, can't she take a hint? "My dad basically deserted me when my mom died, right? Then he cut me out of his life, so it wouldn't hurt so much if something happened to me."

Nail hit directly on the head.

"So, naturally, I've been hurt by this man in my life. So when Derek basically does the same thing, deserting me—"

"He could have had a very good reason, you know." At her incredulous look, I shrug. "Man's not here to defend himself. That's hardly fair."

"*Anyway*, I think maybe I should talk to my dad."

Who is probably feeling much better about life right about now. "Brilliant idea." As long as I don't have to talk to mine.

"You know, maybe you should talk to your father, too," Haydee offers, *so* not helpfully. My daddy issues are just fine tucked away on Mount Olympus, thank you very much.

"My father's not the talking kind." He's the punishing kind. The kind who can't see the pot is calling the kettle black, and then banishing said kettle for not falling too far from the tree. To mix a metaphor or two. "I tried to talk to him once, and I ended up living in Human Land and answering to 'Fairy Godmother.' "

"And maybe you'll be stuck here until you and your dad see eye to eye."

Which means I will be here for eternity. Which makes me pause. And feel a little sick inside.

Thankfully Haydee distracts me—

"If I can resolve things with my dad, maybe everything with Patrick and I will turn out okay."

I slam on the brakes and spin toward Haydee. "How on Mount Olympus do you figure that?"

Haydee

Venus was, of course, furious with me. She was all for me talking to my dad until she realized I wanted to do it to ensure that Patrick and I had a fighting chance at marriage and not to solve my issues with Derek. But really, this isn't about anyone but me. I need to tell Dad how I feel in order to heal.

I waited until the bait shop closed for the night. Derek was still at the beach cleanup, hauling trash to the dump in his truck, so I knew the coast was clear.

My dad was still around, since lights glowed from the office windows. I'm sure he stayed late most nights. Who wanted to go home to an empty house night after night? He didn't even have a cat to keep him company.

But now wasn't the time for any sympathy I might feel for my dad. Now was the time to be strong and tell him how I felt. Because that was the only way I'd get past this. And past Derek. And on, hopefully, to a life where the men in my past didn't affect the men in my future.

I used my key—my father's one acknowledgment that I, in fact, existed in his life—to get in the front door.

"Dad, it's me," I called out as soon as I was inside. No need to give him a heart attack.

He sat at his office desk, tying flies. "Derek isn't here," he said, without looking up.

"I didn't come to see Derek." I set the items I'd been carrying on the edge of his desk, taking a deep breath to shore up my courage. "And the fact that you assume I came to see him instead of you, my own father, only proves how much we need to have this talk."

Lowering the fly, he looked up curiously, though he still didn't say anything.

I quickly went through my pile of albums to the one I wanted in particular. I'd rehearsed what I'd say, how I'd present myself. How I'd convince a man who had once loved me with all his heart to love me again.

Flipping to the page I wanted, my heart stuttered a little. If this didn't work . . .

I clutched the book to my chest and met my dad's eyes again. "You don't have to talk," I told him. "But you do have to listen. And look."

Laying the open photo album on the desk next to the fly-tying paraphernalia, I only had to wait a moment before he registered what he was seeing. His gasp was soft but audible.

"That's what we once were." I poked my finger at the family portrait we'd had taken at the beach the summer before my mother died. Her bald head was wrapped in a pink bandana, and she and I were laughing hysterically at something my dad had said. The photographer, seeing a real moment, had snapped it. It was this snapshot my mother had chosen for our fireplace mantel, not a perfectly posed shot that told no story, showed no love.

"This was our family," I continued, my voice catching on the long unused word. "And you know what? Only one of those people died. There are still two people in that photo, who made up two thirds of that family, and they deserve to go on being loved and cared about. It's what she would have wanted."

Instead of answering, my father just swallowed tightly and turned back to his flies.

"Fine, Dad." I gathered up the remaining photo albums that I'd thought maybe we'd go through together when he realized I was right and we started over again. "If that's how you want it."

I turned to leave but glanced into the open storeroom door, it's contents clearly visible. My eyes welled up when I saw the black-and-white cemetery photo still propped against the wall on the workbench. If I'd had my dad that night, I'd never have had to sit in a cemetery and talk to my dead mother. I'd have never been where Derek could take my picture.

"You know what? *No.*" I whirled around, facing my dad. "I'm tired of being held at arm's length because you're afraid I'll die on you, too. *Mom* died. Not me. I'm still here. I always have been."

He finally looked up at me, his eyes haunted.

"You let me down, Dad." I gestured across the hall, where my father would have had to be blind not to notice the picture of me crying my eyes out while sitting on the soggy ground. "The Christmas after Derek and I were an 'item' as you called it, I lost a baby. A girl. And I couldn't even tell you, because you weren't available to me."

Tears streamed down my face and I did nothing to stem them. I'd been saving them up for a very long time. These tears belonged to my dad, and he was going to have to face them.

"I should have been able to tell you about the baby. I should have been able to come to you for support."

When my dad's expression continued to be one of surprise, it suddenly dawned on me—

"She's buried right next to Mom. And if you don't know about her, that means you never go to Mom's grave, do you?"

He only looked away.

" 'Every day, Maxie. Every day.' That's what you once told her. *Promised her.* Even when she told you it would be silly to visit a patch of grass and a piece of stone. But I bet you've never once been there, have you?"

My accusation was met with only silence.

Sighing, all the fight left me, like a balloon releasing all the air that held it taut and strained.

"I hope you think about all this," I told him, my voice barely audible. "Patrick Butler and I are getting married in three weeks. Although it's entirely possible I'm so screwed up that I'll end up alone anyway, and you'll be all I'll ever have in my life. And isn't that just a cheery thought?"

At the door, I turned back once more. "By the way, I named her Danielle Maxine," I told him, my voice catching on the name I'd agonized over, choosing to honor my dead mother, as well as my baby's father, Derek Daniel Reed, despite the fact that he would never know her. "Just thought you should know."

❧ 36 ❧

Haydee

"Have a great afternoon, honey," Patrick said on the other end of the line. He'd just let me know that he'd been able to secure the Bander Grange for our wedding reception. I wanted to be more enthusiastic, but I couldn't get out of my mind the picture that the bride's side of the church was going to be pretty bare of guests, since clearly my father wouldn't even be attending.

"That's great. I'll call you later and you can tell me about it," I said into my phone. I snapped it closed and slipped it into my pocket before entering the stadium. The proper way this time, through the gate.

The ball field was alive with the shouts of players and coaches, the crash of helmets and shoulder pads, and the grunts of players pushing themselves to their limits, as they put their best skills forward to impress the coaches who would decide their high school football fate.

Standing at the edge of the action, I just took it in for a few minutes, pushing my hands deep into my jacket pockets to keep them warm. To keep them from shaking. It was time to get this out of the way once and for all. I felt freer after talking to my dad (even though it was a completely one-sided soul-baring moment), but to move forward with my life—the one I planned on sharing with Patrick—I needed to clear up *all* of the past. Which meant telling the truth about what happened so long ago. Derek would finally understand why I was so angry, why I could never trust him.

And then my life could get back to normal. Whatever normal would be from this point on.

Still, it had taken me two days to work up the courage to locate Derek and get it over with. Since Derek's truck hadn't been in front of the bait shop, I'd driven around a bit, trying to work up the nerve to call his mother's house to see where he was. Only it turned out I didn't need to. His battered old truck was in the stadium parking lot.

There seemed to be a break in the action, a call for a rest period. It was as good a time as any to find Derek. I had no idea what he was doing here. Reminiscing maybe?

"Is Derek Reed around?" I asked Bob McDermot, the current football coach, who I'd heard was retiring at the end of the year.

Bob pointed down the sidelines a ways, where Derek stood chatting with one of the other coaches.

"Thanks."

Fighting nerves, I waited until he was finished talking and had noticed me. We hadn't spoken since the day I'd accepted Patrick's marriage proposal a little over a week ago. The wariness in his look indicated he hadn't forgotten our last encounter.

"What can I do for you?"

"Will you be done here soon?" I asked. "I, um, need to talk to you. It's important."

After a moment's pause, he shrugged. "Give me a minute."

By the time he'd finished talking with Bob McDermot a few minutes later, I'd convinced myself I could actually do this. That him still being furious about the other day was good. It would keep me from thinking of him in any other way than what he was. Part of a past that needed to be dealt with like an adult.

He jerked a thumb up toward the bleachers. "You come back for an instant replay of the other day?"

I ignored his jab and led the way out to the stadium parking lot. "I need to drive you somewhere."

"Crazy?"

His joke surprised me, especially considering his face gave no indication of humor when I ventured a look.

I unlocked his door, then rounded the back of the Cherokee to the driver's side.

As soon as I climbed in he checked his watch. "Are we going to be gone long? I have a plane to catch to Sri Lanka for a photo shoot."

I wasn't even shocked. "Of course you do. It won't take long."

I turned the key in the ignition and we were silent for three seconds before he took another stab.

"Butler know you're alone in a car with me? It could be grounds for calling off the wedding. In some countries a man can have his fiancée stoned to death for being alone with another man."

"This isn't about Patrick." I hadn't told him I was having this conversation with Derek, because then he'd want to know what about our past was so important that I needed to clear it before moving on. And I really didn't want to discuss this with Patrick. It was too intimate, too personal.

We pulled into the parking lot of our destination just a few minutes later. We could have actually walked from the stadium, but it would have taken longer, and I didn't need to spend any more time in Derek's company than necessary.

"The cemetery?" He shut the car door behind him and gestured toward the fenced-in area that bore the headstones of most of Bander's deceased residents of the past several hundred years. "I've been on some pretty scary dates before, but this it definitely a first."

Instead of responding, I opened the slightly rickety gate and entered the graveyard, allowing Derek to follow me. I could do this. No matter what I thought of his integrity or his trustworthiness, Derek deserved to know he had had, or almost had, a child.

37

Venus

"There are no more stars!" I slam my fist down on the rule book.

Across the store, Curt looks up from where he's spent the last half hour alternately washing the floor-to-ceiling windows and gazing dreamily in my direction. "I see stars when I look at you."

"Knock it off, punk." Thankfully he obeys, because I don't have time for this nonsense. I have a problem to solve.

After much prodding on my part, Haydee finally admitted she'd gone to talk to her father after the beach cleanup. Which hadn't gone well, she said, but she looked as if at least some of the weight had been taken off her shoulders.

Not that that means talking to my father would help me. Because that's just not going to happen. Instead I'm going to break the code of this damn rule book and figure out what's missing from my methods. What I'm doing that's kept me from finishing up my sentence and being set free.

Only there aren't any more starred rules! I've spent all day going through each and every page, checking for any indication that one rule is more important than the others. The only stars I've come across are the ones I've already found. And those haven't gotten me any closer to victory than before I'd read them.

"You know, I could just hang a closed sign in the front window and we could go in the back for a little while." Curt, with his pierced eyebrow and droopy forelock of hair hanging in his face, leans over the countertop and sighs heavily.

"In about two seconds I'm going to hand you the phone," I tell him. "And you better start dialing nine-one-one before you try to hit on me again, because when you do, I'm going to kick your ass."

He sighs dramatically and turns to lean his elbows back on the countertop. "Is it almost closing time? I need to get home so I can put these feelings of dejection into poetry before I lose them."

I roll my eyes behind his back. Good grief. He's easier to control than the others have been by far, but maybe because his emo lifestyle puts him only marginally higher up the depression scale than Haydee's dad.

"You just got here," I tell him. "It's your night to work, remember?" And I was only here because Haydee said she needed to go to the cemetery and didn't want "interference." *Hmmph.* What she calls interference, I call being proactive.

"Maybe when Haydee comes back for you, I should tell her I need to go home to nurture my sorrow," Curt muses, his shoulders sagging under the weight of my rejection.

"She's visiting her dead mother," I snap at him as I turn another parchment page. Visiting her live father hadn't provided any insight into what was wrong with her life, so she'd moved on to the dead. "I really doubt she'll take over your shift so you can go home and pout."

"Hmmm," Curt muses. "She told me she was going to put the past to rest. Sounds more poetic the way she told me. More romantic . . . in a tragic sort of way."

I pause in page turning, my eyes boring into the back of Curt's head, as if I could read his mind to find out exactly what Haydee told him. Only my complete and utter fear of fucking this match up more prevents me from siphoning out his thoughts like a mental vacuum.

"Do you remember her exact words?" I ask. "Without taking any poetic license, if you don't mind."

He spins around and crosses his arms along the tall counter, dropping his chin to rest on them. "She said, 'I'm going to clear my conscience. Put my past to rest.' And something about severing the ties that bind. If it wasn't Haydee we were talking about, I'd think it had to do with a guy."

Blast her with Zeus's lightning bolt! She was going to talk to Derek. I know it. How it fit in with visiting the cemetery, I have no idea, but I have to find out.

Slamming the book shut, I race into the backroom and toss it in my tote bag before going back out to Curt. "I need to get to the cemetery," I tell him. "Where is it?"

"Oh, man, V, it's clear across town." He glances at my feet. "Even in those highly serviceable sneakers, it'll take you a half hour."

"Highly serviceable sneakers? Do you always talk like such a freak?"

There has to be a way to get there. Staring out the front windows for inspiration, I find my answer.

"Isn't that your moped?" I flash Curt my brightest smile and watch his face turn pink as he nods. "Can I borrow it?"

"Do you know how to drive one? I mean, it's kinda hard if you don't know how."

Which of course, I don't. Crap.

But Curt does. He also knows where the cemetery is. And thinks I'm hot.

I flip the store sign to "Closed."

∾ 38 ∾

Haydee

After Derek and I meandered up the path, well groomed by a committee dedicated to beautifying the resting places of our forebears, and headed toward the more modern-day part of the cemetery, Derek broke the silence. "Are we going somewhere in particular, or is this supposed to be a romantic stroll?"

We'd reached our destination anyway. My mom's burial plot was fairly easy to spot with its angel-carved marker, the last thing my father had done for her before turning emotionally comatose. But I needed Derek to see the unobtrusive plaque nestled in the grass beside my mother's angel. The plaque had been all I could afford as a junior in college. The baby wasn't even really buried here—it wasn't common thirteen years ago—but I couldn't pretend she never existed. She deserved to be honored as much as anyone else.

Taking a deep breath, I stepped to the side and indicated what I was here to show him. "You might recognize this spot," I said, my voice quivering. "From the photo you took."

He shot me a questioning look. "Your mom's grave."

"No. Beside it. In the grass." I pointed. "I wasn't here for my mom that day."

Taking a few steps around my mother's headstone, Derek finally knelt beside the plaque buried in the grass.

For a moment, he didn't say anything. Then, he reached out

his hand and tentatively used his fingers to push aside the over-growth of grass that covered some of the words.

He read it aloud. "Danielle Maxine . . . Miller." Only his shoulders moved as he breathed over his daughter's grave. "Who's the fath—"

"Read the date," I snapped, annoyed he'd even think I'd bring him to see the grave of someone else's child. "I may not be able to trust you enough to marry you, but you deserve to know the truth. Why I'm *so* angry with you for walking out on me. Because it wasn't just me you left."

When Derek stood up, his normally sun-touched face was pale and tight. "You knew you were pregnant when I left?"

"No. I didn't figure it out until I'd gone back to school." Sitting alone in the dorm bathroom, clutching the pregnancy test stick so tightly my knuckles turned white. Silent tears streaming down my face as I realized my life would never be the same again.

"What happened, Haydee?"

I closed my eyes and remembered my goal was to be honest. I opened my eyes and faced him. "I thought about getting an abortion. I was alone. I had no one. Not my dad. Not you." The laugh that escaped betrayed all the bitterness and hurt I'd felt back then. "But I kept the baby, and I grew to love her and want her, and when I lost her—" I couldn't begin to put it into words now any more than I could then. I yanked up the left side of my shirt just high enough. "I miscarried at five months. I got the tattoo so I'd never forget." As if I could have anyway.

His eyes flicked only briefly over the tattoo, and he shuddered slightly, probably remembering his crass words about how it turned him on. "It never crossed your mind to contact me?"

"Of course it did." I didn't bother to tell him that his mother had refused to tell me where he was. That I'd begged her to have him contact me, tried to explain it was important. It wouldn't serve any purpose to tell him that. This wasn't about his mother. This was about the fact that if Derek hadn't left me in the first place . . .

I'd left his mother's house defeated. Scared. And I'd never tried to find him on my own.

"You were off making your way in the world." I flung a hand out, indicating what an enormous endeavor trying to track him down would have been. "With. Out. *Me*. You'd made it very clear you didn't want me. Why would you have wanted my baby?"

"My baby, too," he whispered.

He plowed his hand through his hair and moved away, walking toward the trees that edged the cemetery. His agitation was clear, and I didn't blame him. I'd lifted the weight of the truth from my shoulders and dropped it squarely on his in the form of guilt.

"You left, Derek."

He spun around, hands braced at his waist. "So you decided to pay me back by not telling me I was going to be a *father*?"

"It wasn't about payback." I wrapped my arms around myself, as the memories flooded back. "It was about the fact that I didn't want you to be with me just because I was pregnant."

Because I always, always would have wondered if that's the only reason he was there.

"You should have contacted me," he repeated.

"Why?" I grasped the sides of my head, unable to comprehend why this was so difficult for him to understand. "Why would I have put myself in a position for you to break my heart all over again?"

"I wouldn't have broken your heart again."

"What would have changed? I knew what it was like to have a

dad who couldn't stand to look at me because I was a reminder of all he didn't have anymore. I would *not* do that to my child. You'd already lost an NFL career. I would not let my daughter grow up to figure out someday that her father couldn't look at her either, because she was a reminder of what he'd lost. His *freedom*." I nearly spat out the last word.

"My leaving didn't have anything to do with freedom," he said, striding across the grass until he was in my face. "If I'd known about that baby, I'd have been more selfish and stayed. I'd have come back. I'd have said *screw* your stupid plan and *made* you take a chance."

I gaped. "What? What are you talking about?"

For a minute he didn't look like he was going to answer. But suddenly it was as if he saw things clearly. Finally, he got it. Why I couldn't crawl back to him, begging him to love me . . . or the baby . . . when he clearly didn't. Finally.

He finally focused on me. "I get it now. You don't trust yourself any more than you've ever trusted me. Or your dad. Or your mom." He waved a hand toward her headstone.

He was out of his mind. What did that have to do with anything? "You see your dad out there turning his back on life and on you because he was crushed when your mom died. You don't trust, anymore than he does, that people aren't going to leave you."

"You *did* leave me!" I protested, barely maintaining control over the sobs that were building up inside me. "When I needed you most, you were gone, off making something of yourself, because that was more important to you than I was."

"And you were here making something of *yourself*," Derek said softly. "Because I knew *that* was more important to you than I was."

Everything around us became still. Only the sound of our breathing reached my ears. "What are you talking about?"

"I didn't plan on falling in love with you that summer," he said. "But I did. I was ready to ask you to marry me. I even had the ring. But then you offered to give up every dream you had. The dreams that made you get out of bed every day. The dreams you needed more than you needed me. I had to let you do it."

I laughed. "You think you left for *my* benefit?"

"I know I did. It was the hardest damn thing I've ever done." Once again he paced away from me, back toward the cemetery gate, so when he faced me he was out of reach. Like he'd been for so many years. "Maybe my leaving added to your inability to trust anyone. But you didn't trust me before I left. You don't trust yourself, either. And you still cling to that plan, because you don't trust yourself to just take what life gives you and deal with it. Well, you know what?" He let out a strangled laugh. "I was a damn fool to tie *myself* to your stupid plan. If I hadn't done that, I'd have been back here years ago. And maybe we'd have had a chance then."

For an hour, I sat in the grass, propped against my mother's headstone, my hand pressed to my baby's plaque.

I'd been angry with her, too. For leaving me.

Perceptive as he was, Derek hadn't picked up on that one. But he'd picked up on a lot of other things.

I pulled the copy of The Plan out of my wallet and flattened it in the grass beside me, smoothing out the wrinkles until it laid flat enough that I could look at it without touching it.

Had this plan really been my savior all these years? Or my downfall?

I recognized that it was the one thing that got me out of bed some days. Mostly when I'd been younger, when I didn't have the maturity to realize that I didn't need a piece of paper to prod me through life. It had served its purpose then.

But what about later?

When Derek and I had fallen in love, we'd talked about forever. We talked about finishing school, him getting his teaching credentials, me my business degree. We'd get married when our careers were settled, we had decided. I'd forgotten all about The Plan. At least its timeline. I'd still planned to do all the things on my list. Get my degree, buy a house, open my bookstore. Only the order had changed. I'd have done all those things with Derek by my side.

Then . . . I'd panicked.

I hadn't realized until today that that's what happened. Why I'd suddenly decided that we couldn't go to separate schools, that I needed to give up my plans for business school, for my bookstore. That I needed to stay glued to his side. I'd panicked at the thought of being apart from him for even a few months out of the year.

Because what if, like everyone else in my life whom I'd loved, he left me?

I hadn't trusted him even before he left.

I rested my arms across my knees and laid my head down, reading my list and all I'd accomplished. Derek had been right about me not trusting him. But had he been right when he said I'd needed my dreams more than I needed him? Had it been any easier to get through my life, any *better,* with dreams to keep me going?

Or would I have been better off with love?

❧ 39 ❧

Venus

A baby. I can't believe there had been a baby. Damn my lack of mental powers! If I'd known about the baby all along, I would have done things differently.

Okay, fine. I probably wouldn't have done things differently because, seriously, what could I have done that I hadn't already done?

I'd begged. I'd pleaded. Endured the groping hands of the Mr. Wrongs Haydee brought home. Masqueraded as a bum. What was left?

I keep moving about the living room, tape in hand, hanging all the posters I'd had made with the last bit of cash in my wallet. There was one on the front door. The hall closet door. On the back of the couch. And so on throughout as much of the house as I could cover.

Everywhere Haydee looked would be a copy of her plan. The plan that stated she had nine days. Nine days to have a wedding band on her finger or her plan was a failure. But she'd decided to *compromise*. She'd decided to deviate from the plan (which she'd stated in the past had resulted in disaster) and accept engagement. Granted, if she was engaged to Derek instead of Patrick, I'd be less inclined to point out her compromise, but because she insisted on making the biggest mistake of her life, I was more than willing to bombard her with reminders of her failure to follow her sacred plan.

From the back of the couch, Zeus growled under his breath.

"What's your problem, furball?" I hiss back. "If you have something to say, just say it. Because I really can't take any more today."

When he doesn't respond—surprise, surprise—I keep working. When all I really want to do is curl up in a ball on the couch and whimper. Even without using my mental powers, even keeping the wall between Haydee's emotions and mine firmly in place, watching what went down at the cemetery had exhausted me.

I'd come out of my hiding place shortly after Derek left, leaving Haydee alone . . . looking at her plan. Derek had told her exactly what she didn't want to hear. That her plan hadn't actually helped her all these years; it had been her downfall.

But if she believed that, it would be *my* downfall. If she set that plan aside and decided it didn't matter anymore whether she was married by her thirty-third birthday next week, I was screwed. She had to remember why it was so important to her. Because if she compromises on that, then she might advance to compromising altogether—like on marriage in general.

"What's going on?"

I spin around to find Haydee with her hand on the front doorknob, staring around the room.

"Uh . . . um . . . reminders," I tell her, as brightly as possible. Because I can't let her know I was spying on her in the cemetery. "So, um, you don't forget your plan. Isn't your birthday next Wednesday?"

I scoop the cat off the back of the couch, squeezing him to my chest and stroking him across the top of his head as he struggles to free himself. I'm not sure Haydee buys my way of showing that I'm a concerned part of her life, of her family. Finally Zeus has had enough and claws my arm until I let go. I barely resist kicking his behind as he ducks for cover under the coffee table.

"Just trying to be supportive," I tell her. "I was thinking of, um, inviting Derek over for dinner. Maybe to, ah, talk."

Haydee turns and quietly closes the door. "It's over, Venus." She waves her hands at all my hard work. "Derek is over. Patrick is over."

Wait. "What? *Patrick* is over?" Obviously Derek isn't over, because he's still her Prince Charming, but the Patrick thing is news to me.

"I'm going to change my clothes and go break up with him," Haydee says. "It's not right to marry him to fulfill a plan. A plan that is over, too."

"The plan can't be over!" I tell her, ready to grovel if I have to. "It's your life. It's what gets you out of bed in the morning." It's what gets *me* out of bed in the morning.

She passes me right by on her way to the stairs before turning again, one hand on the banister. "Thanks for everything you've tried to do. But I think I can take it from here. It's about time I see what I can do on my own without someone . . . something"— she reaches up and tears the nearest poster off the wall and lets it flutter to the floor—"telling me every move to make."

❧ 40 ☙

Haydee

I decided to talk to Patrick at his office again, where there'd be reminders of why he was a bad choice for me in the first place. I couldn't believe I'd just been here, accepting his proposal, and now—

"Got a minute?"

Bev had sent me back to his office. Patrick's black eye was healing, turning a purple-blue color over the past four days. He'd been on the receiving end of the punch I'd heard thrown in the pastor's office. Venus said there was a good chance that neither he nor the pastor remembered exactly what had happened, and at least Patrick clearly didn't. I'd seen him once and talked to him since then, and he'd never mentioned it. He told me he thought he'd gotten the black eye falling out of bed. I didn't bother correcting him.

"I only have a second or two," Patrick gave me a quick kiss then gathered some files into his arms. "Patients to see, you know. I'm going to have a family to support soon."

I looked away so the joy in his eyes wouldn't guilt me into backing down. I had to do this.

"It won't take long," I promised, pushing the door shut behind me. "I feel like I need to explain."

Patrick set his files down, sensing my serious tone. "Explain what?" His sudden focused attention made it all the harder.

"I should never have agreed to marry you, Patrick."

At his look of confusion, I hurried to continue. "Someone suggested I was, uh, marrying the wrong man in order to get back at the right man. Which is . . . inaccurate." Venus may have had some sort of similar experience—though she hadn't elaborated at all about her marriage to Hephaestus—but she couldn't lay her mistakes at my feet. Derek had nothing to do with my decision to marry Patrick. "But I *was* trying to fulfill the next step in The Plan, and using you like that . . . to meet a goal . . . was wrong."

"Yeah, that hurts a little."

I flinched. My conscience had stopped giving me hives and had starting jabbing me with pins instead.

"However, I knew that going in, you forget," he continued. "You forget how we got started in the first place—the drink at the bar. You feeling lonely and worrying you'd fail to meet your plan's deadline? We talked about it at the beach a few weeks ago. I went into this with my eyes wide open."

Patrick sighed and scrubbed at his face, wincing when his fingers found his black eye. When he looked back at me, his eyes told me everything I needed to know about how Patrick Butler really felt about me. He loved me. He may never have said it, probably because he knew I couldn't say it back, but it was right there in his eyes. "We'll make it, Haydee. You realize that, right?"

He had a lot more faith in me than I did.

I sank into his guest chair since he didn't seem in a hurry to throw me out. "No, I don't think we will. I'll mess it up somewhere along the way. So I'm going to mess it up now before we need Nita's services to get us out of it."

He didn't laugh at my lame attempt at a joke. "I don't understand."

"You're a good friend, Patrick. You're easy to talk to. But I'm not in love with you."

He took a sudden interested in examining his feet. "You're in love with Derek."

How could you love someone you didn't trust? "I have feelings for him, yes. And those feelings make it impossible to have any kind of normal relationship with you."

"You know, if people try hard enough—"

"It doesn't work that way for me." I stood up and paced the room. "I find that no matter how much I want to, I can't just set aside my problems with Derek to marry you. And it wouldn't be fair to even try."

I stopped in front of a photo on the wall. A Butler family portrait, with two proud parents and ten happily grinning adult kids. I traced a finger along the frame.

Would my life have been different if I hadn't lost my mom . . . and my dad? Even if it had just remained the three of us in our family, we'd have still been the same happy family. And I'd not have lost faith in happiness.

But in the last few weeks, despite my protests that I didn't need True Love in my life, I think I'd actually been searching for it anyway. All I'd netted was a series of awful dates, but I'd really been looking for True Love. The love my parents wrote about in their books. That love had always ended with happy ever after in my mom's books. But my dad had showed a different, but no less important, outcome. The bittersweet sadness that was often part of life. And love. It had taken a while, but my eyes had finally been opened to the fact that, no matter whether I got the happy ever after or the bittersweet True Love, I was still willing to wait for it to come again. No matter how long it took.

"You deserve a wife you loves you, Patrick. Not one still fighting demons of the past."

Patrick came up behind me and laid his hands on my shoulders. "Some demons are best not fought alone."

For just a second, I wanted to believe he was right.

But no.

"Sometimes it's best not to drag others down with you." I turned in his arms and backed up toward the door until his hands fell to his sides. Acceptance dawned slowly on his face. "I can't marry you, Patrick."

I opened the door and stepped out into the hall before turning once more. "Find the right girl and it'll all work out for you."

Haydee

"Finally you've come to your senses!" Nita kicked back in the armchair, trying fairly unsuccessfully not to look like she had "I told you so" painted across her forehead.

I'd just given her and Joan the news that Patrick and I were over.

And the news that Derek and I weren't getting together, either.

"I still don't understand exactly what's going on," Joan said, pouring frosty margaritas from a pitcher and passing them around the room. She'd made herself a special virgin drink, of course. "What exactly are we celebrating then?"

The fire appeared to be going pretty well in the grate now, so I swiveled around on my heels and sank down to sit cross legged on the floor. Joan handed me a margarita glass with a questioning look.

"We're celebrating the loss of Haydee's mind," Venus whined from near the kitchen door, where she'd been hovering so she could duck into the other room to sob off and on. She looked like hell. Her secondhand rags completely hid the figure she was so proud of. She hadn't combed her hair since she got out of bed this afternoon . . . yes, this *afternoon*. Her previously perfect manicure was chipped, her nails ragged. Her face was sallow with dark circles ringing her eyes.

I felt a little guilty, but I couldn't live my life for anyone else but myself anymore. Venus would be gone soon, off to find a new godchild, who hopefully would give her what she needed. I had to be able to live with myself for the rest of my life. I didn't know what my screwed-up love life meant for Venus, but I couldn't think about that right now.

I pulled the folded pages of all three copies of The Plan from my back pocket. "Remember when I told you I'd made this plan back when I was in high school?" I asked Joan, who was nursing Baby Braden under a blanket so hopefully Nita would forget what was she was doing. "The goal list I had—the one that said it was time for me to get married?"

Which, now that I said it out loud like that, sounded completely ridiculous. A piece of paper *said* it was time to get married, so I did it? How asinine.

Once Joan acknowledged that she remembered me mentioning it, I continued. "I realized a few days ago that The Plan really just holds me back. I've stuck to this plan, basically an arbitrary timeline that I pulled out of my ass to make my high school guidance counselor happy." I unfolded the pages, looking them over one last time. I fully admit to shaking inside about the whole thing. Eliminating The Plan from my life was like eliminating oxygen from the air that I breathed. I wasn't at all sure I could live without it.

But I had to try.

"Don't get me wrong. Goals have their merits."

"They give you something to look forward to," Joan injected, looking a little worried. Probably for my state of mind. And I couldn't say I didn't share her concern. "Something to reach for."

"And that works if they don't limit you," I said. "I think the problem was limiting myself with a timeline. Maybe I'd have been married years ago and have two kids by now if The Plan hadn't kept me from even thinking of that as an option. I can still do everything on this list without waiting for some supposedly perfect time to arrive. Maybe my store would be more successful. Maybe I'd be happier." My voice wobbled a bit, and I folded the sheets of paper in my hand in half. "And dammit, I want to be happier."

Across the room Venus sniffled. "I've been trying to help you with that for the last five weeks."

No one paid her any mind.

"So you still haven't explained what we're here for," Joan prompted. "And why we have a fire in the fireplace and all the windows open because it's sixty-five degrees out."

This was it. This was the time for me to step out and believe that I could, and would, live the rest of my life spontaneously, as it came, instead of rigidly.

"We're here for a plan-burning party," I finally said, summoning a smile I was having a hard time feeling, but experts always said fake it till you make it. "I don't need it anymore. All the things on this list can be done anyway, but I don't need a piece of paper telling me when to do everything in my life."

With a flourish, I stood, flicking the papers open with one hand, and setting my glass on the mantel.

"To freedom." I took the top sheet and leaned forward to feed it to the flames. It didn't feel so bad. Neither did the next sheet.

But when I came to the last page—the one that had lived in my wallet since I was seventeen, the one most well worn and well read—my heartbeat kicked up a notch. Could I do it? Could I live without it?

Only time would tell.

I balled up the last sheet and threw it into the fireplace, flames licking it black within seconds.

Behind me, Nita clapped her hands. "Hooray! Now we can get back to normal and stop all this nonsense about trying to find a husband—"

"Bite your tongue!" Venus shot back, sounding like she meant it literally. "Haydee and Derek Reed are meant to be together."

"No, Venus," I said firmly, ignoring the part of me that might have wished she was right. "We're not. And we never will be."

"Well, you're still good to go feng shui–wise," Joan said. "When it's the right time."

"Thanks, I appreciate that." I took a tentative sip of my margarita, knowing if I drank as much as I really wanted to of the slushy mixture, I'd have a brain freeze that wouldn't quit. "And just so you know, I still plan on getting married someday." I looked pointedly at Nita, who chose to ignore me by attempting to induce her own margarita brain freeze. "But not right now. And not to Derek Reed." I looked pointedly at Venus, who slumped dramatically against the wall.

"My life is over. I hope you're satisfied."

Spinning around, she stomped up the stairs and slammed the door to her bedroom.

"She takes her job failures very seriously."

❧ 42 ❧

Haydee

A cold nose pressed into my cheek, and I popped one eye open. Zeus's purr rattled as he snuffed at my face, making sure I smelled the same as I had when I went to bed last night.

Apparently satisfied I was who I claimed to be, he hopped down and headed for the door, where he sat and censoriously counted the minutes until I got out of bed.

Which I wasn't sure yet I could even do.

Rolling to my side, I peered at Zeus across the room and waited for the depression to hit.

I had no plan.

For the first time in nearly sixteen years, I had no goal to reach toward. No blueprint of what my day should work toward.

Or *was* this the first time?

I sat up and pulled my knees up in front of me, smoothing the quilt over them as I contemplated what I'd just realized.

That I really hadn't relied on The Plan to get me out of bed for a long time. Until recently. The previous few items on The Plan had been accomplished years ago. Opening the bookstore, turning my first profit, joining the Bander Business Association—I'd accomplished all that at least three years ago. So, for the last three years, I hadn't relied on The Plan to keep me moving forward at all.

I'd been *waiting* on The Plan to give me permission to move forward.

I grinned at Zeus, who was now pacing in front of the closed bedroom door, waiting to be fed. "I'm free," I told him. "I don't have to follow The Plan's timeline anymore. I can do anything I want! Whenever I want."

Which included getting started on all the plans I had for the store. My plan had only ever included a goal to "expand the store." And I'd stuck to the stupid rigid schedule, not bothering to begin any of the ideas that had popped into my head over the years. The new children's section, the book clubs and guest author signings? The online sales, rare-book acquisitions, the coffee bar? I no longer had to wait to get married and start a family before doing any of those things. I was free to start today if I chose.

I jumped out of bed, renewed like I hadn't been in forever. Flinging open the door, I danced my way into the hall, doing circles around the cat who was very unappreciative of my new-found joy.

Rapping my knuckles on the door next to mine, I called out to Venus. "Oh, Fairy Godmother? Are you awake yet?"

"Guh 'way," she muttered, muffled by blankets.

Instead I pushed open the door. "Rise and shine! You can help me step into my new life of freedom from arbitrary timelines and wasted days."

She ripped the covers from her head, and I tried not to flinch. She really had let herself go. Her hair was a matted mess—more than just the typical bedhead. I don't think she'd actually combed it in days. Her skin was dry and flaky from lack of her evening moisturizing routine, which I knew for a fact she followed religiously. I knew it had all been in an effort to do her job, for me. Maybe she'd feel better now that it wasn't necessary.

"What part of 'My life is over' didn't you understand?"

Okay, "better" might be too strong a word. She'd probably have to work up to that. "Maybe it just feels like it's over because you've been focusing on getting back to Mount Olympus before allowing yourself to really live." I had astonishing insight now that I'd figured out my own life. "Maybe if you—"

"Maybe if *you* would admit that Derek Reed is the love of you life," Venus shouted as she bolted up in bed, her blond curls shooting every which way like Medusa with a bad bleach job, "I wouldn't have to *focus* on getting home because I'd already *be* there."

Apparently my astonishing insight was completely lost on her.

"Well," I said, picking up a still-hinting-for-breakfast Zeus, "I'm going to the bookstore and getting started on the rest of my life. You can sulk here in bed all day, but I can't support that by hanging around waiting for you to realize I'm right."

I turned to leave again, then paused. "Just because I don't need your, uh, outstanding matchmaking skills anymore, doesn't mean you're not welcome. Just so you know."

I was halfway down the stairs to the kitchen before Venus bothered to answer.

"Oh, you just *think* you don't need my matchmaking skills!" Feet hit the floor with a thud. "But there's a Prince Charming out there with your name on him, and I'll be damned if I'm going to give up and allow you to make the biggest mistake of your life."

43

Haydee

"Whatcha building, Haydee?" Glenn pushed the flatbed cart of supplies out to the truck I'd borrowed from Hoop.

I flipped down the tailgate and stepped back while he began sliding lumber into the bed of the pickup. "Shelves for the store," I told him, feeling very weird saying it out loud. I felt like I was cheating on The Plan—The Plan I'd followed faithfully for literally half my life.

God, I was totally delusional, wasn't I?

But now that I'd tasted freedom, I couldn't wait to get going. Beginning with an insane urge to pound nails. So, as soon as Venus had shown up at the store to help out on the floor, I'd gotten started.

"It's just shelves for now," I told Glenn. "But eventually I'll have a raised seating area that'll be carpeted. For a new children's section. We'll have weekly storytime and bring in special authors occasionally. Something fun for the kids. You'll have to bring yours in for the opening ceremony."

"Will do." He shoved the last can of paint in beside the wood, then slammed the tailgate shut. "Sounds like something my wife would like, too. She's always wanted to try her hand at writing stories."

"That'll be great." I handed him back the signed invoice. "Thanks for your help."

I rounded the back of the truck and had my hand on the door

when I heard my name called. Turning, I found Derek's mom getting out of the car next to me. The lumberyard shared the parking lot with the Wagon Wheel Restaurant next door. Derek's mom had been a waitress there as long as I could remember.

Since Derek had left and she'd refused to divulge his whereabouts, I don't think we'd done more than share uncomfortable glances when we'd crossed paths. Even though at one time we'd gotten along just fine. Guess we knew whose side she was on. And Derek had probably told her what happened the other day, so I braced myself.

"Hi, Mrs. Reed . . . Mrs. Stedman." I'd never gotten used to her new married name. Though she'd remarried more than ten years ago. In Hawaii. Where Derek had flown the entire wedding party so he didn't have to set foot in Bander.

"Barbara." She smiled tentatively as she closed the space between us. "I think you're old enough to call me by my first name."

Wary of her sudden interest in speaking to me, I just nodded. "I suppose I am. Barbara."

Now that we'd gotten that out of the way, she suddenly looked a little less sure of herself. And a lot more like she regretted striking up a conversation with me.

When the silence finally stretched out to an uncomfortable length, I took the initiative to get us out of it. "Well, it's nice to see you again. I'd better get back to the store."

"I wanted to talk to you," Barbara blurted out. "Derek's out of town for a photo shoot, so it seemed like a good time."

Oh right. Sri Lanka. A few weeks in Bander and Mr. Adventurer was bored already and needed a fix. Once he got a taste of the high life again, who's to say he'd even come back? I'd made the right decision.

"I owe you an apology," Barbara continued.

Confused, I turned back to her. "What for?" Not telling me

where Derek was thirteen years ago? Not telling him I needed to speak to him, even though I'd cried right there in her kitchen, trying to convince her it was important?

Barbara wrung her hands around her purse strap, only meeting my eyes for a few seconds before looking away again. "I told Derek to leave," she finally said.

Oh, was that all? "I never expected him to stay. He's got a career to return to."

"Not recently," she corrected, as I reached for the door handle. "Thirteen years ago. I told him to leave town then."

I turned back to her. I don't know why I was surprised. Though Derek's mom had never given any indication that she'd been unhappy about our relationship at the time, she clearly hadn't wanted me to contact him after he left.

"I thought I was doing you a favor."

There seemed to be a lot of that going around. First Derek tried to tell me he'd left for my benefit. Now his mother?

I leaned back against the truck door. "Maybe you should tell me what you mean, because I really don't understand."

With a heavy sigh, she continued, finally meeting my eyes. "I knew how much you'd come to mean to Derek that summer. He even told me he wanted to marry you."

He'd shared it with his mother? "And . . . and you didn't want him to?"

"Oh no!" Barbara reached out and touched my arm. "I'd have loved having you as a daughter-in-law."

"Then why would you tell him to leave me? Why wouldn't you tell me where to find him afterward? "

"Because I didn't want you to make the same mistakes I had." She shrugged a little. "When I found out you planned to give up everything to be with Derek, I couldn't let you end up being a waitress, when you were meant to be a bookseller."

I shook my head, still not understanding.

"Haydee, when I married Derek's dad, I was about the same age you were when you fell in love with my son. I thought the only way to be with Lou was to give up everything to be with him. Instead of becoming the nurse I'd dreamed of being, I became a waitress. Put Lou through med school. And I was happy doing it. And then he died."

Her anguish was clear, but I didn't try to stop her. Suddenly I knew what she had to say would be important, crucial even, to understanding exactly what had happened to Derek and me.

"I had nothing left. No husband. No career. I told Derek not to let you do what I had done," she continued, her anguish clearly growing. "I told him not to let you give up everything for him. I thought he'd just go back to school, tell you he wanted to wait until you'd both graduated. I never *dreamed* he'd leave for good."

I stared at the dusty gravel at my feet while Barbara paused to let some customers pass by.

"I'm so sorry, Haydee. I thought I was doing the right thing. Even when I figured out about the baby, I never told him—"

My head shot up. "You knew about the baby?"

"I'm on the beautifying committee for the cemetery," she explained, a sad smile on her face. "Who else would be Danielle Maxine Miller right next to your mother's grave? You named her after Derek." A tear slipped down her cheek. "I'd have loved to know my granddaughter. Can you ever forgive me?"

I glanced across the parking lot at the red neon Wagon Wheel flashing atop the building next door. I'd have made a lousy waitress.

When I turned back to Barbara, a tear of my own spilled over its banks. "I'm beginning to understand that a lot of mistakes were made, Barbara. By a lot of people. Maybe we all did the best we could."

~ 44 ~

Venus

"If I break another nail on top of all the other indignities I've suffered the last few days, I shall never forgive you."

Haydee pays absolutely no attention to my anguish at being forced into manual labor. "Grab that end, Venus. It should be light enough for you and Curt to shift while I line it up with the other bookcase."

I slap at Curt's hand, which is edging toward my butt again, and point to the other end of the bookcase so he and his puppy dog eyes will back off. I suspect him of being visually challenged, because he has done nothing but drool down my cleavage this morning—the cleavage that is thoroughly covered with a faded T-shirt sporting a logo for a long-ago oyster festival.

Frankly, I am too anxious to enjoy his attention. I need to be out there fixing the mess Haydee has created for herself, inciting Derek to not give up, to continue to fight for her. But no. I'm stuck here, apparently working on my career as a slave laborer. Which I may have to resign myself to, since it doesn't look like I'm ever leaving here.

Oh, woe is me!! If Curt could comprehend my anguish, he'd have years worth of poems to pen.

"A little more to the left."

Curt and I lift with the knees, as instructed by the Task Master, and finally she's satisfied.

"How long is this going to take?" I ask, breaking for a swig of soda and a mouthful of M&M's. My eating habits are becoming as dreadful as Haydee's. We've been at this for days, with Haydee finally deciding just to go for it all at once, by closing the store until the first stage of the remodel is complete. Thankfully, it isn't all going to be a do-it-ourselves project. She hired a carpenter to build the new seating area for the rugrat section of the bookstore, which he's going to do later tonight. In the meantime, my goddess life is flashing before my eyes.

"I figure the store will stay closed for the week," she says. "Consider all the hard work my birthday present."

It's the only thing she's getting from me for her birthday, that's for damn sure . . . unless I can figure a way to wrap up one Derek Reed and deliver him to her bed on her birthday morning.

A knock on the door finally gives me an excuse to take a break. "I'll get it!"

"Tell them we're closed for remodeling," Haydee reminds me, as if I could forget what all the slavery is for.

My pace automatically slows when I see who's on the other side of the glass door. I'm not telling this one to go away. I don't think Haydee would, either, considering this is his first visit.

I turn the key sticking out of the lock and pull the door inward. "Come on in," I tell him with a broad smile. After all, things are clearly out of control, and if he's come to fix things, I'm all for it.

He looks a bit tentative, but finally steps through the door, his gaze moving cautiously about the room until it lands on Haydee.

Who's just noticed him. She straightens from the shelf we'd just moved, and it's easy to see she's struggling. "Dad?"

Mr. Miller clears his throat, glancing at me once again, and I nod encouragingly until he turns back to a hopeful-looking Haydee.

"I . . . heard my daughter might need some help," he says.

And even I get a little choked up.

Haydee

Thankfully, Venus and Curt decided to take a dinner break, because awkward didn't even begin to describe the feeling in the room.

Dad silently hammered and screwed until the new display unit hung in its new spot waiting for the first-designated author of the month.

"Thanks, Dad. That's fantastic." I took the hammer from him, my fingers brushing his. Literally the first time we'd touched in I can't remember how long. "Would you like a cup of coffee? Do you take cream and sugar?"

"Just black, please. Like always."

Dropping the tools back in their box, I mentally slapped myself. Of course he liked his coffee black. If we had any kind of relationship, I'd know that.

Once we got settled with our steaming cups, the conversation stopped dead. Finally, I couldn't stand it anymore.

"You didn't come here just to help, did you, Dad?"

His face remained impassive for a minute then finally softened. "I figure I owe you an apology."

"I—"

He silenced me with a look I hadn't seen since I was a kid. "Yes. Whatever years we've lost . . . they're my fault. It's one thing to be depressed after losing a spouse, but it's no excuse to lose a child. Especially one who still needs you."

I'd wanted to hear this for so long.

But now I didn't know what to do with it.

"You deserved to have me there for you when you lost the baby," Dad continued, taking my hand.

Tears flooded my eyes and spilled down my cheeks. And when I laid my head tentatively on my dad's shoulder—just like I used to when I was a little girl—he didn't move away.

Which just made things worse. I gave Joan's water element competition for fountainlike output.

Dad handed me a clean rag from the stack we'd been using to dust with. "I promise to try harder, honey." He pulled my chin up until I faced him. "I made the mistake of letting tragedy come between us, when we needed each other most. It won't happen again. I thought maybe we could start by going out to dinner for your birthday on Wednesday night, if you aren't doing something with Patrick, I mean. Or he can come along."

I lifted my head to look at him. He remembered my birthday?

"Someplace nice," he said, hanging his head a bit. "I have a lot of birthdays to make up for."

"That would be nice." Any more eloquence was a bit out of my realm of capabilities at the moment. "And . . . Patrick and I broke up. It wasn't meant to be."

Looking grim, Dad just squeezed my hand. I was thankful he didn't ask me to explain. I was a bit too emotional right at the moment to explain how I'd had to break a good friend's heart.

We sat in silence for a few minutes, with only my sniffling audible. Zeus finally made an appearance, having spent most of the day hiding out in the backroom, away from the noise and chaos of the remodel. He sniffed tentatively at Dad's foot, then sat back on his haunches to stare at him. Venus hated when he did that to her, but Dad seemed to have something still on his mind.

"So, uh, you know Clarice Woods, right?"

I looked up from blowing my nose, confused at the change of subject. "The librarian? Sure, I know her." We talked about what books were popular, what I should order for the store, or she should order for the library. "Why?"

Dad frowned. "We, uh, we sorta have a . . . we're going to have dinner on Friday night."

I didn't gape like a largemouth bass, I'm sure. But close.

"You're upset." Dad stood quickly, watching me warily like he was worried I'd collapse. Or burst into tears again. "I shouldn't have brought it up right now. This is about you and me."

"I'm not upset. Just . . . surprised," I corrected, tipping my head to really look at him. He had more emotion on his face than I'd seen since my mom died. And for once it wasn't anguish or sorrow. "You're really going on a date?" Maybe I should warn him it wasn't all it was cracked up to be.

He flushed and frowned harder, turning to face the store again. Something about the display he'd just hung caught his attention, and he snatched up a hammer before crossing the room to make adjustments to it. "Something just . . . changed lately. Like it was time to move on. It's dinner. No big deal."

Dinner *was* a big deal for a man who'd cut himself off from social activities for the better part of two decades. And the fact that he'd shared it with me made me happier than I thought I would be for a long time. "It's a good idea, Dad. I'm glad you're getting out."

I leaned back against the empty bookcase. Maybe I should offer Venus's services to him. She was kind of jobless at the moment. Maybe she'd do better with him than she had with me. After all, Venus had matched him perfectly with my mom all those years ago.

"I'd even be okay if you got married again," I told him, wondering what had brought about this change, but not willing to look a gift horse in the mouth. "So you wouldn't be alone. You need companionship."

Dad slowly lowered the hammer and turned around. "Marriage isn't just about companionship. Didn't your mother and I teach you better than that?"

Yeah, they had. Mom's books took up a whole row on a shelf across the room, and I could tell you everything about every couple in each of those books. Every struggle they'd fought through to end up together. Every bit of pain they'd suffered—and inflicted. It was never one-sided. I knew a bit about that. Only in my case we hadn't been able to work things out. There was too little trust between Derek and me to ever put our past behind us.

But that didn't mean it had to happen that way to everyone.

I turned back to my dad. "You're right. You did." I cocked a grin. "So, I hope you find passion and excitement and a reason to be happy to wake up every morning."

For a second he looked ready to pass out. Then he laughed. "Okay, you got me there. Guess that's what we taught you. So what about you?"

I stood and brushed the dust from my jeans. "Well, it's been a rough week, but I am excited and happy to wake up every morning now, too." Maybe passion would come later. Gesturing around the room, I couldn't help but feel hopeful. "I have a lot to do and I'm finally moving forward and doing it. Instead of waiting around for 'someday.' "

"What about Derek?"

I feigned sudden interest in my coffee. "I'm afraid that shipwreck is unsalvageable."

"Bet you thought you and I were unsalvageable, too, didn't you?"

True. "That's different."

"You're right, it is." Dad dropped the hammer and pulled me into his arms. Surprisingly, it felt right to be there. "It took us almost seventeen years to get it right. Maybe it'll only take you and Derek thirteen."

～ 46 ～

Haydee

"Coming!"

No way could Venus be back with dinner so soon. She'd headed for McDonald's only ten minutes ago . . . on foot, because she said she needed the time alone to "ponder her mortality." She'd become Ms. Doom and Gloom in the past few days, so I was happy to let her go for a while. It was hard enough to keep a positive attitude myself, despite all the good things chasing away the bad, and I needed a break from her, too. To put my good mood back in place. Which I was doing by going over all the plans for the store that I'd put into motion this week.

Setting aside the building permit applications I'd been going through, I went to get the door.

I was more than a little surprised to find Derek on my porch. I knew he'd come home from Sri Lanka. Venus heard it at the coffee shop and had raced back to the store to tell me right away . . . minus my coffee.

"I wonder if you'd take a drive with me this time," he said. He ran a hand through his hair, which looked like this hadn't been the first time he'd done that today. "We won't be gone long."

It won't change anything, I told my heart, which started racing the moment I'd opened the door. But I owed him equal time to clear up the past.

"I'll get my jacket."

When I met him out on the porch a few minutes later, he led

me out to the curb and opened the door to his shiny new black truck.

"Been helping out Embassy Auto's business?" I questioned, as I buckled into the plush leather seat. Inside I was a quivering mess. I'd pretty much decided he was still driving his old truck because he didn't plan on sticking around Bander. So what did this actually mean?

"I'd have done it sooner, but I wasn't really sure what I wanted."

When his intense gaze became too much, I looked away. The short ride into town was awkward to say the least. And silent. What else was there to say, after all? We'd said everything possible in the cemetery last week.

God, had it only been a week ago? It seemed like a lifetime had passed. A lifetime in which I'd made so many decisions that I'd put off for so long. I'd actually lived more in the last week than I had in the last three years, since I'd completed the last item on The Plan.

When we parked in one of the spots in front of an empty storefront a few blocks down and over from Mount Olympus Books, I finally broke the silence. "You want to shop?"

"Not exactly." Derek hopped out of the truck and came around to my side. He opened the door, but when he automatically reached out to help me down, he pulled his hand back at the last minute.

No doubt about how over we were. I tried not to notice how much that hurt. Because logically it would take time for this wound to heal. Probably longer the more time Derek stayed in Bander. But I'd make it. I would. Determination had become my middle name in the last week.

I followed Derek down the sidewalk a bit until he came to the door of the empty building. It had been a craft store but had been vacant for at least a year or so. For some reason, though it was prime Main Street frontage that should have put it in high demand for businesses, it had remained unoccupied, the windows papered over, no sign to indicate what it might someday become.

When Derek stuck a key in the lock and opened the door, curiosity took center stage and shoved aside my worries about the future and dealing with the past.

"You rented this building?"

We stepped just inside the door and Derek indicated for me to wait there while he moved further down the bank of papered-over windows, presumably to turn on the lights.

When he found them, my question was answered.

"Welcome to the future Reed Gallery. I bought it. A year ago."

The room was beautiful. The colors were of sand and sea, taupe and aqua, the textures of walls and flooring an art form in and of themselves. But the real art was in the pictures. Derek's photos hung around the room and on accordioned three-quarter walls placed throughout. I recognized many of them from the backroom at the bait shop.

As I wandered slowly amidst the sometimes familiar shots, the same or similar to ones that had graced the covers of dozens of magazines over the years, I held my breath. Waiting to see if he'd hung—

"This one's for you," he held out a brown paper-wrapped package.

I reached toward it cautiously, then tore the paper away from it. The cemetery portrait.

Stunned, I glanced up at him.

"It's yours," Derek said. "Do with it whatever you wish. Keep it. Burn it."

I could barely breathe. Of course, now that he knew about the baby, when he was as angry with me as he was for keeping it from him, he wouldn't look at the photo in the same way.

As I reached out to take it from him, my fingers brushed against his. When we touched, I raised my eyes to his. "Thank you. It means a lot to me that you wouldn't—"

"I never meant to sell it, Haydee." He hesitated, then reached up and tucked a strand of hair behind my ear. "I couldn't have."

Clearing my throat to get past the lump in it, I stepped away. I needed space. I walked back to the door and leaned the portrait against the wall so I wouldn't forget it when I left. Which would hopefully be very soon, before I lost it.

"So, gallery owner?" This explained where the pictures would be stored while awaiting sale on his new website. He didn't even really need the Constantine House. Though, being a Bander business owner now, I could see where he might need to drop by and check on things from time to time. "You're laying down a few roots. Looking toward retirement someday?" In twenty or thirty years, when his adventuresome days were over.

It came out sounding more like wishful thinking than I'd have liked. Or maybe that was panic. That I'd never be able to get on with my life as long as Derek stayed in Bander. Because no matter how many times I tried to tell myself the opposite was true, I knew I wasn't over him yet.

And might never be.

Was it possible to move on with a new life without getting over the old one?

"I'm not leaving. I'm not giving up my photography," Derek said from across the room. "It's a great career, and there's no reason I can't keep Bander as my home base for the times in between shoots. Or longer. So I thought I should apologize now."

I shook my head. "We really don't have to do this anymore. We said everything that needed to be said at the cemetery.

We've both made a lot of mistakes, and if we just put it behind us—"

"I lied about leaving so you could fulfill your dreams."

My mouth fell open. If he told me he never really loved me . . . if he told me that summer had all been a lie . . . it would take more than a new plan to get me out of bed in the morning. I sank onto a bench beside the front door. "Then why *did* you leave?"

He took a deep breath, the crevices in his forehead deepening as he tried to figure out what to say. "I left to fulfill my own dream, too."

I shook my head, not comprehending. His dream had been to get a teaching degree and live in Bander . . . coach football.

Unless it wasn't.

He finally looked up at me again. "When I lost my chance at the NFL, I really thought there was nothing left. And then, that summer with you, I really believed you were all I needed."

I braced myself for the let down.

"I found out about the photography internship with Joseph Lazarus before I came home that summer," he continued, pacing a path in the carpet across the room. "I applied for it just for fun, to see if I was good enough."

"You never mentioned it to me." The fact that he'd never mentioned the internship before springing on me that he was leaving for good was one of the things that bothered me the most . . . aside from the fact that he deserted me. "We always told each other stuff like that, even before we . . . became more."

His anguish was clear, but I didn't understand. "When my chances at a football career disappeared, I felt like such a failure." His gaze finally met mine again. "You made me feel like I wasn't a failure. You gave me hope again. If I'd told you about the internship, you'd have encouraged me, told me I was good enough. And then, if I'd failed at that, too . . ." He just shook his head and thrust his hands in his pockets.

"You thought I'd think less of you if you didn't make it. Because you felt you'd already failed at one career."

One corner of his mouth forced itself upward. "It sounded logical at twenty-one. Not so much at thirty-four."

Derek crossed the room and sat next to me on the bench, leaning forward to brace his elbows on his knees. "When we fell in love that summer"—he turned briefly and met me with a smile— "though I'm not at all convinced we hadn't actually been in love for a lot longer than that . . ."

I smiled sadly back. There was every possibility he was right.

He went back to examining the floor. "When we fell in love that summer, we made plans. I really wanted all those things—to come back here after college, to teach, coach. To marry you. I wanted all those things like I'd never wanted anything since high school. But then everything happened at once. I decided to propose and then you offered to give up everything to come to Seattle with me. And then I talked to my mom." He paused a minute. "She told me she finally confessed to you what happened. And that she eventually figured out about the baby. I can't believe she never told me."

"Don't blame her," I told him. "She did what she felt was best . . . for both of us, it looks like."

Derek straightened and sat back on the bench so he could look at me. His face betrayed every bit of the struggle he'd gone through so long ago. "So, when Joe Lazarus called and said he'd chosen me for the internship . . . I realized how much dreams really did mean. I wanted you, but I knew I'd be no good to you without finding out what *I* could do. I *wanted* to go. I wanted to prove that I had more in me than just the ability to teach history and watch the next generation's NFL hopefuls do what I couldn't do. And when I realized how much it meant to me, I understood how much your dreams meant to you."

"That still doesn't explain why you never told me when you did get the internship," I said. "You know I'd never have tried to hold you back. We could have just put things on hold awhile. Maybe things would have been different. I wouldn't have been so angry at you for leaving. I . . . would have told you about the baby."

"Would you?"

"Of course! The only reason I didn't tell you was because I was mad."

"So if I'd told you about the internship, you'd have sent me off with your blessing . . . and then what? You'd have called me back a month later to tell me we were having a baby and you wanted me to turn down the internship? Or would you have *not* told me because you didn't want to hold me back?"

I looked away, my eyes falling on a portrait of an aborigine child, whose big dark eyes held secrets of a life none of us would ever know, captured by the talent of Derek Reed. *Would* I have held him back after sending him off to take the chance of a lifetime? He'd lost his NFL career. Would I have taken away his photography career, knowing what it would cost him? I hadn't wanted him to come back to be with me just because of the baby. Would it have been different if I'd known about the internship?

I turned back and shrugged. "I don't know. Maybe not."

"I don't think you would have. My mom was right about that much. She didn't know about the internship when she told me to back off. So she really was only doing it for you. And she was right. I couldn't ask you to give up your dreams, any more than you'd have asked me to give up mine. And frankly, I'd become resentful of your plan. It gave you drive and determination. Something to look forward to. Which I hadn't had since I blew out my knee. I convinced myself that your plan was more important to you than I was. That by accepting the internship, I was giving you what you really wanted. A chance to live out your real dreams, which didn't seem to include me. The Plan is the most important thing in your life. I get that."

I laughed just a little. "I burned The Plan last week."

At his surprised look, I explained. "The Plan wasn't the problem . . . it was the timeline I'd set for it. To get married at thirty-three? Just a random age I pulled out of thin air to satisfy my counselor."

Derek smiled. "Yeah, I'd have been back here years ago, if you'd wanted to get married at, say, twenty-five. I only stayed away so I wouldn't interfere."

I frowned, confused.

"The internship only lasted a year. I just stayed gone the rest of the time because I knew I couldn't be this close to you and not try to get you to throw out The Plan."

"Really?"

"Why do you think I bought this place a year ago? I was waiting for you to 'come of age,' so I could come back for you."

He laughed, but I couldn't join in. I felt like I was getting my heart broken all over again. "We both made a lot of mistakes, I guess. A lot of things we should have said . . . and maybe not said."

Derek shook his head. "I've spent the last week trying to rewrite history. Second guessing all my choices. All your choices. Would we really have done anything differently? *Should* we have?"

My friend Joan would have said no. That everything happened for a reason. That if we told ourselves, even through the worst times of our lives, that whatever happened was exactly what we needed most . . .

"Maybe the important thing is not our mistakes of the past, but what we do with those mistakes. How we learn from them." I swallowed and held my breath waiting for Derek's response. Because I finally knew what I wanted more than anything.

What Venus, my crazy fairy godmother had known I wanted all along.

When Derek's fingers touched my face, I shivered. Then I turned to meet his lips with mine. Within seconds, we ignited in a bonfire of many years' worth of suppressed passion. When I pressed my palms into his chest, I felt his heart beating as wildly as my own. I breathed the air he breathed. I felt . . . for the first time in years . . . that everything, *everything* was right.

When we finally parted, breathing hard, I kept my eyes closed, savoring the moment. Almost unable to believe it was real.

"There's one thing that was never a mistake," Derek whispered, tipping up my chin so I would open my eyes and look at him, and know the truth in his words. "I loved you then, and I love you now, more than anything in this world." He briefly glanced at all the photos around the room before looking back at me. "I would give up every experience I've had, every bit of life I've captured on film, to not have broken your heart and walked away from you. Because I broke my own heart in the process. And all that I've ever done was empty without you."

❧ 47 ❧

Venus

"Back off!" I shout, waving the fast-food bag at the horde of rabid men following me onto Haydee's front lawn. I dashed up the steps to the porch before turning toward them again. They'd been collecting around me like flies on a carcass ever since I'd left McDonald's. I shake the bag at them again, menacingly. "Don't make me use this."

"But Venus," one of them pleads, leading the pack hot on my Ferragamo . . . er, Keds heels. "Venus, I need you."

"You *need* to get a grip on yourself. In fact, if you'd take matters into your own hands *literally* . . ." I stare out at the sea of pathetically needy faces, "*all* of you, you wouldn't be acting like such a bunch of love-sick horn dogs."

Whirling, I stomp toward the front door eager for the peace and quiet inside. I'd left the house with such a simple mission: to locate Derek and lure him back here to the house. Yes, using my "feminine wiles." At this point, I truly didn't care about any stupid rules. I needed to make this match work, no matter what it took. Why I felt the need to suddenly become the perfect fairy godmother is beyond me.

So, anyway, I left the house looking for Derek. I was going to lure him home and then get him in the house with Haydee. I'd have figured out how to disappear without him following me when the time came. I just knew I needed them in the same room. They had to work out their problems. I could not be stuck here forever!

But I never found him. I finally gave up when my stomach growled and I remembered telling Haydee I was going out for food.

And now this disaster! I don't know what's going on, but I'm sick and damn tired of it. Zeus wants me to fail. That's abundantly clear. There's no other reason for the disaster after disaster that's befallen this match.

"Veeeennuuusss!" Another man has fallen to his knees on the porch steps, only to be jumped by three other guys who want their shot at me. Ugh!

Upon Zeus, I'd never have guessed I'd wish guys would *stop* noticing me! But it's like I've turned into the Pied Piper . . . only of men instead of rats. Except that the Pied Piper could just stop playing his fucking pipe and the rats would leave him alone.

I can't figure out how to turn me off!

It's like . . . like . . . *Zeus,* I can't even say it. It's like my beauty is a . . . curse.

The door slams into the wall when I fling it open. I'm through it and shutting it behind me before any of my admirers can react. Except for Patrick, who's been following me since I ran into him outside Mickey D's. He manages to get inside and shuts the door behind him, locking it before turning around, a sly smile on his face.

"Playing hard to get is very attractive, Venus. I know you want to be with me and not with those other losers. You sense that we're meant to be together, don't you? Just like I do."

"I sense that you're losing your grip on reality, bub." The bag of dinner is making my stomach growl as I hold it up between us like a burger-and-fry-scented shield. Albeit a flimsy shield. I need help getting rid of him. Maybe Haydee can distract him long enough for me to leave the room. That's all it should take for him to remember he's in love with her and not me. "Haydee!"

"Venus, please." Patrick stalks me, pushing me backward into the living room, unaffected by the fast-food bag. "We're meant to be together."

"Last week you thought you were meant to be with Haydee. Remember her? Dark blond? Green eyes? Your engagement ring on her finger. Just. Last. Week?"

Deaf to what I'm saying, Patrick lunges for me, wrapping his fingers around my upper arms just as I trip over Furball Zeus, who happens to be lying on the foyer floor watching this disaster through slitted eyes.

"Go get Haydee, boy!" I encourage, really hoping for once that Zeus really is my nosy father spying on my every move. Surely he'll see I need some divine intervention right now and, well, *intervene*. Instead he just continues to lay there and twitch his stubby tail.

"Venus. Goddess. I adore you." Patrick starts up again.

"Stop it. Right now. You don't love me."

"But I do! You're my sun and my moon. My light and my shadow."

Knowing that no matter what I say, he's apparently not going to listen, I go for the physical and try to wriggle away, but his grip is too strong. Much as I used to be all for the wicked scoundrel/damsel in distress sex games once upon a time, now, not so much. "Let go. Now," I demand in my sternest goddess voice. "Just take your hands off me before things get ugly . . . uglier."

"Never, my love. Not if you pierce my heart with the sharpest blade. Not if you dig it out with a dull spoon. Not if my heart stops beating and there is no defibrillator—"

"Oh. My. God. Stop with the bad poetry. What has gotten into you?"

"Love. Only love, my precious."

Where in Hades is Haydee? I only left an hour ago and she

was in her office working. What in the world could be occupy-ing her? "Oh, Haydee?" I try again. "A little help out here?"

As Patrick leans toward me, lips parted, I know what's going to happen next. He's going to kiss me, and I, the Goddess of Love and Beauty, am going to vomit.

Just as his lips are about to touch mine, I jerk my head to the side. His lips glance off my cheek instead.

That's it. I'm through. I'm sick of them all. Manhandling me. Putting their paws all over me. Trying to suck face at every op-portunity.

"No more Ms. Nice Girl," I announce, shoving my hands into his chest and heaving with all my weight. The look on Patrick's face is pure despair, as he falls back a few steps, panting with . . . with . . . whatever demon has taken hold of him.

"Venus?"

I whip around at the sound of Haydee's voice. "Thank Zeus you're here! Get him off me . . . Wait? Derek?"

For the briefest of seconds, I think I hear Zeus's choir of vir-gins singing in my head. Derek's here! In this house! With Haydee! They've made up and admitted their undying love for each other.

The next second, the choir of virgins hits a sour note. Shit. I'm still here, which means things aren't quite right with them.

And Derek's here. In this house.

In *my* presence.

"If you want to keep him," I instruct Haydee, "take him and run!"

Instead of following instructions, she and Derek just ex-change a look.

And Patrick resumes his begging with an eyebrow wiggle. "Come on, Venus, let's go play. I'm a *doctor*."

"Eww! You're a dog doctor."

"What's going on Venus?"

Afraid to take my eyes off Patrick in case he makes a move, I tell Haydee what I can, which is absolutely nothing. "I have no idea. I can't seem to control them." A quick glance at Derek shows me he seems to be able to resist, though the hand around Haydee's shoulders appears a bit white-knuckled.

Patrick's hand suddenly lands on my breast, and I lose it completely. I slap him hard across the face. "Hands off! I'm not your plaything. I'm not your next conquest. And I'm sure as hell not your True Love, so get it through your thick delusional skull."

"But . . . but you are!" he cries. "You are my True Love, Venus. You have me under your spell. Your spell of love. I'll never be complete without you." Again he reaches for me, taking my left hand in his and falling simultaneously to his knees on the hardwood floor.

Damn. That had to hurt.

"Patrick?" Haydee takes a step toward us, but to Patrick there's no one else in the room but me.

"Please, Venus. Don't make me live without you. Say you'll marry me," he begs. "Say you'll be mine forever. I'll be your slave. I'll do anything you say—"

"I say no!"

Wrenching my hand from his and tossing the burger bag onto the hall table, I press my fingers into my temples.

Think! I think. Something is really, really wrong with this picture. Men don't talk like he's talking. Not *real* mean anyway. Pansy, fruity men, maybe. Men who really *are* under a spell, like Patrick said.

Wait!

Turning back to the still kneeling Patrick, I narrow my eyes at him, as if squinting will tell me what's going on. Those brown eyes of his look kind of dazed, fully focused on me, to the exclusion of everything else around us.

"Did you say 'spell'?" I ask.

"*Your* spell, my love." Patrick crawls toward me on his knees, which probably isn't doing his kneecaps any favors. "I need you to be with me always. Forever."

There has to be a way to get through to him.

"I'm celibate," I try.

"You'll be my queen and I will be your lowly page, for whom your every wish will be a command of love."

"I'm a virgin," I test.

"You gird my loins with dreams of sweet, sweet love."

Last try. "I'm a *lesbian*."

"We are soul mates destined to spend eternity entwined in each other's arms."

He's obviously not hearing a thing I'm saying. And it's not because of his apparent undying love. It's like . . . it's like he said. He's under a *spell*. He's reacting the way men (and even *gods*) reacted in the past . . .

When. I wear. The *girdle*.

I glance down at my gawdy T-shirt-covered chest. I seriously don't think it's my still awesomely fantastic breasts that have Patrick, and every other guy in town, declaring their devotion. It's got to be the . . .

I reach down and brush at the gold flecks clinging to the shirt I'd pulled from my drawer just an hour ago, picking one of the larger specks up and bringing it closer to my face.

"Venus, please." Patrick's still practically prostrate on the floor, but I'm too interested in this gold flake . . .

which is far too large to be from my makeup or my gold body glitter. It looks alarmingly like—

"Ve-nus!" Patrick's keening cry draws my attention. "Please. I'm begging you."

"Wait. Right. Here." I turn to Haydee and Derek, who remain at the kitchen door gaping in obvious confusion. "I think I know what's wrong."

Without waiting for an answer, I run into the dining room. The Golden Girdle is still sitting on the table where I left it this afternoon, its box crumbling around it. I'd been deciding what to do with it before I left to find Derek.

Lifting it carefully out of the box, I give it a shake. Little, and some not so little, flecks of gold flutter to the tabletop like little golden—magical—snowflakes . . . that apparently retain their magic even when no longer part of their original form.

This has been the problem all along. The damn girdle! It was in my dresser drawer and has probably been dusting half my wardrobe the entire time I've been here.

Wrapping it around my waist, which looks beyond ridiculous with my neon green soda-logo T-shirt, I head back into the living room to test my theory.

Patrick is still right where I left him on the floor. Haydee's trying to convince him to get up and leave, while Derek leverages him off the ground.

As soon as I'm within Patrick's sight again, this time wearing the girdle, he goes crazy.

"Venus. Oh, my one and only Venus—"

"Give it a rest—"

Unfortunately, I'd quite forgotten the girdle will make Derek unable to resist me either.

"I saw her first!" Derek dumps Patrick back on the floor with a thud and dodges around Haydee to get to me. "The most beautiful woman in the world. She's mine."

"Venus?" Haydee's panicked voice rises above the pandemonium.

"It's a girdle malfunction!" I tell Haydee, as Derek makes kissy-kissy noises at me and Patrick grabs him around the ankles to pull him away. "It's been falling apart all this time and getting the magic dust all over my clothes. That's where all the crazy Casanovas are coming from."

Derek makes another lunge for me, but I side-step just in time as Patrick makes it off the floor and tackles him around the waist. "Mine!" They crash to the floor again like a couple of toddlers duking it out over a favorite toy.

"Derek wasn't affected because the magic was weaker in the flakes by themselves. And he's so in love with you, it counteracted it." Strong emotions for someone else or the complete lack of strong emotion—like with Haydee's depressed father that night at the bar—block the magic of the girdle. I catch Haydee's attention again. This is important. "Even *Derek* can't resist the full impact of the girdle itself, though. You have to get him out of here."

Haydee barely catches a lamp knocked over in the pushing and shoving match, just as the riot going on outside the house reaches peak proportions. There must be thirty guys all trying to get through the front door shouting, "Venus! Venus! Venus!"

As Patrick and Derek continue wrestling out their frustrations, Haydee looks ready to bash them both over the head with the lamp.

"How do we stop them?"

I'm not sure we *can* stop them. At least not while I'm wearing the girdle. "I have to get rid of this thing!" I shout at Haydee over the ruckus. "Keep them occupied for a minute."

Like that's going to be a problem. Testosterone poisoning has taken over their systems and they are no longer even thinking about me.

Dashing into the kitchen, I fire up the Seal-A-Meal. Works for pancakes, so it'll work for this. While it heats, I stuff the girdle into one of the stiff plastic bags. The stupid thing has been the bane of my existence ever since Heph gave it to me. It got me into trouble then, and it got me into trouble now.

It's not my beauty that's cursed. It's this damn girdle.

When the element gets hot I shove it into place and clamp down on the Seal-A-Meal lid. Within seconds, the girdle is vacuum-packed, air- and, hopefully, magic-tight.

I still have too much gold dust on my shirt to test the theory that the magic from the girdle is what has had the men all over me, but Haydee has them sitting in separate chairs, held into place by her steely stare and don't-mess-with-me-when-my-hands-are-on-my-hips stance.

"I have to change clothes," I tell her, trying to sneak past.

At her nod, I continue toward the stairs, but Patrick's still under the influence enough that he escapes her and comes after me again.

Deciding to play along a minute, I move closer instead of farther away like I'd rather do. He looks like he's going to die of pure bliss when we finally get close enough to touch.

Walking my fingernails up Patrick's chest, I put on my best pouty look. "Will you wait for me while I go freshen up?"

"Anything for you, my love. Anything you desire."

"Really? Anything?" It's my best Marilyn Monroe breathy airhead voice. She taught me how she did that for the cameras. I hooked her up with Joe and taught her how to, well, no need to get into the sexy details. Suffice it to say, old Norma Jean put my lessons to good use and earned herself an Oscar . . . in the bedroom anyway.

"Absolutely anything." Patrick strokes the back of his hand down my face . . . and my damn good acting skills prevent me from flinching, while my every instinct is to slap him silly.

"Good." I push away from him and step back, keeping my hands on his chest, though, so he doesn't go back into that whole needy, touch-me-now-before-I-perish thing again. "You go outside and make sure all those other naughty boys have gone home and then wait for me on the porch swing. When I come downstairs, I'll give you a little treat."

"Oh, my darling. Please, you must agree to marry me. I know that you're the only woman I'll ever love."

"Yeah, yeah. Save it, sweetie." I pat him on the chest firmly and head for the stairs, calling to Haydee over my shoulder. "I'll have to borrow some of your clothes. Everything of mine has the girdle dust on it."

"Hey, Venus!"

I turn around to find Haydee planted on Derek's lap, where he's vacillating between staring at her adoringly, and looking like he's ready to toss her onto the floor and come after me.

"If this works," she continues with the first genuine smile I've seen from her the whole time I've been here, "you may get your wish after all."

✎ 48 ✎

Haydee

As soon as Venus was upstairs and Patrick outside—where I could hear him issuing instructions to all the other Bander Romeos to clear off or he'd call the cops—Derek visibly relaxed.

"Haydee?" He was still a little dazed, but it only took him a second to forget his confusion, and realize that, no matter how I got there, having me on his lap is right where he wanted me. "Have I told you how much I love you?"

I grinned back, putting the vision of him fighting with Patrick over Venus out of my head. I may not have understood all that magic stuff, but it wasn't really important for me to, was it? As long as I understood what was real. Which was this man, at this time, in this place.

"Yes, you've told me." I slipped my arms around his neck. "But you can tell me again."

"I'll buy the Constantine House for you."

"Really?" I grinned. "Good thing, because that might have been a deal breaker for me."

He ran a finger along the flesh below my rib cage, and my arms sprouted goose bumps. "Also, while I was gone, I got my teaching degree. I start teaching history at Bander High in the fall . . . and take over coaching when Bob McDermot retires. I'll still schedule photo shoots, summers and holidays, but maybe with a few more employees at the bookstore, I could convince you go to with me."

I pressed my breasts into his chest and kissed the tip of his nose. "Keep talking, Big Boy. I'm liking how you tell me you love me."

"I have a few other ways to tell you I love you." He grinned slyly and placed a kiss just above my low-cut neck line, where my heart beat only for him. "And I don't think I can wait much longer."

From my position on his lap, there was no mistaking how serious he was about not being able to wait much longer. Frankly, I felt that thirteen years was far too long myself.

"The sooner the better." I leaned forward to kiss him, when there was a throat-clearing behind us.

I turned to find Venus at the bottom of the stairs. My arms tightened around Derek, just in case she'd been wrong about the Golden Girdle thing. But he just leaned forward and breathed into my ear, "Maybe we should wait until we're alone."

Feeling a little self-conscious, I climbed off his lap, then noticed Venus had come downstairs carrying her suitcase . . . and wearing the one designer dress I own, a black satin Nicole Miller cocktail dress I'd saved for months to buy.

It was a small price.

"You were right," I told her, nodding my head in Derek's direction. "Maybe you're not such a bad fair . . . *matchmaker,* after all."

Instead of saying I told you so or you're welcome, even, Venus dropped her suitcase and crossed her arms over her chest before frowning at me . . . and then really frowning at Derek. "Don't you have something else to say to her?" she demanded.

I turned to Derek, bracing myself. What else could he say? We'd pretty much cleared thirteen years' worth of toxic air in the last hour.

He glanced at me, a tad guiltily I thought, then back at Venus. Who raised her eyebrows and patted the front of her hip.

"Oh." Derek glanced at me again, then back at Venus. "How did you know—?"

"It doesn't matter how I know," she snapped, checking her watch. "All that matters is that I've got places to go and people to see . . . and a schedule that's about two thousand years behind."

When Derek opened his mouth, presumably to question the "two thousand years" comment, Venus just made a hushing noise. "Do it," she pushed.

"I was going to wait for her birthday—"

"She has dinner plans with her father for her birthday."

Surprised, Derek turned back to me. "Really?"

I shrugged and grinned. "It's been a good week."

"It'll get even better," Venus butted in again, "if someone would get the show on the road so I can leave."

"Which means Haydee and I will be alone?" Derek got up from the chair. "That works for me."

His grin was wicked and sexy all at the same time. He raised one eyebrow at Venus, and I held my breath waiting for him to decide she'd cleaned up pretty well and was maybe the better choice.

"Fine," she said, raising her hands in surrender. "Don't let my presence stand in your way." She picked up her suitcase and retreated.

At which time, Derek dropped to one knee in front of me. And produced a ring from his jeans pocket. "Haydee Miller, it's been way too long since we did the right thing. Will you be my wife?"

Before I said yes, I glanced up at the person without whom none of this would have come about, I'm sure.

Venus wiggled her fingers, which were becoming transparent, at me. I opened my mouth to call to her, but she just pointed vehemently back at Derek, who still knelt at my feet waiting for my answer.

"Absolutely," I said, my whole being feeling, well, whole, for the first time in as long as I could remember.

He slipped the ring on my finger, and when I looked up again to show Venus the diamond testament to the love she'd brought together. . . . she was gone.

❧ 49 ❧

Venus

Is exhaustion a disease? If so, I think I'm infected.

I've never had a Love Life Makeover take so much out of me, twist me in so many knots. I think they're getting progressively worse. Like I'm being tested to the very limits of my endurance.

Last makeover, I spent so much of the time feeling sorry for myself, wishing to be noticed again and not to feel so invisible. But for these past six weeks, I'd have given *anything* to be invisible . . . literally! I need to disappear, because truly, I don't care how much I want to get back home. How much I long to see my friends and family. My children. Ares. Upon Zeus, even Heph would be a welcome sight at this point in time.

But it doesn't matter that I long for Mount Olympus more than my next breath. I have nothing left to give anyone.

I'm tired of thinking about love. Tired of fending off admirers. (In fact, if no one shows any interest in me ever again, it's possible I'd be okay with that!)

As I notice my form beginning to fade, the fatigue grows even heavier. Despite the happy ending unfolding across the room. Despite the fact that Lawrence Miller might be getting a second chance at love with the librarian lady. Despite the fact that, while I was upstairs changing, I'd glanced out the window to check on the Romeos and discovered Haydee's employee Kim and Patrick having a very serious conversation on the lawn. He was the only guy not still pounding at the front door to get my attention. Guess you never know where or when True Love might strike.

However, despite all that, I know I can't do it anymore. I can't put out (figuratively) day after day after day, forcing happiness on people who don't even know they want it. It's not fun anymore.

I need a vacation. I can see through my hand to the suitcase handle I'm holding. Why can't I just pack my bag with a bikini, or maybe a less attention-getting one-piece, and a pair of flip-flops and just go? I hear Tahiti is nice this time of year. Only that's probably full of hot men who'd just want my body, so maybe some backward little town in the middle of nowhere. Yeah. That'd work.

A vacation.

A vacation where I don't pick a godchild. Don't set up anyone with their soul mate. I just rest. Maybe work on my tan. And rest. For a long time.

Maybe, if I'm on vacation long enough, Zeus will forget about me.